MURDER ON THE CHRISTMAS EXPRESS

ALEXANDRA BENEDICT

Poisoned Pen
PRESS

Published by Poisoned Pen Press, an imprint of Sourcebooks
P.O. Box 4410, Naperville, Illinois 60567-4410
(630) 961-3900
sourcebooks.com

Originally published as *Murder on the Christmas Express* in 2022 in Great Britain by Simon & Schuster UK. This edition issued based on the hardcover edition published in 2022 in Great Britain by Simon & Schuster UK.

Cataloging-in-Publication Data is on file with the Library of Congress.

Printed and bound in the United States of America.
VP 10 9 8 7 6 5 4 3 2 1

To Katherine Armstrong—
editor, friend, and brilliant quizzer

Faster than fairies, faster than witches,
Bridges and houses, hedges and ditches;
And charging along like troops in a battle,
All through the meadows the horses and cattle:
All of the sights of the hill and the plain
Fly as thick as driving rain;
And ever again, in the wink of an eye,
Painted stations whistle by.

Robert Louis Stevenson,
From "From a Railway Carriage"

Games Within *Murder on the Christmas Express*

Game 1: Anagrams

Anagrams of my favorite stories and poems (plus a song!) involving trains are hidden throughout the book. Can you track them down?

"Adlestrop"—Edward Thomas

"Charon"—Louis MacNeice

"From a Railway Carriage"—Robert Louis Stevenson

"Ghost Train"—George Szirtes

"The Marshalling Yard"—Helen Dunmore

Murder on the Orient Express—Agatha Christie

"Orient Express"—Grete Tartler

"The Railway Library"—Robert Crawford

The Signalman—Charles Dickens

Stamboul Train—Graham Greene

"The Stopped Train"—Jean Sprackland

Strangers on a Train—Patricia Highsmith

The Trains—Robert Aickman

Train Song—Tom Waits

Violet—S. J. I. Holliday

"The Way My Mother Speaks"—Carol Ann Duffy

Game 2: Pub Quiz

There will also be a Christmas Express Pub Quiz at the end of the book.
As a warm-up for the pub quiz, try this one:
Q: Can you name six of the many Kate Bush songs hidden in the text of *Murder on the Christmas Express*? (Not anagrams, just hiding in plain sight, and sometimes not even hiding!)

Prologue

December 24th

Meg wouldn't let him see her cry, not this time. She ran out of the club car, aware of the phone cameras turning her way. Her eyes stung as she stumbled down the corridor to their cabin. The train seemed to whisper to her: *he doesn't love you, he doesn't love you, he never loved you.*

Fumbling for the key card, she checked behind her. Grant wasn't following. Part of her wanted him to. Wanted the fight that felt like love, and the peace that followed when he'd sobered up and begged forgiveness. The rest of her knew what could happen. What had so nearly happened before. And she wasn't going to die tonight.

Inside their club double, she locked the door and curled into a fetal position on the bed. She held a pillow to her chest and rocked. Her heart felt pulled apart like a Christmas cracker, and all that was left was a scrunched-up joke.

She thought about going to see that woman, Roz—the ex-detective who looked like Kate Bush. Maybe she could help.

Then her phone buzzed.

And again.

She looked at the screen—she'd been tagged in a video, and the notifications were stacking up in the hundreds. Both the train and her heart seemed to fly faster. The video had been posted a minute ago. Someone had filmed the whole argument between her and Grant, from the whispered accusations and shouted denials to Meg running out.

She watched the comments appear in real time. As usual, she couldn't stop herself from reading them:

Lindyhop2010: I'm TeamMeg!

Meg4Eva: 🖤 🖤 😄

InkedAndPrimped: He's fit—she should suck it up. I would! 😉

DinosaurSenior: LEAVE HIM, MEG! Come and sit on my face instead!

TaintedProphets: Don't trust him, take it from me

Nastasha_Roberts: She's a basket case. She's on something. You can always tell.

ICD3adp30pl3: Fake news. All staged. They're both beards and the rest are crisis actors.

Meg checked Twitter—#megrantlovespat was trending.

She could feel her rosacea flaring to match her humiliation. She knew what Grant would say: "Turn it into money." He was like Rumpelstiltskin—he could spin anything into gold, especially if it made her feel pale and brittle. By tomorrow night, he would have sold the story to one of the weeklies, and she'd be on the cover with him, smile never touching her filtered eyes.

Not this time. Not after what he'd whispered to her when she was on that table. People would ask why she hadn't spoken up before, or left him. Those people were lucky, because they'd never been abused. They didn't understand that, after being starved of love, you longed for stale bread crumbs.

It didn't matter what anyone said, not anymore. She would reclaim her story. Tell the truth. All of it. Everything she had been hiding and saving up in video clips for so long. Now was the time to release them, and herself. And, maybe, she'd speak up for the many people who couldn't. Start her own hashtag: #Megtoo.

Meg got out her compact and regarded herself in the mirror. Her dark pupils reflected her face. Kohl ran down her cheeks, making tracks in her foundation. She got out the latest batch of promo samples she'd been sent to test and repaired the worst smears of makeup, covering the red patches that showed through the foundation. If she was going to ugly-cry on camera, she was going to look pretty doing it.

Ring light on, filter applied, Meg typed into her phone the brands that would flash over the beginning of her live stream on Instagram. She had secrets to spill, and today was the day. A Christmas present for her followers and a piece of coal from Krampus for Grant. It wouldn't hurt her career either—the clock never stopped on TikTok, and this would get back some of the attention she'd lost. She had to stay calm, be authentic while promoting brands. Her mentions would explode, and her wavering sponsors would be secured.

She took as deep a breath as her lungs would allow. Picked up a can she was being paid to sell, placed it to her immaculate mouth, then pressed the button marked *Live Stream*.

Lowering the can, she smacked her lips as if she'd tasted something delicious. "Hi everyone. Told you I'd be back later. Things haven't gone according to plan. As you've probably already seen, Grant and I have been arguing again. I'd never normally let you see me like this." She pointed to her eyes, goth-smudged and swollen. The flurry of people watching was already turning into a blizzard. This was her moment. "I'd normally fix myself up and carry on. But not today. Today I'm going to tell you the secrets that lie behind my relationship with Grant."

This would be enough to hook them for now. Time for more promo. She talked on about being resilient, just like the makeup that remained on her face despite the tears.

And then when she felt she might be losing her audience: "So this is what I have to tell you. I've already started, in snippets I've got secretly recorded, but now feels the right time to tell the truth. Behind the makeup and photo shoots, the stories in *Hello!* and other places, lies—"

The train jolted, jerking to one side. Brakes screamed. The bathroom door flew open and slammed against the wall. The railcar tipped slightly, veering. Meg crawled into the corner of the bed, holding tight to her phone. "What's happening?" she asked it, as if anyone watching would know or could help.

The train screeched to a stop.

The decorations she'd made and put up earlier swung and fell over her. Designer bags shunted around the cabin. Her jewelry box fell from the sink, along with a new eyeshadow palette, which scattered pigment in shades of heather and smoke across the floor. The compact mirror slid off the bed, cracking as it hit the wall.

Meg stayed where she was, waiting for the world to settle. Down the corridor, she could hear screams and shouting from nearby cabins.

In a few moments: stillness. She pulled down the window, letting in a blast of air. Looking down the curved track, she couldn't see what had happened, only the thick, winter dark. Other windows were opening.

"Well, I bet you weren't expecting a train crash," she said, turning back to the camera on her phone. "And neither was I, though my life has been one for a long time. But Grant will be here soon, so I need to tell you. I need to speak." She took a deep breath and looked directly at the camera, knowing her eyes would be wide, her pupils huge. "He was amazing at first. The ultimate romantic. My therapist called it love-bombing. But soon he—"

Meg stopped. The door was opening. A foot was in the door. Grant's. She felt relieved at first, saying, "Grant, oh it's—"

Then he walked in, closed the door. He had that look on his face. "Please, don't—" But the words turned to coal dust in her throat. His hands reached for Meg's neck.

She stepped back, fumbling her phone and turning off the recording by mistake. She dropped it on the floor, and his heel smashed down on the screen. She raised her hands to her face. She didn't need to be psychic to know. This *was* the night she died.

Chapter One

December 23rd

It was the night before the night before Christmas. Not one car was stirring on Regent Street. The traffic jam hadn't budged in ten minutes. The taxi meter still moved though, racking up pounds and minutes.

"What time's your train?" the taxi driver said, turning down the radio and craning around.

"Nine fifteen," Roz replied, eyes fixed on the clock. It was 8:50 p.m.

The driver tutted. "With this traffic? It'll take a Christmas miracle to get to Euston in time. You'll have to catch the next one."

"It's the sleeper," Roz said. "The last before Christmas. I have to get up to Scotland. My daughter's gone into labor, six weeks early."

The driver's eyes flicked to the photo on his dashboard of two small toddlers. A look of pain crashed across his face. She felt the urge to ask him about it, then put the thought aside. Not her circus, not her monkeys. She had her own mess of a life to clear up.

"I'd go another way," he said, "but everywhere's chocka. Accident on Charing Cross Road. Knock-on effect all the way up to Regent Street. Are there no trains other than overnighters?"

"All sold out," Roz said, holding up her phone. "I checked."

She lowered the window, hoping that the outside would distract her from the worries inside her head. Cold air burst in. Shoppers bustled past, muffled in scarves and hats. The London night sky had the lilac promise of oncoming snow. It reminded her of her daughter Heather's hair. Roz should be with Heather right now, holding her hand, bringing her snacks, filling up the birthing pool, whatever else she could do. She should've anticipated premature labor, but then she should've done many things in her life and hadn't. She'd promised at the start of Heather's pregnancy that she'd take early retirement from the Met and move back to Scotland a few months before the birth. The plan had been for Roz to help shore up the house to get ready for the storm of a new baby. But then Roz had chosen to tie up one last case before leaving, and now Heather had gone into premature labor. So, Roz wasn't there for her daughter. Again.

She checked her phone. No new WhatsApp messages from Heather or her fiancée Ellie. And the app for the sleeper train still showed it leaving on time.

The driver turned the radio back up. "December Will Be Magic Again" was playing. Kate Bush's voice soared and fell, as brittle and strong as snow. Roz used to love the song, but December hadn't been magic for a very long time.

Above her, the famous Regent Street angels spread their lit wings. They reminded her of Hannibal Lecter flaying a police officer in *The Silence of the Lambs*, then hanging him on the cage, a flensed angel. Probably not the festive associations they were going for. In the absence of celestial beings, she'd have to get to the station on her own.

"I'll jump out here," she said, grabbing her bags. "What do I owe you?"

The taxi driver stopped the clock. "Twenty-four pounds sixty," he said. He shrugged an apology.

Tapping her credit card on the machine, Roz added a tip and prayed to the Mastercard god that it would go through. A moment that felt like forever, then the receipt chugged out.

"Thanks," Roz shouted as she heaved her bags out of the taxi.

"Hope you all make it," the driver called out. He glanced again at the picture of his children and made the sign of the cross on his chest.

Chapter Two

Rucksack clumping against her back, squat suitcase at her side like a rolling Passepartout, Roz headed up the street to Oxford Circus Underground Station. Euston was only two stops away on the Victoria Line, then a quick walk across to the overground. Even so, it was going to be tight. She'd decided to take a taxi to avoid dragging her luggage around London and onto the Tube, but here she was, walking up Regent Street at its busiest. It was like being in a computer game, but instead of dodging zombies, she was trying to avoid shoppers such as the man coming toward her, holding rolls of wrapping paper like a Jedi forgetting he was wielding light sabers. Her suitcase squeaked as if sharing her anxiety.

She checked her watch as she stood on the escalator at Oxford Circus. Ten minutes till the sleeper left. A busker sang "Driving Home for Christmas," and she thought of seeing her new granddaughter's face. And what Heather's face would do if Roz missed the train.

On the platform, Roz dragged her suitcase through the crowd and onto the Tube. She stood by the doors, breathing in as they tried to close. The railcar smelled of sweat and coffee and clashing perfumes. The woman crammed next to her looked up at Roz. They shared the traditional Tube-commuter grimace that acknowledged the enforced intimacy.

Roz's arms were pinned to her sides so she couldn't look at her watch, but still she felt time running away from her. Claustrophobia closed in. She took a breath, trying to fend off a flashback. Too late. She was thrown back into the memories, as if the rape was happening now, not over thirty years ago. Of him on top of her as she begged him to stop. The smell of his Marlboro breath as he spat on her face.

"Are you okay?" the woman next to Roz said. She was eyeing the emergency cord. If she pulled it, Roz would never catch the train.

"I'm fine," Roz said, trying to hide her panic. She should've left even earlier. If all had gone according to plan, she would've been at the station an hour before departure. She should've foreseen an accident, or anything that could keep her away from her daughter. She was good enough at that herself.

Please let it be delayed, she thought, praying to God-knows-what. *Let it be late. Let there be snow on the tracks, a leaf on a window, whatever.* The darkest part of her even thought of a passenger on the line. But she didn't wish for that.

When the Tube train stopped at Euston, Roz squeezed out onto the platform, dodging commuters and shoppers. The escalator would take too long, so, holding tight to her suitcase, arm muscles screaming, she puffed her way up the stairs. As she entered Euston, she looked at the clock on the board.

21:18.

Her heart was a lift about to plummet, but she held the doors. All wasn't lost, not yet. She scanned the information board, trying to catch her breath.

21:15 Fort William. DELAYED.

Relief surged. She looked around the station. A baubled tree reached for the ceiling. Carol singers ding-donged merrily in the center of the concourse. Queues of people clutching snacks and paperbacks stretched out of shops. A man with reindeer antlers on his head waddled along pulling suitcases strained to bursting. All the emotional shades of Christmas were there, from people meeting loved ones off trains to the woman on her own, red parka hood up, trying to stopper sobs.

Roz felt the urge to go over to her, offer a hug, a tissue, a chunk of the whisky tablet—a sweet that was like fudge but Scottish, drier and better—she'd made that morning. Then she reminded herself of Heather's frosted words: "Don't you think it's time you looked after your family instead of everyone else, Mum?"

Turning away from the weeping woman, Roz instead went over to the information desk. She needed to know when the sleeper would be leaving. Last thing she wanted was to settle in for the wait, fall asleep, and miss it.

An elderly man at front of the queue was trembling. The bunch of roses and eucalyptus in his hand shook with him. "Aren't you supposed to put on coaches if the train is canceled?"

The woman behind the desk must've been no more than thirty, but her face was already lined, as if every customer complaint had etched its mark. "If alternative travel has been found, sir, then it will be on the board."

"What am I supposed to do?" he said. "I have to get up to Manchester. My family is expecting me."

"I'm so sorry, sir," the woman said. "Snow is causing safety issues on the line."

"But other trains are running."

"Judgments have to be made. Some lines will have more issues than others. Age of the tracks, the trains running, weather in certain places."

"But it's Christmas," he said in a small, high voice. Roz suddenly saw him as a young boy, learning for the first time that life wasn't fair.

The railway tracks across the woman's forehead doubled as she frowned. "I wish there was something I could do," she said, and Roz believed her. "You'll have to talk to someone at our head office. It arranges transit on occasions like this."

The man nodded slowly and walked away, now looking much older.

Roz hoped it would be a long time before her incoming granddaughter knew the injustices of the world. She checked her phone. A new WhatsApp had arrived from Heather:

HEATHER: Still in early labor. Already scoffed all the flapjacks Ellie made. She's making more in between my contractions. Wish I had some of your tablet. You on your way?

Roz thought about how to reply. Should she say that she had tablet in her bag ready to hand over the minute she arrived? Or maybe that she remembered the early stages of labor with Heather, how scared she'd been. How alone. How she tried not to access those memories at all, and how Roz's heart hurt for her daughter, then and now. Or maybe she should say sorry and all the other words that had been kept in their tin and never opened. What was the emoji was for that?

This wasn't the time though, and WhatsApp not the place. Instead, she tapped:

ROZ: Train delayed so I'm still at Euston. Eat all the flap-jacks! Be with you soon as. Love you, Mum x

Roz should've sent tablet up to Heather weeks ago. She had no idea why she hadn't. At work, her brain had been great at seeing how things came about. She could connect the railcars from what seemed to be an otherwise baffling and scattered train of events. But her own life? No chance. She didn't even have the excuse that tablet needed to be made fresh. Her tablet lasted at least a couple of months. She had tried to leave it longer once, to test whether it could last a year, but within a fortnight she had nibbled it to nothing.

"Excuse me, madam?" The woman behind the desk—Natalia, according to her wonky name tag—was talking to Roz. "Can I help you?"

"Have you got any more information on the sleeper to Fort William?" Roz asked. "It says 'delayed' but not when it's expected." The word "expected" reminded her of Heather and her labor. And of Roz's own labor. She shunted away the memories. She couldn't think about it. Not now.

Natalia tapped into the computer. A look of relief smoothed her face. "You're in luck. That's the only leg of the sleeper running. Usually the train splits at Edinburgh to go to different parts of the Highlands, but today the other routes are considered too dangerous."

"Lucky for me, then."

"And it looks like it'll be here within an hour or so." The crinkles of concern returned. "You're not getting off at one of the smaller stops, are you? Due to the delays, some of the little stations will be missed out."

"I'm going all the way to Fort William."

"Then you're golden," Natalia replied. "You'll be home for Christmas." Her smile was catching, spilling from her face to Roz's.

Natalia's smile deepened then faded as she looked past Roz and saw the frown on the next customer's face. Roz thanked her again, hoping that Natalia's Christmas improved from here.

As Roz crossed the concourse, she passed a drunk city twat in a floppy Santa hat. He wolf-whistled at a young woman dressed as an elf. Her face flushed and her shoulders slumped.

Roz knew his sort, as did so many. That feeling of being reduced. It had happened to her so many times, and worse. She'd joined the police to try and stop it happening to others. And she'd failed; her last case showed that more than anything.

She gave the young man her best inspector's stare.

"Fuck off, Grandma," he said, his face twisting into a snarl.

"I'm about to become a grandma, little boy, and proud of it. What would yours say if she saw you now?"

He paled. Looked down at the scuffed floor.

"Thought so."

He gave one last sneer. As he shuffled off, the elf turned to Roz and glared. "I can look after myself, you know." Then she walked away, tiny bells on her hat and shoes tinkling.

And that was exactly why Roz needed to leave the Met and this circus city. Let the monkeys look after themselves.

Chapter Three

A cappuccino cooled in the killer's hand. And the killer's hand shook. They knew that wasn't good enough, that they'd have to pull themselves together. The murder had to happen. The victim mustn't be allowed to live.

They watched people rush across the concourse, all wanting to get home. Many seemed worried about the delays and cancellations, or maybe about a fraught family Christmas that would meet them at the end of the train line. The killer wished that was all there was to worry about.

The killer tried to calm themselves by going through the plan. They had been on the Fort William sleeper three times recently—they knew the train, the terrain, and the stops like the premature lines on their face. The killer had never left anything to chance in their lives, not since they'd met the victim anyway, but there were too many variables to control. Too many people on the train. But it would still be the easiest way to get near the victim. They would be alone at times, vulnerable. And stuck on a train overnight with their killer.

Knowing that didn't help though. This would be the first time they'd killed anything other than the swarm of fruit flies that beset their bananas last summer. Now the killer felt like they had fruit flies in their stomach. Did all assassins feel like this? What if the killer got scared? What if, when it came to it, they couldn't commit murder?

But that was all it took. Commitment. And the killer had no problem with that. Not commitment to a cause, at least. They hadn't been able to fully commit to a person since, well... That was the reason they were here, after all.

When they'd arrived at the station and saw the train had been delayed, they'd almost turned around and gone home. Imagined Christmas without death on their hands, only on their plate. But then they'd seen the victim. Checking their likes on social media, looking at themselves in shop windows. The smile on their face that the killer knew was as fake as their tan and the lash inserts that fell out on their pillow. The killer had no choice but to kill.

They walked to the whistle-stop to stock up on snacks. On long train journeys, it paid to be prepared in case no food arrived. Once, the killer had had to subsist on a tangerine and a squat tube of Pringles from London to Edinburgh. Today, they bought a cheese and pickle sandwich, some nuts, and a Cadbury chocolate bar. They wouldn't be thinking of calories today. It was nearly Christmas after all, and there was murder to commit. They also bought a book then headed for the first-class lounge to wait for the train. They would fit in and smile.

A young couple walked by, swinging their clasped hands. They laughed and talked about the party they were off to. Christmas for them would probably be full of light and love and cinnamon kisses. The murderer-to-be was sure that they, along with the law, the police, judges and juries, the soaps and tabloids, would say it was wrong to kill at Christmas. But then they didn't know the victim's secrets. Not yet. When they did, they'd be sure to cheer the killer, and wish them a very merry Christmas.

Chapter Four

The first-class waiting lounge was bigger than Roz expected but still almost full. Spotting an armchair free near the back, she wove her way round the funky-shaped chairs and tables. Many of the voices she heard were Scottish, making her feel homesick in a way she hadn't been for years. She had long ago grown used to being in London, where the East-End-meets-Essex accent was as ubiquitous as weed smoke. Here, though, with the accents in different tartans, she already felt at home.

Reaching the chair, she put down her luggage, then explored the lounge. There were showers and changing rooms; tables of "free" crisps, biscuits, fruit, and pastries; and machines dispensing tea and fancy coffee. So, this was how the other half traveled. She loved trains but had never been first class before. Everyone at the police station knew she'd always wanted to go in a sleeping car and had bought her this ticket as part of her leaving present. Bucket list item well and truly ticked.

After helping herself to a coffee and muffin, she settled down, making sure she had a clear view of one of the departures screens. She took out her phone—her message had been seen but not replied to. She wondered whether Heather was having another contraction. Ellie would be there, giving Heather back rubs and having her hand squeezed till her bones groaned. Roz should be there too.

Roz got out her Mirror Cube from her bag to distract herself. She closed her eyes and just held it. The 3D puzzle was made up of different-sized pieces, each covered with looking-glass vinyl. She had twice been Inverness's Rubik's-cube "Young Champion" in the late 1980s and had never lost the urge to put everything right. As she started twisting, the voices outside and inside her head faded. The only noise she heard was the small click of shifting pieces as they found their place. All she thought about was how each reflective element related to the whole. She felt as smooth and calm as a mirror, her mind blank and unoccupied.

"Can't you leave it, Meg, just for one moment?" A voice cut through Roz's clicking. The man was a few seats away, talking to a gorgeous, glamorous-looking young woman applying mulled-wine-red lipstick that matched her nails. She was in her midtwenties or so, and had the sharp cheek, wrist, and collarbones of someone who picked at their food. Her face, though, was contoured to suggest even deeper shadows.

The man was the kind of handsome that didn't interest Roz. Gym-honed, tall-boned, tanned skin as smooth as paté. Her eyes slid off him as if he were greased. Designer bags surrounded the couple. "We're supposed to be going on holiday together, not with the whole world," he said. His legs, in sausage-skin-tight trousers, seemed to be going for a world record in manspreading.

"Keep your voice down, please," Meg whispered, glancing around to see who was looking. Roz bent her head to peer in her bag and pulled out a little cellophane twist of her homemade whisky tablet. She slowly unwrapped it—this way she looked busy. People never thought you were listening if you weren't looking at them directly. Roz had long ago perfected the art of watching and listening without appearing to, training herself to notice the tiniest things before people even spotted her. And as she was getting older, people noticed her less and less. She was being erased by age.

Another, younger, woman—in her early twenties Roz judged, although many girls looked older than they were—and her teenage brother weren't even trying to disguise their interest in Meg. They were sitting at the table next to the coffee machine, staring at her, mouths open.

Meg froze when she saw them, then smiled and waved. The young woman's hands went to her chest and she nodded slowly, as if she had been blessed by their attention. Meg then dabbed concealer onto the deep shadows under her eyes and put on a huge pair of sunglasses. She held her phone out on a sticklike contraption that fixed it in place, microphone clipped on. The phone itself was surrounded by a ring light that gave it a halo.

Meg smiled again, at the camera this time, and it was as if her presence was amplified. "Hi, everyone," she said. "Just thought I'd let you know—the train is delayed so you're going to have to wait for our train sleepover a little bit longer. Hang in there, put on comfy jammies, get your favorite festive drink and snacks, and we'll be seeing in Christmas Eve together *in no time.*" She sang the last three words, her voice soaring, while making the peace sign, head on one side.

The young woman next to the coffee machine sang along, out loud. She was also holding up a phone, probably filming the whole thing.

Roz popped the tablet in her mouth, then quickly googled: Meg, "in no time." She crunched through the grainy tablet and, as the spiced sweetness dissolved on her tongue, she read through the first page of results. Most were stills of Meg Forth winning a TV singing contest, holding a trophy, surrounded by glitter falling like snow, but there were also videos on YouTube and TikTok. Looked like she'd won the contest by singing "In No Time," a soaring pop ballad about loss of love and youth that Roz remembered hearing on the radio. The song had stayed at number one for weeks, then Meg had released an album that briefly hit the top of the charts before disappearing.

Meg had resurfaced a year later as a beauty and travel "influencer" and tabloid sidebar regular: Meg Forth flaunts her curves and shows off her new man, reality TV star Grant McVey. Grant, it seemed from Roz's swift Googling, had won *Britain's Best Boyfriend*, a short-lived TV show in which he and nine other men had tried to woo a bamboozled woman called Freya. Grant had won the hearts of the voting public, and later broke Freya's. He'd since been on a number of reality shows and met Meg on one of them. They'd split up a few times since due to, reading between the headlines, Grant's drunken nights and wandering eye. On the covers of magazines, Grant was always looking at Meg with adoration. Now, in the first-class lounge of Euston, he glowered at her, his fingers drumming on the table.

"I promise, no more till we're on the way." She reached out and held his knee. Meg's tone was low, reassuring. The kind Roz used when trying to appease people she knew would escalate a situation. "This is a break for us too. I just need to check in with followers regularly to show off my sponsors. But my priority is *you*." She then leaned forward and whispered something to Grant that Roz couldn't hear.

He nodded slowly, but his jaw clenched in anger. Reaching into his inside jacket pocket, he took out a huge brown vape stick in the shape of a cigar and a bottle of vape juice. He carefully refilled his e-cigar, then inhaled slowly. The vape stick hissed and crackled like a death rattle. Grant huffed a stream of vapor into Meg's face.

Meg laughed slightly but turned her head away. The look that crossed her face looked very much like fear. She opened her handbag and took out some white paper and a pair of sharp scissors with winged handles. She started cutting, curving the blades carefully. It was one of those paper doll chains, like Heather used to make. As Meg moved the paper around, Roz glimpsed a purple bruise on the inside of her upper arm. The kind of bruise Roz had seen in many cases of domestic violence.

But she shouldn't leap to that conclusion. And none of that was her business. Roz leaned back in her chair, took a sip of her drink, and tried to switch off the curiosity that had very nearly got her killed several times in her twenty-five-year police career. The coffee was good, even if she'd let it go too cold. And the muffin had that solid, nubbly top that came off in one piece, like a chocolate-chipped thatched roof. Roz never knew why the term "muffin top" was used as a term of disparagement. Same with "bingo wings." As far as she was concerned, they were positive: if you had a muffin top it meant you had eaten well; and if you had bingo wings i meant you'd won at bingo. And both of those things meant you'd lived.

"Bet you can't beat me."

"How much?"

Raised voices snagged her attention. Four kids, university students by the look of their striped scarves, were sitting round a table, holding cards in their hands. Roz couldn't see which game they were playing.

"I bought this for my parents' neighbors," one said, pulling out a cylinder of single malt Scotch from her rucksack and waving it with a magician's flourish in front of the other young woman's face. "You win, and it's yours. You could give your aunt more than that mug you painted." She smirked.

The young woman sitting next to her lowered her head. She had brightly colored hair, two plaits running like rainbow train tracks down to her shoulders. She looked older than the others, and yet younger too.

"Leave her alone, Beck," said the young man opposite. Tattoos of ivy crept from underneath his dark blue sleeves.

"You can shut up, Blake." Beck rolled her eyes.

"What is it with you?" the androgynous goth sitting next to Blake said. "Can't you find a way to not be unkind?" That, plus their blue-black hair, made Roz think of ravens, and also back to her teenage years of kohl and funereal lace. It was a look she loved and could return to now that she had retired.

"Sam, Sam, like most of life, you just don't get it. I'm helping her. Aren't I, Ayana?" Beck said to the other girl. Ayana barely nodded. "How else is she going to get on the team? And of all of us, she's the one with the most incentive to win the prize money."

"I need it too," Sam said. "If we won, I could do a master's."

"Sure, but think of poor Ayana. I don't think her mum and dad's market stall can stretch to dinner at an Italian restaurant, let alone MA tuition fees. And it's not like she's going to get funding or a sugar daddy to pay for her."

Ayana's head lowered.

They must be trying to get on *Geek Street*, Roz thought. It was an addictive quiz show that was a mixture of *University Challenge*, *Love Island*, and *Big Brother*. Teams from different universities lived in a studio made to look like a hall of residence, boning up on subjects and boning each other before competing at the end of each week. The public loved watching the nerds socialize, fall in love, and, best of all, fight—the *Mail* called it "Swots in a Box." Teams were whittled down until the eventual winners were given scholarships for research degrees. It was hard to get on the university teams; the students must be competing for the last places. It wasn't her choice of how to spend Christmas, but each to their own.

"I think," Sam said, staring with some fascination at Beck, "that you might be the most horrible person I've ever met."

"Good job I'm clever, then. Gives you all a chance to coast on my brilliance."

"Wow" was all Sam said in reply.

"Of course," Beck continued. "That means the three of you will be fighting it out for the remaining two spaces on my team. I should have left you all to it, instead of agreeing to come on this stupid trip. Still, as we're here, we might as well practice. I'll throw in a box of chocolates and the necklace I'm giving my mum."

Ayana blinked several times, took a deep breath. "And if I lose?"

"To be honest, I don't think you've got anything I want. But let's say your handbag."

Ayana pulled her handbag closer. It was made of red leather that had been worn to a mix of cracks and smoothness. She wrapped its faded straps around her wrist. "It was Mum's," she said.

Beck blinked and tipped her head on one side. "But you think you'll win, don't you? So, it doesn't matter. Or perhaps you don't think you should get on the team after all? Perhaps you should just nominate yourself as the substitute, and we can get this over with?"

"I can do it," Ayana said, so quietly that Roz hardly heard it. Roz wondered what kind of card game this could be. Not Snap, that was for sure.

"I can't watch," Sam said and stood up, tall as a goth poppy. They willowed over to the toilets.

Beck shuffled her cards, picked up the first one, frowned, then turned over the next. Roz didn't like the way she smiled. "Ayana Okoro," Beck said, in the low and showy voice of an eighties quiz show host. "You must name a capital city for every letter of the alphabet."

A quiz. Roz loved a quiz. She'd been on the station pub-quiz team for years and was known as one of the best and most competitive quizzers, until the third gin of the evening kicked in and she started giggling, finding everything a hoot. She stored up facts and images in the same way that she hoarded toiletries from hotel rooms.

"Ask her something else," the tattooed boy said. His voice had urgency inked into it.

"Shut up, Blake," Beck snapped. "You've got sixty seconds, Ayana. Your time starts…" She took a small sand timer from her bag and turned it over. "Now!"

"Ankara," Ayana said, her eyes closing as she concentrated. "Beijing, Caracas, Damascus, Edinburgh…"

As cities passed from Ayana's lips at high speed, a baby wearing a reindeer onesie crawled into view, heading toward Roz. Their little antlers wobbled as they pulled themselves up on Roz's table leg.

"Hello," Roz said. The baby gave a two-toothed grin and let go of the table. Roz reached out an arm, grabbing the little one as they almost fell. The weight of the baby made her heart feel swaddled.

"Thank you," a man in his thirties or so whispered, running up to her and scooping up the baby. "This is Buddy. He's developed a turbo crawl."

"Hello, Buddy," Roz said.

Buddy grinned again as he was tucked into the sling across his father's chest.

"How old is he?" Roz asked.

"Seven months." His voice stayed quiet, even though the baby was clearly awake. "Somehow, we have to keep him, our toddler, Robert, and our older kids out of trouble all the way to the Highlands." He gestured toward the tables where his eldest children sat. The boy, a teenager, Roz guessed, was wearing a Metallica T-shirt, bless him, and the young woman a striped dress. She was still staring at Meg in awe. Behind them, an older woman wrangled a wriggling Robert into a jumper.

"Your two seem enthralled by the celebs."

Phil glanced quickly over to Meg and froze. He was staring straight at her, but not with the same adoration as his children, instead something that looked like fear. He turned back to Roz. "You know what young people are like."

"You're on the sleeper too, then?"

He looked away from Meg and half smiled. "Yes, up to Fort William, though I reckon it's called the sleeper just to spite us." The deep shadows under his eyes suggested he hadn't gotten a solid night's sleep in a long time.

"Anyway, I'm Phil, and my wife is Sally."

"Phil!" Sally called over, "Some help needed here." Antagonism, or maybe just extreme tiredness, simmered in her voice.

Phil gave an apologetic smile to Roz, then hurried over to where his toddler was now throwing packets of sugar over the floor.

"Ulaanbaatar," Ayana continued, "Vaduz, Warsaw…" She stopped, her lips moving as if trying to close around a capital beginning with "X." Roz started to search for one, then realized that's what Blake had been worried about. There wasn't one.

Sam returned and stood, hovering, between the tables.

"Time's nearly up," Beck said, her face settling into that smirk again. Roz's mind clicked through ways to remove it.

Then the pieces settled, reflecting the answer.

"She's already finished," Roz said.

Beck turned to look at her, face contorted into the prettiest of snarls. "What?"

Roz smiled back. "You meant the Scottish Gaelic alphabet, right? Which doesn't have an X, Y, or Z." Five years of Gaelic lessons from her aunt and a fascination with languages had been good for more than road signs and impressing dates. The women she'd dated, though, had been generally more impressed than the men.

"Which means she has completed the task in time!" Sam clapped their hands.

Blake smiled, so did Ayana. "Thank you," she said.

"That's cheating," Beck said.

"And how is it fair that you meant, but didn't say, the Gaelic alphabet? You knew we'd be assuming it was modern English." Blake folded his arms.

"Then you shouldn't presume anything. Ayana wouldn't get help like that in the TV studio. We are supposed to be operating under—"

"Who said she didn't know already?" Blake replied. "Give her the stuff."

Emotions stormed across Beck's face. Her chin jutted as she handed Ayana the whisky and a box of posh chocolates. She was reaching for her suitcase, presumably to get the necklace, when Ayana said, "Not the jewelry. You should give it to your mum." Her voice cracked, and Roz could hear the unsaid under the skin. She knew Ayana wouldn't be able to give anything to her mum again, just like Roz couldn't to hers.

"How generous of you," Beck said, but she was staring at Roz. Roz held her gaze until Beck glanced away, then got up for another coffee.

As Roz approached the table of food and drinks, stepping through a maze of suitcases, she saw the same woman who'd been crying on the concourse. She was younger than Roz by at least ten years and was stuffing complimentary biscuits, crisps, and fruit into her rucksack like it was a canvas stocking. Her thin fingers trembled. Realizing Roz was watching, she jumped. A guilty Santa in a red parka. She didn't return Roz's conspiratorial smile.

"Don't worry," Roz said, picking up several packets of shortbread and then, after holding them up, placing them in her pocket. "You're not doing anything wrong. I should know, I'm a—" She stopped. Tried again. "I *was* a police officer."

The woman's eyebrows showed her surprise, although Roz wasn't sure if it was the legality of her actions or that Roz had been on the force. She then gave Roz a half smile and went to get a cup of tea.

The nearby door of the first-class lounge opened. A man in his sixties, with hair the color of city-grayed snow, helped a very elderly woman walk slowly through. She looked as frail as paper chains.

"We don't have tickets to let us in the lounge," he said to the woman behind the desk, who checked everyone's tickets as they entered. "But our train's delayed, and Mum needs somewhere warm and comfy."

"I told you not to make a fuss, Tony," the elderly woman said. Her voice was strong and deep. "It's only an hour or so."

"You're in pain, Mum." Tony's face contorted, looking in as much distress as his mother.

"Never let someone know how much discomfort you're in, Tony," his mum said. Roz wondered what she had been through to have to say that. Not that she disagreed. In Roz's experience, showing vulnerabilities only led to people exploiting them.

"I'm afraid we can't make exceptions," the ticket checker said. She fiddled with her fingers, clearly uncomfortable.

Tony placed his hands in the prayer position. "I was hoping that as it's Christmas…" He left the sentence hanging, hoping it would be filled with a gift.

"Nothing I can do."

Tony turned to go, and Roz saw he was wearing a cat carrier on his back. Through the sheer mesh, a huge tortoiseshell cat blinked at Roz.

Roz walked up to the desk. "I'm happy to give up my place for…" She left a space for the older woman to say her name.

"Mary. And before you say it, I'm not looking for a room for the night. Just a wee sit-down in the warm. But Mousetache here"—she pointed to the cat—"is really used to better treatment."

The ticket checker looked from Roz to Mary to Mousetache. Roz could see she was relenting. From the sound of his purring, Mousetache thought so too. In her peripheral vision, Roz saw Grant by the buffet table, listening to their conversation. Maybe he wasn't so bad—maybe he'd give up his place too, so Tony could stay here with his mum.

Grant came over. "You should've bought a proper ticket if you want to come in here," he said. "Your mum can't be feeling that rough if you haven't put her in first class. Or you don't love her. One of the two."

"That's not how it works," Roz said. She could feel her anger rising. "Not everyone can afford it."

"Then they can't have it." His hands were on his hips. Muscles strained against his designer shirt. "We work hard for these tickets. It makes a mockery of us if you get it for free. It's stealing."

"No one is thieving anything," Mary said to him, eyes spiked like holly leaves. "This young lady has graciously given me her seat. And you, boy, should learn some manners."

Grant seemed to grow taller. His shoulders shifted in their shirt. He took out his vape cigar and took a drag.

"You can't vape in here, sir," the ticket checker said nervously.

Grant exhaled vapor that smelled of sweet Christmas spices. "My mistake," he said, with a grin people sometimes described as wicked when they meant charming. Roz knew, though, that he was in no way charming. "Won't happen again."

Meg hurried over and placed her hand on Grant's flexed bicep. "Come and help me get things from the buffet, would you, love? Don't think I can do much with these nails." She waggled her slender fingers with their dark red acrylic extensions. Seeing as she had been operating a camera phone and making paper decorations earlier with no problem whatsoever, Roz reckoned this was a well-practiced distraction.

Grant rolled his eyes but followed Meg over to the table. She started picking up random packets and placing them in his hands. He looked down at them then, loud enough for everyone to hear, said: "Are you trying to kill me?"

Meg looked up, startled.

Grant dropped several packets of crisps and held up a small bag of peanuts. "You know I can't eat these. And if they're for you, then we need separate rooms. No, fuck that, a different train."

"Do you mind keeping it down?" Beck shouted across the lounge. "We're doing something actually important over here."

Grant didn't even turn to look at Beck, just said "Mind your own fucking business, bitch," and stared at Meg.

"I didn't mean…" Meg said. "I didn't know they were there. I would never…"

Grant threw the bag of peanuts, hard, in Meg's face. Meg backed away, her hand going to her temple. Grant advanced toward her.

Roz marched over, standing between Meg and Grant. "I suggest you stop there, unless you want to be charged with common assault or even battery."

Grant's laugh was full of derision. "Come on, it's nothing. What's it got to do with you anyway? And why are all you women giving me grief?"

"I used to be in the police," Roz said. "I know the law." She also knew that the law and the people who enforced it were inadequate. It was partly why she'd had to resign. Too many victims not getting justice.

Another passenger strode over. "How about you go back to your seat, mate, and stop throwing things at people." The man was in his early fifties, thinner and taller than Grant, and shabbily handsome. Next to Grant and Meg, he stood out like a run-down old house in a row of new builds. He seemed oddly familiar, and Roz felt a strong pull toward him.

Grant eyeballed the man in silence. Then walked away, shaking his head.

Of course he listened when a man spoke up. That was how those sort of men operated.

Tony pointed at the announcement board over the reception desk. "Our train's arrived."

Roz checked—the sleeper was here. People in the room also stood and started to gather their luggage. Looked like many of them were off to the Highlands tonight.

Including the shabbily handsome man.

Chapter Five

Meg watched as Grant picked up her suitcase and slung it over his shoulder. It was stuffed with all the clothes, wigs, and cosmetics she'd been sponsored to wear over Christmas, but he made it seem as light as his jacket. He forged ahead, pulling his own suitcase behind him. Meg had once asked, laughing, why he had a bulletproof case when he didn't wear a bulletproof vest. His reaction was the reason why she hadn't asked, or laughed at him, since.

"Wait up, baby," she said. She tried to dodge her way through the crowd but couldn't help knocking into people. She had little spatial awareness at the best of times, but when carrying fancy shopping bags, she had no chance.

He stopped and turned to her. His eyes had no softness in them. "You should get your face on. There may be press when we get near the platform."

Which meant there definitely would be photographers, and that he'd called them. Their relationship with the press was circular—photos of them looking happy, photos of them in crisis, photos of Meg looking sad and fatter, photos of Meg happy and thin again in her "new body."

"I've already got enough makeup on, I think."

"I'd trowel on some more." He kissed her face and held her chin.

Looking deep into her eyes, he whispered, "I know how you don't like to look old."

Meg felt like a Coke can crushed under his feet.

She watched as Phil left with his beautiful family. She felt a pang of sadness. Grant had never treated her like that.

"What are you waiting for?" Grant asked, gesturing to her face again, already looking past Meg to the other passengers. His eyes landed on one of the students, traveling up and down her body.

Meg bit the inside of her cheek but did as directed, opening the door to the toilets and escaping inside. The latest batch of samples were soon laid out on the tiny shelf in the cubicle. She was constantly sent freebies and promos in the hope that she'd mention them on Insta or TikTok. And she did, when she could. She liked to help small companies, especially ones with natural products. The more handmade and homespun the better.

They were unlikely, though, to turn back the clock to before she started worrying about wrinkles. Not that she could remember such a time. She was twenty-four and had been freezing her forehead for years to fight the frown lines, but she still feared them appearing. One of her earliest memories was sitting on the floor, watching Mum as she put her hands on either side of her face, pulling back the skin and saying, "I used to be so pretty. So young. Never get old, darling."

Meg quickly tested the new eye products—drops and peptide-rich mascara, from a wild-grown cosmetic company—and finished by dotting a shimmer of white shadow in the corner of each eye. That should make her look more wide-eyed and awake.

Grant hammered on the toilet door. "Hurry up, the train's boarding."

Meg took a last look in the bathroom mirror. Her face would have to do.

Chapter Six

The atmosphere in the scrum waiting to get onto the platform was both bristly and festive. Nearby, a busker played "I Wish It Could Be Christmas Every Day" on an electric harp while people jostled behind Roz, impatient to stop being patient.

Near the front of the queue at last, Roz got out her phone to see if there were any more messages from Heather. Nothing. Just ahead of her, Sally and her family were signaled through onto the platform by a stressed-looking guard. A man moved quickly behind them, his head down.

"Can I see your ticket, sir?" the guard shouted after him as another security guard chased him down. The man was escorted away, taken right past Roz as she showed her ticket. His eyes darted back and forth as if still desperate to find a way through. Everyone wanted to find a way home for Christmas.

Roz's sleeper car was over halfway down the train: her step count today was going to be mighty. Her rucksack was getting heavier and heavier, and her suitcase had developed a plaintive whine to add to its squeak.

As she neared her railcar, she heard the quizzers from earlier already in the sleeping car next to hers. The four of them were standing outside two interconnecting rooms.

"Dibs on the top bunk," Beck said.

"But…" Ayana said.

"What?"

"Nothing."

Beck looked round to see Roz standing behind them. She was holding Ayana's red handbag and raised it to show Roz. Roz doubted she was carrying it out of kindness—Beck must have dared Ayana again. And this time won.

"Oh, no, are we in your way?" Beck asked sarcastically as she moved with exaggerated steps into their cabin. Roz hadn't intended to enter the train here, but now she would, just to inconvenience Beck.

"Sorry," Blake said, as both he and Sam backed away. Roz grinned at them both and glared at Beck.

"Thank you," Ayana whispered as she flattened herself against the wall when Roz walked past her. "For earlier."

Roz smiled. "No bother."

In her little cabin, Roz placed her case and coat on the bed and looked around. Decorated in plaid with blue and orange accents, the room was mostly taken up with a double bed. The gift bag, waiting for her on the white duvet, contained a sleep kit of toiletries, eye mask, and ear plugs. There was a sink under the window and a tiny toilet that doubled as a shower room. Perfect.

"Trust you to get on the wrong railcar," Sally said from the corridor outside as she and her family passed Roz's door.

"I was only one out," Phil said, with the weariness of one who felt he was always in the wrong. They all trudged to the end of the railcar to enter the same sleeping car as the students.

Roz's first reaction was to be glad they weren't next to her in case the baby kept her awake all night, then guilt surged like a sea loch tide. She'd have to get used to the sounds of a baby again.

Lying down on the bed, Roz phoned Heather. She had to know what was happening.

After five rings, it was answered. "Everything all right, Roz? Are you on the train now?" It was Ellie, Heather's fiancée.

"I'm in my wee cabin," Roz said. "We should be leaving soon. How's it going?"

"Contractions still ten minutes apart. Have been for a few hours. The midwife is on her way." Roz could hear Heather pacing and swearing in the background.

"How is Heather?"

Ellie laughed softly. "She's bored with waiting. Reckons that if the little 'un's coming early, then least she could do is hurry up. Says it's like a dinner guest who arrives by six but hasn't brought wine or gossip."

"That's the problem with babies. They don't bring their own bevvies."

A timer went off. "Flapjacks are ready. Better go."

"Give Heather my love," Roz said. It didn't feel like nearly enough.

"Will do." Just before Ellie rang off, Roz heard "Wish You Were Here" playing in the background. It was on Heather's birth playlist. The only soundtrack Roz had listened to while giving birth was of her own bellows. Heather had shared her playlist to Roz via Spotify a few weeks ago. It consisted of Eno, Pink Floyd, Atomic Rooster, Yes, Deep Purple, and Goblin among others. The idea of giving birth to *Suspiria* or *Profondo Rosso* felt profoundly wrong, but then Heather's musical predilections were far away from Roz's love of Kate Bush and Fleetwood Mac. They were more like those of Roz's mum, Liz, who had basically brought Heather up. But that wasn't the point; Heather was the one giving birth. Roz had even messaged, saying Love your Preg Rock playlist, but Heather hadn't appreciated the pun. She must have got her lack of humor from her dad. Whoever he was.

Memories of being pregnant had swelled when Heather told her she was going to have a baby, along with flashbacks to the birth. It's said that you forget the pain of delivery—that hormones eat away at the horror and leave you with the oxytocin-soaked awe and all-consuming love. Nature's way of ensuring further pregnancies.

Roz, though, had yet to forget. Even now, though she knew she was on a train, she could feel those memories pressing in on her. She had managed to keep them beneath the surface for so long, but since Heather fell pregnant, Roz's flashbacks had become far worse. Each day, she remembered a detail of her daughter's birth. The peppermint-cream-colored delivery room where she labored for hours before having an emergency C-section. The stain on the ceiling tile above her head that looked like a scar. The heartbeat monitor strapped to her belly setting off alarms. The kindness in the midwife's eyes that curdled into fear. The smell of bleach and blood.

And then there were the other memories. The ones that were attached like an umbilical cord. Those flashbacks were far worse. Louis, a rape counselor Roz had often contacted to help survivors, always said "trauma sticks to trauma." And lying down, unable to move due to a paralyzing drug, while her body was hurt and entered by a stranger... Of course the birth trauma had attached itself to the rape.

Roz's chest tightened, as she felt herself plummet into the memory of that dark room. She picked up her mirrored cube, twisting away the memories. She had to stay in the present, not get dragged under into flashbacks. She was here, right now, a forty-nine-year-old on a sleeper train, not a young pregnant woman raped on a night out or that same young woman in a maternity ward.

She focused on the picture of Fort William on the wall above the bed, at the hills that had always called to her, no matter how far away. She was heading north, heeding them at last. And she was going to her daughter and her daughter's daughter. If Roz had anything to do with it, she was going to make December magic again. Somehow.

Roz popped the cube in her handbag, picked up her card key, and opened the door. Time to have a very late tea. As the whistle blew and the train began to move, the man who had tried to get on without a ticket ran past her. He couldn't have bought a ticket as it was sold out, so he must be a stowaway. But this was not a circus train, and he was not a monkey. She continued on to the club car.

Chapter Seven

Meg sat cross-legged on the bed, looking around the cabin. To cheer herself up, she'd given it a literal glow up, stringing fairy lights across the sink and up over the curtains, as well as decorations she'd made herself. She'd finished the train of paper women, complete with skirts and drawn-on buttons and Christmassy patterns. She'd also made paper chains. Her mouth was still dry from licking the gummed edges, but it'd been worth it. The double cabin now had an orange glow, as if she were sitting in her own pumpkin carriage. A very suitable way to be taken all the way to Scotland to get married. Not that Grant knew that yet. She was going to spring it on him later. Maybe that would make him love her more.

"Do you like it?" she asked Grant, sweeping an arm around the room.

"I love it," he replied, but he wasn't looking. He was at the door of their cabin, filling his e-cigar, then putting spare bottles of vape juice in his jacket pocket. "I need a drink."

"Wait," Meg said, rootling in her handbag, "for the final touch." She pulled out a crumpled paper bag and wafted it back and forth, smiling.

"What's in there?"

"It's why I went to Colombia Road early this morning." She plucked the bunch of mistletoe from the bag, held it over her head, and patted the bed with her other hand. She wasn't moving till Grant came over and gave her a kiss. It was tradition.

Grant sighed, but smiled anyway, even if it was a bit patronizing, like she was a child he had to placate. He walked across the tiny space, leaned over, and kissed her, hands stuffed in his pockets.

Meg bounced on the bed, legs still crossed, like she was levitating, something she'd also tried on *Celebrity Ashram*. She loved Christmas so much. It was the time of year when, as a child, she could pretend everything was going to be okay. It was all about that magic when hostilities briefly stopped and candles were lit, and there were board games and distracting toys and food enough to quell arguments. There had even been a twenty-four-hour ceasefire between her mum and dad, like in the First World War, where the two sides played football on Christmas Day, then continued trying to kill each other on Boxing Day.

She stood on the bed, ducking under the ceiling, and balanced the mistletoe on top of the painting of a mountain. It looked like white-berried holly on top of a Christmas pudding, and hung as a blessing over their bed.

"Good evening and welcome to the delayed 21.15 sleeper to Fort William," said a bass voice from the speaker in the corridor outside. "Calling at Crewe, Preston, Glasgow, Dunbarton, Rannoch, and Fort William for definite. Due to the delay, ongoing snow, and expected storm, we won't be calling at all our usual stations, so please check with a steward about how to undertake connecting trains to your required destinations." The man took a deep breath before continuing. "If you have tickets to Watford Junction or our other highland routes, Inverness and Aberdeen, then I'm afraid you'll have to get off the train and find alternative arrangements. We're sorry for the delay and hope to make up time on the way, but again, weather conditions may make that difficult. Passengers in cabins can order room service and have first-come-first-served access to the club car, where a light dinner and drinks will be served. Those seated can also order from the steward. Please settle yourselves into your cabins or seats, familiarize yourself with the facilities, and enjoy this beautiful journey."

The train then started with a gentle jolt. As Meg clapped her hands in excitement, the mistletoe fell from the top of the mountain.

Chapter Eight

The club car was buzzing when Roz entered. It was too hot and smelled of coffee, whisky, and a not-unpleasant mix of tatties, Mackie's crisps, and cheese. Four orange and blue booths with tables took up one side of the railcar, and seven tiny triangular tables lined the other like a toppled Toblerone.

The booths each sat four people, six at a squish, and the strip of beige plaid covering the headrests gave Roz a reminder, if one were needed, that she was heading home. Three of the booths were full: the quizzing students were in one (Quizlings, Roz thought she'd call them, notes and revision cards on the table); another contained the family Roz had met in the first-class lounge; and in the adjacent booth, a couple shared a clootie dumpling, feeding each other spoonfuls of the fruited pudding across the table. Oh to be in love.

Roz felt a pang of envy and looked around, as casually as she could, for the shabbily handsome man, but he wasn't there. She was surprised by the strength of her disappointment. Ayana looked up as Roz passed. She smiled, then checked to see if Beck was watching.

Roz went up to the bar at the end of the railcar and ordered food and a scotch from a steward called Oli, a youngish fellow with a big wonky grin. She carried her drink over to one of the few free triangular tables and sat on the moveable spinning chair. From here, she could look out of the window at shadow-smoked London while simultaneously seeing a reflection of the whole club car. She took a sip of whisky. It tasted of chocolate, peat, and Highland toffee. A hint of smoke lay over her palate like the ghost of a steam train.

She breathed out. Everything was going to be okay, she told herself. She would get there and begin to make everything up to Heather, however long it took. At the table next to her, a gentleman in a green plaid suit sat reading a book of Christmas poetry, his long thin legs crossed like a cricket. He had the look of someone who both recited Dickens and really knew how to party. Not that it was kicking off in here, not yet. Like ice cubes in second-best whisky, dinner being served and the childlike excitement of being on a sleeper reduced the temperature of the room and diluted the strength of feeling. But ice cubes disappeared, and even a watered-down drink knocked back had the same effect on the bloodstream. Roz gave it ninety minutes before it was Hogmanay wild in here. She wasn't sure that the railcar could take it.

At one time, Roz would have welcomed a party atmosphere. Joined in with an abandon that had made her mother despair. Her late teenage and early university years were filled with clubbing and pubbing, a blur of beds filled with boys or girls or girls and boys. She couldn't remember the names or faces—they had vanished into locked memory vaults—but she could recall so clearly the electricity in the streets on a big night out, before the assault had stopped her from ever clubbing again.

Decades of being on the force had also shown her evenings like that led to blood. One way or another. She could sense it in the train already, as if trouble waited for them at the end of a long tunnel. The club car would be a limbo space. A nowhere zone where anything went, the same way that a stag or hen night, or any trip to another town, always led to vomit on pavements and values left at home. Roz had been on duty too many bank holiday Mondays and full moon Fridays to ever relax when that feeling was in the air.

For now, though, she had peace. And, most importantly, cheese. Oli had placed the platter in front of her. Pale hunks of Orkney and Arran cheddars hunkered like standing stones on the slate. A Hebridean Brie looked pleasingly squidgy, and the Mull of Kintyre blue was as pale and vein-threaded as Roz's thighs. Cheese was for life, not just for Christmas, but there was something particularly festive about a cheese board. The spices in the chutney, maybe, or perhaps there was something primal about the way everyone came at it with knives—a sacred and communal whittling of the cheese wheel of the year. This board, though, was just for her. As she cut a slice of cheddar, popped it on an oatcake, and dolloped on apple chutney, her stomach rumbled in casein anticipation.

"Do you mind if I sit here?" The woman in the red parka stood next to Roz, pointing to a spare seat next to her.

"It's no bother," Roz replied. "Help yourself."

The woman placed down her drink and sat, still wearing her coat. "Sorry about earlier," she said. She was in her thirties or so, hair high-lighted in salt and caramel. "I was embarrassed."

"You should see me at a buffet breakfast. I make enough cobs to last for days."

"I'm Ember." She stuck out her hand and Roz shook it. Ember's hand and grip were both soft.

"Roz." Her tummy burbled again.

"Please, eat," Ember said. "I won't disturb you."

Roz took a nibble. The cheese had just the right amount of bite, and the oatcakes made her think of the ones her mum used to make. The recipe for them might even be in her cabin, right now. Roz's mum, Liz, had died that September, leaving Roz with a lot of guilt, a house in Fort William, and a handmade recipe book.

The recipe book was in one of Roz's bags, filled with recipes Liz had invented and clippings from magazines, with her commentary on food and life and love. It was her diary, her memoir, a foodie Book of Shadows. Liz had kept the book close to her chest and heart, only sharing a photocopied recipe or two with Roz on special occasions. The recipes for tablet and shortbread were two of the few she'd given to her daughter, and Roz had always prized those rare pages and their wisdom, sometimes related to ingredients (*always use freshly grated nutmeg, never from a jar. And make sure the nut isn't old—if it looks too much like a testicle, discard immediately,*); sometimes equipment (*it is wise to have a spatula to hand at all times. It is not only essential in baking but also useful for swatting away flies and unwanted attention from men.*); occasionally on gardening (*I've found that growing basil in between tomato plants keeps the bugs away,*); but mainly her notes contained advice for everyday living (*learn to say sorry, early and often, but only if you've done something wrong, and only if you mean it. While I'm here, you should know, Rosalind, that I'm sorry if I've ever been offhand with you, or not loving enough. And for any trouble you have with me when I'm even older and more infirm.*)

Roz knew the book, shipped to her London address after the will was read, would contain her mum's thoughts leading up to her death. Which was why Roz had yet to read it.

She would have to though. And soon. It most likely contained ideas for food that Roz could make over Christmas. When Roz didn't know how to express love, she made food. And when she didn't know how to feel, she ate it.

Ember plucked a slender book out of her handbag—*Murder on the Orient Express*. It was years since Roz had read it. She'd adored Christie as a teenager, but once she'd become a cop there'd been more than enough murder.

Ember saw her looking. "I've been dreaming of going on a sleeper train since I first read this."

Roz laughed. "That's like watching *Don't Look Now* and booking a lagoonside honeymoon suite in Venice."

"Why do you think I'm wearing this coat?" Ember's smile, however, contained the smoke of sadness.

The image of her in the station came into Roz's head. "Are you okay?" she asked, before she could stop herself. "I saw you crying earlier, on the concourse."

"I was worried the train would be canceled, and I wouldn't be able to go home."

"Is that all?" Roz asked.

Ember met Roz's reflected gaze in the window, then looked away. "I've also had some romantic bad luck. It's nothing though."

"By that do you mean it's not nothing, but you'd rather not talk about it?"

Ember laughed. "Yes."

"Fair enough. I keep trying to tell myself to keep out of people's bins and business. Force of habit on the force. Where were we before I poked my nose in again? Ah yes, the train! I've dreamed of going home on the sleeper for years. Tomorrow morning we'll wake to winter sun on the lochs."

Ember lifted her drink. "To sleeping on a sleeper." They clinked glasses.

In the window, Roz saw Meg and Grant enter the club car. Meg slipped into the remaining booth while he stalked to the bar, taking a wedge of banknotes from his wallet. "My girlfriend's hungry, have you got anything without bread, potatoes, or tomatoes? She's a 'picky eater.'" He placed the last words in air quotes. "Oh, and champagne," he said in a voice that didn't need to be so loud.

Oli pointed out three different brands, and Grant glanced over at Meg before choosing the most expensive.

Roz rolled her eyes. Ember laughed—a little too loudly, according to the look Grant gave her. She gazed at the floor in response.

"Don't mind him," Roz said, also loud enough to be heard. "He's a prick without any standing."

Grant's mouth opened, then closed. He glared as he went back to his table, bottle in one hand, flutes held like sparkling knuckle-dusters in the other.

Ember stared at Roz. "How do you do that?"

"Do what?"

"Speak out. Speak up for people."

"I try not to. It gets me in trouble."

"But that doesn't stop you?"

"I wish it would. The words run out the door before I can close it. It's why I never got higher than inspector."

"So speaking up doesn't work either," Ember said, nodding slowly.

"At least it feels like doing something rather than nothing."

"I've never done enough."

"Give it a go. But remember it gets you in trouble."

Ember nodded, and their conversation died down.

Roz stared out of the window. The movement of the train made the lights of every building seem connected, as if London was strung up with fairy lights.

Roz refocused to look at Grant and Meg, reflected in the window. He was glancing her way, top lip curled. Meg stroked his arm, then pointed to the bottle and put her hand to her chest in thanks.

Phil was slowly making his way out of the booth, holding his sleeping children. The baby was fastened to him, and Robert was draped over one arm like a chubby coat. "You take your time," he said to Sally.

Sally held up her drink. The table lamp behind her gave the glass an amber glow. "I intend to."

"And Aidan, Liv, don't stay up too late," Phil said to his older children.

Liv crossed her arms. "Dad, I'm twenty-one in three days."

"You'll need your sleep to deal with Granny."

"What's that supposed to mean?" Sally's voice was sharp.

"Nothing," Phil said, holding up his free arm as if surrendering.

"Dad means Gran's a nightmare," Liv said, folding her arms. "He doesn't want us to set her off. Good job that doesn't run in the family, eh, Mum?" Her sarcasm was snowdrift-thick.

"Anyway," Phil said. "Time this pair were in bed and for me to get a bit of sleep. There's at least two whole hours before the baby's next bottle." He started edging crablike toward the door, facing away from the booths as if trying to avoid someone.

"Mr. Bridges?" Meg called out as he passed her table. The excitement in her voice was clear. "Phil?"

Phil froze. His mouth opened, but he said nothing. The baby shifted his head against Phil's chest as if he heard his dad's heartbeat speeding up. The conversation in the club car turned down in volume as everyone listened.

Meg scrambled out of her booth. Behind her, Grant folded his arms. His jaw moved side to side.

Phil turned round, his back now to Roz. His shoulders were trying to disappear behind his ears.

"How long has it been?" Meg said. She was standing in front of Phil. Her elfin face was just visible from where Roz was sitting. Meg looked up at him with the kind of intensity that didn't appear in the tabloid photos.

"Seven years, I suppose," Phil said. "We've been in London that long."

"Are you still teaching?"

Phil hesitated a moment, then shook his head. "I was at a university till recently, but we've decided I'll take a career break until these two are both in school and nursery. They keep me busy."

"I bet," Meg said. "They are so cute!"

"They take after their mother," Phil said, nodding over toward Sally. "You remember Sally, don't you?" Roz caught the faintest breath of warning in his tone.

"Of course," Meg said, smiling but not turning to acknowledge Sally in the booth.

Sally didn't smile. Her eyes were fixed on Phil's face.

"And I know how well you've been doing," Phil replied. "Can hardly pick up a newspaper or go online without you being there." His laugh went on too long.

"You'll be looking forward to being back in Fort William for Christmas, then?" Meg asked.

"Oh, yes. It's beautiful this time of year."

They were saying the boring things people do in social situations, packing the distance between them with muffling snow. Roz, however, could sense black ice beneath.

They were staring at each other. An atmosphere of strain built in the club car as people tried to work out what was going on. Roz wanted to cut the tension with the cheese knife.

Robert stirred over his dad's arm, dropping a well-loved toy giraffe on the floor. "Best go before this one kicks off," Phil said.

Meg bent and picked up the giraffe and tucked it next to Robert. Grant came out of the booth and stood behind Meg, placing his hands on her shoulders. His long fingers were hunched at the knuckles, resting like spiders on her clavicles.

"Is this the teacher you told me about?" Grant asked.

Phil froze again.

"Not exactly what I was picturing."

"Leave it, Grant," Meg said.

Grant was not going to leave it. Men like him never could.

"You told me he had terrible skin. Said it was like braille. Hairy, warty braille." Grant's voice was all sneer.

"I didn't say that, I promise." Meg was blinking at Phil, pleading with her big eyes. "I just said your skin used to be a bit…" She trailed off. Phil put his spare hand up to his face.

Grant rested his chin on the top of Meg's head and wrapped his arms round her, all the time staring at Phil.

Roz felt the air in the room tighten with testosterone. She had dealt with so many Grants. It'd take hardly anything for him to spill like a pint knocked over by an innocent passerby. And it wouldn't be Grant who ended up in hospital.

Grant moved Meg to one side, literally manhandling her, and stood a few inches away from Phil.

Roz could feel Ember looking at her, most likely wondering if she was going to do something. Roz, though, stayed seated. If she intervened, things would be more likely to escalate. You had to trust your gut. And her gut had served her well, both metaphorically and literally. She used to hate her tummy in her teens. Had tried to grab the tiny amount of fat showing in the mirror to show how gross she was. Now, Roz had grown to rather like her belly with its new menopausal flesh fluff and stretch marks that reached from her navel to C-section scar. She'd grown a human in there. Had an appendix taken out. Digested late-night kebabs and trauma.

But then, if you didn't say anything, sometimes it gave bullies carte blanche to continue.

"Bit weird to hang around with an old teacher, isn't it?" Grant said. "Creepy."

"I'm not that old," Phil said. "Not even forty yet." He didn't sound convinced though. Roz knew what it was like to feel old before your time.

"And how old was he when he was teaching you, bae?"

Roz was aware that "bae" was a term of endearment, either an abbreviation of "babe" or meaning "before anyone else," an acronym she hadn't been able to apply to anyone for a long time. Grant though, said "bae" as if it stood for "better accept everything."

"Are you going, Phil, or not?" Sally asked. Her voice was sharpened, puncturing Phil's paralysis.

"Yes, of course," he said and shuffled to the door.

Meg watched as he left. Her large eyes reflected the lamplights. The look on her face wasn't quite readable. If it were a train, it'd be somewhere on the line between fear and regret.

When the doors had closed behind him, Meg and Grant went back to their table. Meg's head was bent in supplication. She would somehow end up in the wrong and would clearly pay for it, in silence or worse.

Sally slammed her hands on the table. "Let's get the party started. I intend to get very drunk."

Liv placed her hands over her face. "Mum!"

Roz smiled. It wouldn't be long before Heather found out what it was to be an embarrassing mum. It couldn't be avoided. And it happened a long time before the cliches of cringing teens. Heather had been five when she'd said to Roz, then twenty-six, "Stop it, Mummy, you're making my face hot," when Roz had been clowning around at the school sports day.

Sally held out an empty glass. "Oh, shush, Liv. You're old enough now to see your parents as human."

"I'll go," Aidan said, grabbing his mum's wineglass and edging out of the booth. He looked glad of an excuse to get away. "And no, I won't drink any, don't worry."

Roz's phone buzzed—Heather was calling. The noise in the railcar faded as if placed behind a screen. None of this mattered compared to what was happening at the end of the line.

Roz stood and, accepting the call, hurried toward the door. "Everything okay, love?"

"Me again," Ellie replied on the other end. "And no, everything is not okay."

Chapter Nine

Roz stood alone in the jostling hinterland between railcars. Her heart felt just as shaky. "Has something happened?"

"Jean, the midwife, isn't happy with the way things are going." Ellie's voice, usually so strong, had a tremor. In the background, she could hear the distress in Heather's voice as she talked with the midwife, whose low, reassuring tones flowed like the warm water that filled a birthing pool.

"What's wrong?" Roz felt her own voice quiver in her throat.

"The baby's heartbeat is too slow."

Roz's heart started running as if to make up for her granddaughter's. "What about Heather?"

"Not good. She says she's just tired." There was more behind those words. The pressure Ellie was bearing pressed against them.

"But you think it's more than that?"

Roz heard a door open and close. Ellie must be in the hallway, where she could talk without Heather hearing. "Jean is worried about Heather. She doesn't like the way she's shivering. And her blood pressure is too high. She also thinks the baby is in distress." Ellie audibly gasped for air, then swallowed. "It could be that the placenta has abrupted, or there's a problem with the amniotic fluid or umbilical cord—basically the baby may not have enough oxygen."

"So now what? You all go to the hospital, right?"

"I'm going to drive us to Inverness maternity."

"And Heather's not too upset about it?" Her daughter had been set on a home birth. She'd written out the birth plan, from the essential oils to be used (lavender, clary sage, neroli, mandarin, and peppermint), to the temperature of the water and the reflexology points that Ellie was to press at certain times. Heather had gone to hypnobirthing classes and had been practicing the breathing and visualization techniques before bed every night. She had always been a planner. But childbirth couldn't be contained by a spreadsheet.

"She objected to start with, but me and Jean talked her around. She'll be in the best place if anything…" Ellie trailed off. Nobody wanted to say the words out loud in case they came true. As if just puffing air from your lips to form a word gave them life.

"It'll be all right, Ellie," Roz said and tried to listen to her own words.

Ellie's voice was muffled by tears. "I'm going to throw some stuff in a bag. You talk to Heather."

Roz waited, hardly breathing, as she heard the door open again. She looked out of the window into the dark. The houses passed in shadow. Only at night did the suburbs look as sinister as they really were.

"Roz?" Heather rarely called her "Mum," not since she'd learned Roz's name at age four. Sometimes, when Heather was really annoyed with Roz, she called her Rosalind. It hurt.

"I'm here, love."

"I wish you *were* here." Heather was short of breath, the words coming in bursts. The request for video came through and Roz accepted. Heather appeared on screen. Her face was red and puffy, almost unrecognizable. Her eyes were glazed, and she was shivering so much the camera shook. All Roz wanted to do was hold her. Behind her, the living room was lit by candles.

"They want me to go into the hospital, Roz." Heather snuffled and sniffed, the way she always did when trying not to cry.

"It's for the best, love. Just in case." Roz hoped she was keeping her voice calm.

"I wanted it to happen here."

"I know. But your baby needs you to make sure she's going to be okay." Roz winced as she said this, knowing that her own baby needed her and she couldn't be there.

"I've already failed her," Heather said in a voice so low Roz hardly heard it.

"No," Roz said with a defiance she didn't expect. "You haven't failed at anything."

"At the prenatal classes, they said the baby will be stressed by the hospital. That it's not a good start for her heart."

"That's bollocks," Roz said before she could stop herself. "Woo-woo nonsense. Her heart is hardly in a good way at the moment."

Heather started to cry. And Heather very rarely cried.

"I'm sorry, darling, I didn't mean—"

"I have to go," Heather said. And then she cut the call.

Roz stared at the phone. She called back, but Heather didn't answer. Roz recorded a voice message: "So sorry, love. Last thing I wanted to do was upset you. Just know I'll be thinking of you constantly, and I'll be there soon as this stupid train can get me to you. Sorry again. Just ignore me." She didn't press stop at first, then didn't know what else to say apart from, "I love you."

Roz's own heart felt like an unwrapped, unwanted present. She'd messed everything up. Again. Her stupid runaway train of a mouth.

Outside, fences and gardens and rectangles of light flashed by. Roz knew in theory that she was the one moving, but it never felt like that. That was the magic of trains. The world seemed to pass you by while you were still, yet somehow you got where you wanted to go. If only life were like that.

Looking out of the window helped. While the most important thing in the world to Roz was still what was happening in a basement flat in Fort William, she became aware of thousands of parallel lives. All those people in just-glimpsed houses, on their sofas, in the bath or in bed, watching telly or porn, happy or otherwise, some crying, others dying. Like every small part of the train, each life was integral. Essential. At the Met, when Roz had wanted to get perspective on one of the many disastrous aspects of her life, she had looked at the folder of unsolved crimes. In there she would see that her problems were at least shared by others. She'd often also find another case to try and resolve. Anything to stop her thinking about the man who attacked her. If she couldn't find out who he was, at least she could put away others of his kind. But the conviction rate was getting worse, and some of the perpetrators were themselves in the Met.

She was probably passing a crime, or several, right now. Each box of a window with its blinds or curtains closed could contain an atrocity. Schrödinger's casement.

But concentrating on others had meant she'd been a terrible mother. Anyone who said that you could successfully juggle a vocation with parenthood had never tried juggling. Juggling was hard. She'd tried to learn once from a YouTube video. She ended up with balls everywhere and her twenty-years-in-the-Met carriage clock in pieces on the floor.

Roz needed to walk off some of the pent-up worry. She went through the automatic door into a sleeping car and strode down the corridor into the next one, and then the next. Voices floated from the cabins as she passed—Phil singing "Silent Night" to his children; a man talking on the phone.

Beyond the cabins were the seating and luggage cars. The train had been sold out yet it was sparsely populated, only about twenty people in total. Presumably because the train would usually carry everyone up to Edinburgh before it split into four, a number of carriages going in different directions. Now it was only going to Fort William, and passengers intending to travel to the other regions would still be in London.

Farther up, Tony and his mum, Mary, were on either side of a table, seats reclined slightly. The cat box was on the seat next to Mary. The top mesh was unzipped, but Mousetache seemed perfectly happy staying where he was, occasionally being given little snippets of ham by Mary. He purred continuously, as if that was fueling the train.

An open tin of Quality Street lay on the table, the chocolate and toffee wrappers glistening like jewels.

"It's our savior!" Tony said. "Coming to see the plebs?"

"Hardly. I needed a walk," Roz replied.

"Would you like a sweetie?" Tony asked, jiggling the tin. The chocolates danced.

"Leave the ones with nuts in," Mary said. "They're my favorite."

Roz respected the straightforwardness. They were Roz's favorite too. Maybe Mary could sense that in her. There was a certain squirrelishness to Mary: her dark, bright, hardly blinking eyes. The quick way she turned her head. Roz couldn't see from where she was standing, but she wouldn't put it past Mary to have a bushy tail.

"Otherwise, help yourself," Mary continued. "Especially the fruit or coffee creams, they are abominations unto the bouche."

"I like those ones, Mum!"

Mary shrugged and grinned.

Mousetache yawned and placed his massive paws over the top of the backpack, poking his head out. She stared at Roz, then chirruped and tutted. Roz had never felt more judged.

"What kind of cat is he?" she asked.

"Half Maine coon, half Siberian. Although he thinks he's a sheepdog," Mary replied. She stroked Mousetache's head, causing the cat to close his eyes in utter pleasure. Roz wondered what that felt like. It was a long time since she'd been touched.

Mary tried to stretch out her legs and winced in pain.

"There are still some seats in the club car," Roz said. "Should give you a bit more space."

"Are we allowed in?" asked Tony.

"Of course, we are," Mary said. "If there's room, even us second-class citizens can sit with the elite."

"They don't call it second class anymore, Mum."

"Doesn't matter what they call it," Mary replied. "Still class stratification. We're the stratum of the train, responding to the bumpiness of the terrain, while the plane above us is smooth."

"Mum used to be a geology lecturer," Tony said in explanation.

"I still am when given gin and a chance," Mary said. Her eyes shone.

Tony reached for his mum's hand. The look between them was made of decades of sediment and love.

Roz's heart couldn't take that tonight. "I'll leave you to it," she said. "But do pop along to the club car if you fancy it. Before it gets too rowdy. Although there's already been conflict, so I can't promise it'll be without drama."

"In which case, I'm definitely coming," Mary said. She looked at Mousetache, who stuck his tongue out. Roz couldn't tell if that meant agreement or rebuttal.

Roz walked back down the train corridors, holding on to the walls as the train shunted and bumped. When back outside the club car, she looked again at her phone. No messages. No voicemail. Nothing.

Just as she was thinking of phoning again, the automatic door from the sleeping railcar opened. The man who had gotten on the train without a ticket stood in front of Roz. He had dark, or possibly dirty, blond hair that hung in straggly tangles to his shoulders. From the look of him, he'd slept in his tattered brown coat for several nights, if he'd slept at all. He held a plastic bag as if all his precious things were inside. He couldn't have been much more than forty, but his eyes were saturated with sadness and were shadowed underneath.

"Sorry," he said, bowing his head. "I was looking for the toilet." There was an urgency in his voice that didn't show in his body.

In the railcar beyond, Roz could see a ticket inspector coming this way. The man was obviously trying to avoid him. She had two choices.

Roz stepped back, pointing to the toilet. After all, maybe he had to get home for Christmas and had no other way. "There you go," she said, pressing the button that slowly opened the doors.

The man looked at her in thanks, then slipped inside, pressing the button to close the door several times as it if that would aid the process. If Roz were a toilet, and she'd felt like it at times, the number of times she'd been shat on, she'd close the door *really* slowly just to spite people who did that. Although in this case, seeing as the guard was the other side of automatic door now, maybe she'd hurry up.

The steward came through into the vestibule, his eyes fixed on the closing loo door. He was a big man of about sixty, with hair the color and thickness of porridge. His name badge said "Beefy," which only led to more questions.

"I was just going to ask," Roz said, mainly wondering what her brain would come up with, "if our arrival at Fort William will be delayed tomorrow morning? Or whether we'll make up time on the way?"

"Hard to say," he replied. His voice had the Thames running through it. "We can't go up to our highest speed as there's ice on the tracks. And the forecast has shifted—looks like there'll be more snow than originally thought. The train should probably have been canceled along with the others. But the driver said it was fine on the way down, so…" He sighed in a way that suggested his opinions rarely held weight. "Long as I get back to London tomorrow, I don't mind." He looked at the toilet again.

"You'll be wanting to see my ticket," Roz said. "It's in the club car, in my bag. Come with me, I'll show you." She gestured toward the door and, looking baffled but still doing as he was told, Beefy shuffled through the door. As Roz followed him, she was aware in her peripheral vision of the toilet door slowly opening. When she looked back, she saw the stowaway hurrying back down the corridor.

Chapter Ten

Meg reached for Grant's hand across the table. Very gently, hardly touching, she traced the lines on the palm of his hand. They were scored deep into his skin, his heart and head line tracking across but never meeting. She wished she could remember what that foretold, and what it could mean for their relationship, but couldn't. Ma had died before she'd passed on all her knowledge of palmistry and other kinds of divination; not that Ma believed you needed specialist equipment or even any more than the basics. "You can divine the past, present, and future from anything. All you need is the gift, Megan," she had said. "And you have that. You've just got to remember to connect to it."

She tried to connect with her gift, to read the future written on Grant's hands, but it was like one of those painted fake train tunnels in cartoons. She crashed into a brick wall and couldn't see any future. She'd take out her tarot cards later, see if they were any more instructive. She needed to know what lay on the tracks ahead.

A ticket inspector stopped at their table. He was large, had thick white hair, and smelled of toast. "Sorry to disturb you, Miss Meg," he said. He then did a little bob of a bow. His face changed color from chenin blanc to rosé. "But I was wondering if I could have your autograph? It's for my daughter, Charlie."

"Meg doesn't do Charlie anymore," Grant said, laughing loudly.

Meg smiled but otherwise ignored him. "Of course, I will," she said to the guard. She checked his name badge—a fellow celeb had told her on a game show to always find out the names of people looking after you, and use them—"Beefy. That's a great name!"

Beefy beamed. His teeth needed fixing, but there was something very endearing about the way they were at odds with each other. He then presented a piece of paper that he had been hiding behind his back as if it were a bouquet. "Here you go." He also handed her a pen.

"I've got my own special pen," she said and took her inscribed bright pink fountain pen out of her Anya Hindmarch bag. "How old is Charlie?"

"Eleven next week. My only kid and she's amazing." His eyes shone, and Meg felt a pang of jealousy. He clearly adored his daughter. She wondered what that must be like for Charlie.

Meg wrote, *Happy birthday for next week, Charlie! Keep watching! Love you!* Then she swirled her signature around the page, adding XOXO because Beefy had been so sweet.

Beefy picked up the paper as if it was the most precious thing next to his daughter. He held it at the very edges, between his hamlike hands. "That is perfect. Thank you so much."

He then turned to Grant, and his smile dropped. A steely look came into his eyes. "Tickets please, sir."

"You don't want my autograph, then?" Grant asked with one of the laughs he did to cover insecurity. It was not a laugh Meg liked to hear.

"Sorry, mate," Beefy said with a shrug. "No room left on the paper."

Grant grabbed the A4 sheet and turned it over. He then grabbed Meg's pen and wrote his signature. Meg shivered as she heard the pen scratch on the paper, sure that he had ruined the nib. He then handed the paper back to Beefy. "Now it's really valuable."

Beefy turned the paper over to the side with Meg's signature, but you could still see Grant's bleeding through. His face was now Shiraz red. "I really need to see your tickets now, sir."

When Beefy had gone, Meg looked out of the window. It was like a reverse snow globe: she was trapped behind the glass, looking out at the snow falling everywhere but on her. Seeing Beefy's love for his daughter made her think about having kids herself. Not yet, although she didn't want to wait too long, obvs. One day soon though. Maybe becoming a father would help Grant settle down. Maybe he'd stay by her side.

"You're so beautiful when you're thinking," Grant said to Meg. His eyes were so soft and full of love. Everything else melted away. "I like it when it's just us. When I don't have to share you with the world."

"I like it too." And she did, mostly. Connecting with her audience, though, reached a part in her that craved more. Maybe that's why he flirted, and cheated, with other women. To feel a connection she couldn't give him. In this moment though, they were one. When she looked at him again, he was staring out the window, as if he too was trying to scry in the snow.

"Come over here," he said, holding out an arm. He was looking at her with such warmth and affection.

Meg scuttled around the booth and sidled along to Grant. She leaned her head against his shoulder. These were the times where she felt that maybe, just maybe, everything would be okay.

And then she saw what he had been looking at. It wasn't her, it wasn't the snow, it was the reflection of the student who had shouted at him across the first-class lounge. Who'd told him to be quiet. And the look in his eyes was no longer one of love.

Chapter Eleven

Roz's face flamed as the shabbily handsome man walked into the club car. From her position by the window, she was able to get a good look at his reflection. He had the burnished look and paler crow's-feet of someone who spent their working life outdoors. He looked vaguely familiar, but she had met so many people in her career it was hard to say if that was because he was criminal, civilian, or copper. She looked for a wedding ring, then wondered what was up with her. She was never normally like this.

He sat down at one of the little tables, two away from Roz. He looked into the window and caught her staring, and smiled. She couldn't help grinning back. Ember was also watching their exchange, a smile on her face too. Although hers was small and sad.

"How's the cheese board?" he asked Roz, pointing to her nearly empty slate. His accent was patterned with Paisley, therefore becoming 33 percent more attractive to Roz.

"Impeccable," Roz replied. "Watch out for the pickled onions. At first they tickle, then they kick."

"I've never met an onion that's bested me yet." He paused, then said, "I'm Craig, by the way."

"Roz."

"Can I get you another one of those, Roz?" He nodded at her empty whisky glass and moved toward the bar.

Roz raised it in assent and felt her spirits lift with it. Maybe she'd find a way to forget the memories and concentrate on the present after all.

"He seems like one of the good ones," Ember said.

"Maybe," Roz replied. She knew you could never really tell.

At the Quizling table behind them, Blake was waving his mobile phone. "I've made a Christmas round. It's got music in it." He pressed his screen and "Stay Another Day" by '90s heartthrobs East 17 played through the speaker. People looked around, and he guiltily turned the music down.

"Let's be clear though," Beck said, convincing Roz that she was destined for a life in Tory politics. "That is *not* a Christmas song."

"Please don't start all that," Blake replied. "You'll be saying that *Die Hard* isn't a Christmas film next."

"It isn't," Beck said, folding her arms.

"'Stay Another Day' *is* Christmassy though," Ayana said, so quietly that Roz had to strain to hear. "Bells, furry hooded coats in the snow in the video. And it's about death. I think all that sums up Christmas pretty well."

"Death doesn't sum up Christmas," Beck said, her scoffing laugh as loud as Ayana's voice was soft.

"It does for turkeys," said Sam, holding Blake's hand.

Blake nodded. "Excellent point, Sam. Winter festivals have always acknowledged death. It's about holding on to the light at the darkest times, a flickering hope that the long nights will shrink and, even though we can hardly imagine it now, dawn will come, and so will summer."

"I hate summer," Sam said.

Ember, clearly listening, gave a slight nod in agreement. Roz imagined that Ember wore her coat all year long.

"You don't like anything," Beck said to Sam.

"That's not fair or true," Blake replied. "Sam likes rain. And trains. And they *love* facts."

Sam laughed. "Almost as much as I love you," they said to Blake.

"You don't have to flaunt your preferences," Beck said, edging away.

"You have a problem with your friends being gay?" Sally asked.

"One, they're my colleagues, not my friends," Beck said. "I wouldn't choose to be here. Two, Sam's not gay, they're bi or pan. Three—"

"Then why are you on this trip?" Roz interrupted. "If you're not friends."

"The university gave us a grant to study together in preparation for the TV show. Three of us will definitely be on it, the remaining one will be the backup, the substitute," Ayana said.

"It's like a swimming training camp before selecting the British team for the Olympics," Beck said. "We're using a holiday rental. And as I was saying, I don't care about people being gay. I'm talking about Sam being sapiosexual. As a quiz team member, it's unsettling. I don't want to answer questions and worry that they're getting off on it."

"I promise you. That is *not* happening," Sam said, shivering slightly as if at the very thought of being attracted to Beck's brain. "And it's not all right to out me. That's not your call."

"You're the one shoving it in our faces."

"What is being shoved at us exactly?" Roz asked. "My face doesn't have anything in it, sadly. I'm going to rectify that with more cheese." She took a large hunk of cheddar and chewed it slowly.

"It's not about bodies and gender identity for me, it's all about brains. I'm specifically attracted to people who are clever, wise, or knowledgeable, as well as a preference for decent human beings," Sam said. "And Blake is all of those."

Blake beamed.

"I think my followers will be fascinated by that," Meg said. "Can I interview you?"

Sam smiled shyly. "Sure."

Grant's laugh was loud and wrapped in cruelty. "As if your followers are clever, wise, or knowledgeable."

"You must admit, it's not pleasant to be on a quiz team with someone turned on by facts," said Beck.

"I'm attracted to specific people, not abstract facts," Sam said carefully. "Although facts are great. For example, to return to the topic in hand, a YouGov poll in 2017 had only twenty-four percent of people think 'Stay Another Day' was a Christmas song."

Beck looked confused to be backed up by Sam, but her slow grin showed she was also taking it as a win.

The door slid open, and Mary and Tony appeared; Mousetache was stretching out of the open backpack, his paws on Tony's head, as if checking out where they could sit. He had a point. There were no seats together. All but one of the single seats, and all of the booths, were taken. Although the booths weren't full, some only had two people in.

Mary looked so fragile, holding on to Tony. She was like a glass decoration that had been in the family forever, every year aware that this might be the one where they would end up broken.

"No room, I'm afraid," Beefy said, looking around.

Roz felt a stab of guilt. She'd encouraged Mary and Tony to come here, but had been so pleased to see Craig she'd forgotten all about them. The people in booths avoided looking at Mary. At least most of them did—Grant was staring at her with disgust. The students bent their heads, Blake's quiz questions so hushed that Roz could no longer hear them.

And then she had an idea. She quickly surveyed the railcar, counting passengers and available seats. In her head, she rearranged everyone, clicking through permutations like a Rubik's Cube until everyone had a seat. When she'd managed, she realized that Ember was looking at her.

"You're going to do something," Ember said.

"I like things to be fair," Roz replied.

Ember smiled properly. "So do I."

Roz stood. "Excuse me, everyone." A few looked her way, but that was all. Maybe she needed a ribbon of friendliness, fun even, with which to present herself. "It's Christmas!" she shouted, channeling Noddy Holder. "And we have two people here who could do with a festive drink and a nice sit-down. And one of them is called Mary."

"You will be surprised to learn that I'm not a virgin though," Mary said. "Far from it."

"Mum!" Tony said.

Mary grinned and said, "Not that it matters anymore. I am offered neither sex nor respite by gentlemen callers."

Roz warmed to her even more. Tony shook his head fondly. Ember laughed, then placed her hand over her mouth as if her palm could reabsorb her mirth.

"Are we really going to turn them away?" Roz asked.

"You won't leave it, will you?" Grant said to Roz. There was threat in his voice.

"I don't see how there's room," Beefy said, looking around. "Priority goes to clubroom peeps, and no one can stand, for health and safety reasons."

"There's plenty of space for everyone," Roz said. "We just need to rearrange ourselves."

A murmur of discord rumbled like a train around the club car.

"We don't want to put anyone out," Tony said.

"I do," Mary replied.

"Quite right, Mary," Roz continued. "My suggestion is that we have a club-car Christmas quiz. We obviously have a team in our midst who are preparing for something quizzically magnificent and need our help. There are big booths and extra chairs. So I reckon we split into four teams of four or five and squidge up." She pointed to the table of quizzing students. "One of you could head up each team, as you're the experts." She nodded her head while maintaining eye contact with Beck, hopefully allowing Beck to infer that Roz was deferring to her as leader.

Beck, possibly subconsciously, bowed back. "That could work." She was already scanning the room, sizing up people for her team.

"I'm here for a romantic trip with my other half, not to make friends or answer stupid questions," Grant said. Roz thought she caught a glimpse of fear on his face and, for a moment, softened toward him. She pictured him as a boy, shrinking from answering questions in class.

"I think it's a great idea," Craig said. "That way everyone can sit down, and we all have a laugh."

"So do I," Meg said. She was looking at her phone, and Roz

wondered whether this was because she wanted to avoid Grant's disgruntled gaze, or whether she was thinking about the live stream potential of a quiz.

Roz was aware of her own motivation, other than to move everyone around to make room for Mary. A quiz would at least distract her from thinking about Heather and the baby, of Ellie driving them all in the car through a vortex of snow. It would also allow her time to get to know Craig.

Beck clapped her hands. "Okay," she said, taking over. "We can have four rounds, each led by one of the four of us. Obviously, we wouldn't be able to contribute to our own questions, so our teammates will be without our help for those." She pulled a face of commiseration, as if being without her input was the worst thing to happen to anyone in her vicinity. "Don't suppose we get to join in?" Oli asked Beefy.

Beefy looked like he'd love to say yes. Instead, he shook his head. "Can you imagine what Bella would say if she caught us?"

Oli sighed. "I know."

"Who's Bella?" Roz asked.

"The driver," Oli replied. "She's fierce."

"So, who is in which team?" asked Sam, looking at Roz.

Roz had seen eyes that pleaded less in a greyhound rescue center. "I'll join you." She turned to Ember. "You want to come with me?"

Ember looked down at the carpet. "This isn't really my thing." She was gripping the toggles of her coat, her face extra pale.

"Give it a try. You can always slip away, if you'd rather," Roz whispered back to her.

Ember nodded.

"And I'll be the fourth," said Craig, moving to stand behind Roz.

Roz felt her face heat up again. Maybe it was menopause rather than a pathetic crush on a stranger, but, for once, she didn't think so. She bent her head and picked up her chair, placing it at the end of Sam's table.

"Fine. Then I suppose I'll have Tony, Mary, and...what's your name?" Beck said, pointing at the man with the book and the green plaid suit.

"I'm Nick," he said. Roz tried to place his accent but got stuck choosing between Greek and Nordic.

Beck gestured with a royal dismissal. "The rest of you can sort your-selves out."

Roz shifted her chair so that she had a good view into the other booths too. She wondered how long into retirement it would take her to lose the urge to check all entrances and keep an eye on everyone. Ember sat down on one side of her, Craig the other. She could feel his proximity; the small space between them seemed to pulse. He handed her the glass and, when she noticed their fingers touching, had to tell herself off for feeling like a teenager.

As everyone else formed teams and switched seats, with Ayana giving out pens and paper, Phil came back in, baby still papoosed on his chest. He looked around the railcar in confusion at all the movement, then spot-ted Sally, who had sidled into the first booth, opposite Meg and next to Aidan. Roz wondered which one of them had decided to sit with the other, especially as Grant was at another table with Liv and Blake. It looked like Phil was wondering that too. He was frozen in place, staring at Meg and Sally as they took the pens from Ayana. He swallowed twice before speak-ing. "Sally, love, have you still got my glasses and the extra milk in your bag? I dropped one of my lenses in the cabin and now I can't see."

"Have you left Robert on his own?" Sally asked, her eyes wide.

"He's locked in the cabin, sparko, and it's not like I'll be long," Phil replied. There was, understandably, a slight edge to his voice. He held up the child monitor with a color picture of the sleeping child on the screen. The toddler's soft snores snuffled through the speaker along with the lilt of a lullaby playing in the room.

Sally searched through her large handbag, pulling out nappies, wipes, crumbs, Mr. Men books, two tampons, various tinctures in brown bottles, and a topless lipstick before she got to a glasses case covered in Peppa Pig stickers. She then found a little carton of infant milk and handed them both to Phil without saying anything.

"Night, then." Phil waited for a response from his wife but none came. Slinking out of the room, he looked over at Meg, and a weird look came over his face. He no longer seemed quite so benign.

Chapter Twelve

The killer glanced over at Meg. Everything seemed to come easy to her. Flirting. Laughing. Talking.

The killer saw through it though. Of course, they did. They recognized everything about her. They knew how much effort it took to be perceived as at ease. No one else knew what it took to contour that smile. In many ways, the killer admired the performance. Admired it as much as they hated it. This wasn't the real Meg. The real Meg was underneath the extensions, the serums, the shading, the microblading. The killer wanted to cut out the filler, peel off the mink lashes, let her forehead wrinkle, her crow's-feet crow.

Meg thought that her followers loved her, but they only wanted the avatar, the filtered vulnerability. They thought she was just like them, but more so. That's why they always wanted more, and she would give herself to them, live stream herself until there was nothing left but a dry riverbed. She needed to be left alone. To be treated as she deserved.

The killer wanted to take Meg away from all this. And they would.

Chapter Thirteen

It was gone eleven o'clock but didn't feel like it. Outside, lights in houses were turning off, one by one, but inside the train they still blazed. Roz had lost track of where they were in the country. She had the sense that they were no longer rooted to time and place, only this space.

Everyone now settled in seats and teams, Beck stood, cleared her throat, and put her hands on her hips like a principal boy. "You all need a name for your teams. I've decided ours is the Cracker Team." She waited, slight smile on her face. Then, when no one responded: "As in 'crack team,' but for Christmas." Beck waited a bit longer. Still no response.

"I think everyone gets it, Beck," Blake said.

"You all try it, then. I'll give you two minutes to choose your name." She glanced at her watch.

Roz took a big glug of whisky as suggestions for team monikers floated above the booth.

"The Wise Women!"

"Merry Quizmas!"

"The Noel-it-alls!"

"Agatha Quizteam!"

Roz checked her phone. She loved a pun as much as anyone, but there were other things on her mind. She had sent a message asking

Ellie to let her know when they reached the hospital, but there was nothing yet.

"Phones off and away, everyone," Beck said, pointedly. "There'll be no cheating on my watch."

Roz snapped her neck around to Beck. She could feel her eyes burning. "I need my phone on. I'm not going to cheat."

"What if something's urgent?" Craig joined in.

Beck blinked and nodded. "There are exceptions for emergencies, of course." Her head girl certainty dropped for a moment, then pinned itself back in place. "Let's start with the Christmas round." Her voice was loud again, marshaling the club car. "Seeing as Blake's gone to all that trouble."

"I'd have written different questions if I'd known," Blake said from the adjacent booth. "It was meant for us."

"Are you saying we're stupid?" Grant was sitting between Blake and Liv. His chin jutted upward. Craig rolled his eyes.

Blake's eyes widened, and he edged away from Grant. "No, never. Just that it might not be as fun. I could think of easier ones."

"I don't think anyone's grasping the situation." Beck's voice gained an extra edge. "Whoever gets on the team goes on TV, you do know that, don't you? And if we win, we'll get on other programs. We could be set. If we're not training properly, what's the point?"

"How about if Blake reads his questions, and then also creates a few more for us quizzing civilians?" Roz asked.

Beck's eyebrows raised, but she nodded. "Fine."

Blake stood, squaring his shoulders. He adjusted a nonexistent bow tie. "Question one."

Sam leaned forward, the tip of their nose only six inches from the table, their pen poised above a piece of paper.

"Who," Blake read out, "wrote the melody for 'The Twelve Days of Christmas' in 1909?"

Beck sighed elaborately, conveying how very easy that was, and was about to speak when Mary said in a loud voice, "Frederic Austin." Her r's were as crisp and rolled as pastry around a sausage.

"Mum!" Tony said. "You're not supposed to tell the whole room."

"Be quiet next time," Beck hissed at her. "Or write it down."

"I'm sorry," Mary said, the flash in her eyes showing quite how unsorry she was. "I didn't think it would matter. I'm so used to people not listening to me." Mary had sculpted passive aggression into an art form.

"If you could whisper answers to each other from now on," Blake said. "Then it's fair on every team."

"How did you know that?" Ember called over to Mary in awe.

"I'm eighty-nine. I know stuff, and I've seen stuff. I've read plots in thrillers that are boring compared to my life."

Roz and Ember burst out laughing. Tony covered his eyes, feigning embarrassment, but smiled. Even Beck's mouth twitched.

"Question two," Blake continued. "Which Christmas song was played by two astronauts in a broadcast from space in 1965? For an extra point, name the astronauts. For an extra, *extra* point, name the instruments; and for an extra, extra, *extra* point, name which instruments they each played."

Liv was sitting with her arms folded at the edge of the seat, looking away toward the bar. This probably wasn't the way she'd wanted to see in Christmas Eve. And Roz didn't blame her.

Sam stood up so they could look over the booth at Blake. "That is a wonderful set of questions." They shared a look that could light a Christmas pudding.

"How are we supposed to know that?" Sally called out from the booth nearest the door.

Ayana nudged her and whispered something—presumably the answers—in her ear.

"Never mind," Sally said. She then drank half a glass of wine in one go. Beck wrote down answers on her sheet of paper, smugness showing through her foundation.

"Question three," Blake called out. "What Christmas dinner staple is less commonly known as *Brassica oleracea*, variety *Gemmifera*?"

"Too easy." Beck wrote again on her paper.

Roz glanced at what Sam had written down on their piece of paper. "You need to add an 's,'" she whispered.

Sam looked up, confused.

"You've put 'Brussel sprouts.'" Roz kept her voice quiet, so much so Craig had to bend his head close to hers. "But it's 'Brussels sprouts,' as they were thought to be cultivated in Brussels. In Belgium, they're called *spruitjes*, or *choux de Bruxelles*, depending on where you are and who's serving."

"Thanks," Sam whispered, meticulously adding an "s."

"You know a lot about sprouts," Craig said, his voice low. His eyes were the color of whisky and ginger ale. "And an impressive working knowledge of Belgium."

"I like facts. I'm not great with faces, but facts stick. Faces change, after all. And you can't beat a day trip to Bruges."

"Belgium makes the best mayonnaise, chips, and chocolate."

There was something in Craig's tone that made her think that was an invitation. She imagined being on the Eurostar with him, off to sample the best *moules frites* and feed each other truffles. God, she had to get a grip.

"And detectives," Roz said instead. "Belgium makes great detectives."

"Ah, well, I know quite a few good detectives in the UK too," Craig replied. He was smiling, as if he meant her. "Your parents must be proud."

"Not really. My dad died before I was ten, and Mum always hoped I'd work for myself, as she did. Said it was best to rely on yourself and nobody else. But I'd had no idea what to do."

Mum had been a florist, supplying the hotels of the Highlands. She was as accustomed to avoiding the spikes of rose plants as Roz became at dodging her mother's barbs. She had grown herbs in their garden that she added to the bouquets and always included heather in her arrangements. Another reason why Roz had so named her daughter. "When you work for yourself, you can sleep with your boss with impunity," Liz had said, oversharing as ever. "And you never need worry about unfair dismissal or sexual harassment. And no one else will eat all the biscuits."

"Maybe you could be your own boss now you've retired," said Craig, bringing Roz back from her past. "You've got years and years of life to live."

"Maybe. Still got no clue as to what I'd do."

"I know what you mean. I think about retiring and doing something else with my life, starting again. But knowing where to start is the hardest part."

"What do you do now? You're not in the force, are you?"

"Why do you ask?"

"You seem really familiar. Thought I might have met you in the Met, at a case or something."

"Maybe we did—I'm in the CPS."

Roz's heart sank as if into cold snow. She knew he was too good to be true. Her disappointment must have showed in her face as he held up his hands. "I know, I know. The CPS and the Met. We're mortal enemies."

"True. And that must be where I recognize you from. Must have seen you around court."

"Maybe, although—"

"Really sorry," Sam said to them, looking mortified to even ask. "But do you mind being a bit quieter during the questions?"

"Sorry," Craig and Roz said at the same time.

Blake continued to quiz the teams, from question four—"What is Santa Claus known as in Japan?"—to question ten—"What is the third of the elf 'food groups' listed in the film *Elf*?"

"We'll take a break here," Beck said at last. "Then we'll get onto *my* round."

"Talking of rounds," Roz said to Craig, Ember, and Sam as she stood up and stretched. Her back gave a satisfying crack. "Can I get you all a drink?"

Craig was about to answer, then his hand went to his shirt pocket. His phone was lighting up and vibrating. "Sorry, got to answer this." He edged around the table and headed for the door. Just before leaving, he turned around to look at Roz, guilt clear on his face. And there you had it—not only did he work for the Crown Prosecution Service, cats to the police service's dogs, he clearly had a partner who was probably checking in, asking how his day had been. Roz sighed. It was just her luck to be attracted to an unavailable man.

In Blake's booth, Grant was taking up most of the space, his arms across the back of the banquette. He took a deep inhale on his vape cigar and puffed it into the air.

"Can you stop doing that?" Beck snapped, standing up to glare at him over the booth wall.

Grant inhaled again and blew smoke-ring vapor kisses her way.

"Steward! Tell him he can't vape on the train," Beck shouted over.

Barman Oli tuts, loudly. He was trying to serve the queue that had formed at the bar at the same time as chatting with Meg. "You really can't, I'm afraid, sir. Against policy."

Grant laughed. "Looks like Little Miss Quiz is going to get her own way for now. But not forever." Next to him, Liv giggled and he laughed harder. "I'm going to pop out for a moment, go back to my room." He waggled the cigar as he edged his way out of the booth, obviously hoping to vape when on his own. When he got to the door, he waved to everyone. Only Aidan, Liv, and Meg waved back.

"I need some air," Ember said when he'd gone.

"I'll come with you," Roz replied. They left Sam to go over their answers for the third time and went out into the section between railcars. The window was slightly open, and they breathed in menthol-cold air.

"I don't know how Meg can bear to be around him," Ember said.

"He's a stone-cold charmer, all right. One day she'll work out she deserves far better. And he'll realize that he's not as big, clever, or attractive as he thinks."

"Do you really think so?"

"No. But we can hope." A new message buzzed through, from Ellie: We're at the hospital. Please call. I don't know what to do.

"Fuck," Roz said. "Sorry, I have to go." She started off down the corridor toward her cabin. She needed to be alone.

Chapter Fourteen

Meg leaned against the bar and smiled into her phone. Her audience numbers were increasing on her live stream as much as the amount of alcohol in her bloodstream. Each new viewer was champagne fizzing inside her. She was aware that Grant was coming over and that he didn't look happy, but she couldn't think of that now. "I'm having the best time on the sleeper train to the Highlands. We're in the middle of an old school quiz and, in our break, Oli here, master mixologist, is going to show us how to make festive cocktails."

"I'm only a steward," Oli said. He didn't know where to look into the camera, but he had an engaging shyness.

"Don't undersell yourself," Meg replied. "You're the king of the club car, and I am the queen. Let's own it!" Meg felt Grant's hand on her, tightening into a steel grip around her upper arm. She would pay for saying Oli was king later.

"Aw, thanks." Oli's smile was charmingly crooked. One of his teeth was askew, and Meg liked it so much she almost wished that she hadn't had hers fixed. But then that would be all people saw. Her wonky teeth, the bump in her nose, the bit of fat on her tummy that wouldn't go away no matter what she didn't eat... Once all of that had been changed, people saw the real Meg.

"So where do we start?" she asked Oli, encouraging him to get going. Things needed to happen swiftly on a live stream. You couldn't leave them waiting. And she should get this over with quickly, so she could defuse Grant.

"We're going to make my own invention," Oli said. He glanced at the camera, then away. He wasn't to know that what people loved was the feeling that they were plugged into you. That just for a moment, they knew you better than anyone else. They saw the whites of your eyes and fell in love.

Oli's confidence, though, grew throughout the live stream. By the end of it, no longer timid, he was tossing the shaker into the air à la Tom Cruise in *Cocktail* and only dropping it occasionally. "The trick is to never use a cheap brand just because you think it'll be hidden in the mix. Always get the best you can afford."

At the end of his spiel, Oli presented her with a drink he'd concocted named "The Beauty Sleeper." It was surprisingly delicious, a nightcap of whisky, crème de cacao, lavender syrup, and cream, with a pillow of frothed egg whites on top and a sprinkling of nutmeg. It even managed to make her feel a little sleepy.

"I'll have another of these before Grant and I go to bed," she said to the camera with a wink. Maybe that would appease him. "Say goodbye, Oli."

She turned the camera so they were both in shot.

"Goodbye, Oli!" he said. He was a natural.

"Keep an eye out," Meg continued, "for a round of the pub quiz that's rocking the club car!" She waved and watched the heart reactions float up the screen like bubbles in a glass.

"That went well," she said to Oli when she'd ended the live stream. "You should have your own show."

Oli's cheeks and neck went the color of maraschino cherries.

Grant took her to one side. "You sure you should do another stream?" he asked. He seemed full of concern as he stared at her, his focus shifting from one of her eyes to the other. "Perhaps you should leave it for tonight. You look so tired, babe."

Meg looked away. "I'll fix my face. I've been given a new concealer I need to test anyway."

"I'm only thinking of you," he said, holding her shoulders. "I know you like to look your best on camera."

She nodded, but was too ashamed to meet his eye. No wonder he looked at other women.

"It's gone midnight!" Sally shouted from the booth at the far end.

Grant pulled her in for a kiss. "Happy Christmas Eve," he said, loudly. "Just wait till later," he whispered, and his tone told her it was more of a threat than a promise.

Chapter Fifteen

December 24th

Roz paced in the tiny space between her bed and bathroom, dialing and redialing.

At last, Ellie picked up. "Heather's got preeclampsia." Shock had turned her voice monotone. "She's being prepped for an emergency cesarean, and is scheduled for surgery at three a.m."

Roz tried not to think of a scalpel cutting open her daughter, but the image came anyway. "Why not have the surgery now? Isn't sooner better than later?"

Ellie's voice tightened a notch. "The surgeon is stuck in snow on her way in, and everyone else qualified is already in surgery."

Roz felt anger swell. The unfairness of it all. "How is Heather?"

"She's telling jokes. Trying to make light of it."

"Of course, she is. She's like Frankie Boyle with a bob."

"Wonder where she gets that from." Ellie did deadpan extremely well.

"Can I talk to her?"

"She's busy at the moment." Ellie couldn't stop a sob coming out. "Signing the forms." Roz knew them well, the documents that got you to say you understood the risk of the surgery, the possibility of things going wrong.

"Oh, Ellie."

"It's not helped by the doctors and midwives coming around, trying to not look worried about her and failing."

Roz had been to emergency situations and seen nurses put on the cheery demeanor, the no-nonsense voice, the no-fuss charm, and then crumple when they went into the staff room. Roz herself had attended traffic accidents early on in her career, and held hands and sung lullabies to people as they passed, or told them a final bedtime story. One October afternoon, near Halloween, Roz had been first at the scene of a city center hit-and-run. The victim was a young girl called Tara. She had lain on the pavement, holding on to life and her fluffy rabbit with a weakening grip. The only story Roz knew by heart was *Goodnight Moon*, and by the time she had finished reciting it out loud, the ten-year-old's eyes were fixed and dilated, and Roz was crying on the tarmac.

"I have to go," Ellie said. "I'll let you know when we're going in." She took a deep breath and Roz visualized her drawing in strength, knowing that she had to be the resilient one.

Roz sat on her bed and stared at the picture of Fort William. She wished Heather the fortitude of the mountains and the tenacity of the plant whose name she bore. Roz had often said to her daughter, "You can grow despite inhospitable soil, over and around anything—even having me as your mother."

Heather had laughed every time but never denied it. She would need to be every bit as resilient as the heather that grew around the family house.

Roz got under the covers, still dressed. She reached for her mirrored cube and started clicking. It was the only thing she could control. There was nothing else she could do.

Chapter Sixteen

Meg yawned and checked her watch. 2:00 a.m. The club-car crowd had been whittled to the hard core, and the quiz was still going, even though the bar had closed. Meg didn't mind. She'd had enough espresso martinis, even though Oli was now an expert at making them. All she wanted was to put on her new PJs, courtesy of some brand or other, take a selfie in them (with matching eye mask), then cuddle up in the cozy double with Grant.

But Grant had no intention of going to bed. He had bought a decent bottle of whisky before the bar shut, and Sally had ransacked her rucksack for wine. Besides, Meg still had at least one more live stream to do. Maybe two or three if she was really going to make the most of the trip. Her followers were staying up to see her arrive at Fort William, playing along with the quiz, joining in on sing-alongs. She hadn't expected such a response, but she supposed she had been talking for weeks about going home for Christmas, and the welcome she was hoping to get from her estranged dad. She dreaded it. Dad would turn up at the station, but only because her management team, encouraged by Grant, had paid him two grand.

"Answers to round six." Beck was sitting on the bar, back still ramrod straight. "For those of us still playing and bothered, question one was: What is the Greek word for the Fates? Extra points for their individual names and what they did. And the answer to this extremely easy question is, of course, the Moirae. And for those extra points, their names are Clotho, who spins the thread of life; Lachesis, who measures the thread of life; and Atropos, who cuts the thread when it's time to die. I, of course, got them all right."

Meg took out her compact and saw that Grant had been right. Her skin looked gray in this light, and the bags under her eyes looked like they could carry half her makeup collection. She needed to patch herself up again and get a bit more energy. It would take more than concealer and caffeine at this time of night.

Meg remembered that she had just what she needed in her suitcase. Standing up, she peered into the next booth. Grant was playing thumb war with Blake. Blake's tongue was sticking out as he concentrated. Meg felt relief run through her. He had drunk enough now to be Charming Grant, the one everyone loved and wanted to be around. The maverick who made things happen. The star of reality TV. Soon, he would tip over and become Arsehole Grant, the star barred from countless clubs. She had half an hour remaining, or maybe an hour, until Arsehole appeared.

"Just going to the toilet," Meg said to him.

He held up his other hand in acknowledgment but didn't turn away from the thumb war. The young woman—Liv, Phil's daughter—who had recognized her in the first-class lounge, then asked her for selfies on the train, was looking at her with such an intense look. Bless. She wasn't that much younger than Meg, but Meg felt ancient in comparison. Especially as she'd snogged Liv's dad.

Meg felt a rare sense of freedom as she walked down the corridor. No camera, no followers, no Grant. She pirouetted to the end of the corridor, suddenly remembering Mum taking her to see *The Nutcracker* in Glasgow the Christmas Eve before she died. She must have known that would be their last Christmas together, but Meg hadn't. If she had, she wouldn't have complained about getting the wrong present or made any of the other tiny mistakes that haunted you when people died.

As she took out her key, Meg saw Tony walking, a little wobbly, from the toilet back to the seating car. She followed him to make sure he got back to his seat.

"You doing all right, there, Tony?" she asked, taking his elbow.

"Best night in ages," he said. His accent had been soft when she first heard him, but now it was as thick as midges on marshland on a damp day in May.

They went through the automatic doors into the seated railcar, Tony giggling as he teetered into the wall. "Ssh!" he said. Mary was sitting at the first table, leaning on the headrest, eye mask on. Mousetache was curled up on her lap. The cat opened his eyes and stared at Meg, then at Tony, before slowly closing his lids again. "I haven't seen Mum so happy in a long time," Tony whispered as he plonked down on his seat. "I'm no match for her brain, you see."

"Absolute nonsense." Mary peeled off her eye mask. "You're perfect. Always have been."

Tony's chin quivered. He held Mary's hand and she squeezed his.

"Now, Anthony, drink lots of water," Mary continued. "Take two ibuprofen, and wake me up for breakfast." She squeezed his hand once more and pulled her mask back over her eyes.

"You should get off the train at Edinburgh," a man called out. He was standing at the far end of the seating car, looking their way.

"What?" Meg said, wondering if he was talking to Tony.

The man walked down the aisle toward Meg, his unblinking eyes fixed on hers. His clothes were crumpled and unclean. He smelled of old sweat. She didn't want to judge, but already had. "Get off when the train stops, while you still can."

"Why?" she asked, backing away.

"You're in danger," he said. "Get away from him. He's malignant."

"Who? Grant?"

"You know I'm right." His gaze was clear, pure. He had a purpose. There was also something familiar about him, but she couldn't say what.

"Who are you?"

His laugh was sad and quiet, as far away from Grant's as it could possibly be. "A friend. I'm just trying to protect you."

"Hey, mate," Tony said, looking from the man to Meg in confusion. "What's going on? Is he bothering you, Meg?"

The man turned to Tony and shook his head as if coming out of a dream. "I'm sorry," he said. "Don't mind me." He then turned away and went back to his seat.

"Do you want to do something about him?" Tony asked.

The man covered his head with his coat.

"No," she said. "I think he just needs to sleep. Reckon we all do."

"Thank God for that," Tony replied. "Else, I'd have had to ask him outwith, and that's hard to do on a train." His words slurred, shunting together.

Meg smiled. It felt good to be back with people who used Scottish words like "outwith," it sounded so much better than "outside." She said goodbye and, with one last look at the man under the coat, went back through to her cabin car.

In her room, it didn't take long to get what she needed. She had to be Insta-ready, Gram-fabulous, TikTok-tastic, and every other ridiculous PR phrase that had been thrown her way. She swabbed on foundation, contoured, applied the new natural eye drops and eyeliner, and burnished her cheekbones with seasonal highlighter to a golden sheen. She also had a line of cocaine that she'd hidden from Grant. He disapproved of her taking drugs, said he didn't want the "beautiful lining of her nose" to be destroyed, even though he often did drugs himself. She had, therefore, enjoyed hiding the coke in the lining of her suitcase.

She had sewn it in though, and would have to cut it out of the lining. She rifled through her bag but couldn't find her winged scissors. She hoped she hadn't left them in the first-class lounge. Using a slanted pair of tweezers instead, she picked at the stitches until the lining gave way and the packets of cocaine were exposed.

After snorting a line and then rubbing the remnants of the coke into her gums, she returned to the club car. She hoped Grant would put her bright eyes and newfound perkiness down to eye drops and love.

Chapter Seventeen

The killer looked out of the window as the train approached Edinburgh Waverley. Snow covered the platform in bridal white. The killer loved this place. The people, the hills, the spikes and spires that poked into a purple sky. It was never fully dark in this gothic city, whereas soon the train was headed for the Highlands, where, at that time of year, light was feasted on by night.

"We are now arriving in Edinburgh," Beefy said through the tannoy. "This isn't a scheduled stop but, as we will be no longer calling at some smaller stations between here and Fort William, including Arrochar and Tarbet, Ardlui, Crianlarich, Bridge of Orchy, Corrour and Roy Bridge, you may wish to disembark here. Due to worsening weather conditions, it's probable that farther stations may become inaccessible due to snow. We are terribly sorry for the inconvenience, but I'm sure you'll understand that safety comes first. We'll be at the station for ten minutes or so while we decouple several railcars. We'll then be continuing our journey to Fort William."

Those passengers still in the club car looked at each other, weighing up what to do. The killer smiled and shrugged, exchanging rueful looks and shakes of the head. None of them had any idea what the killer was planning. The victim wasn't in the club car, but they had no idea what or who was about to hit them. Murderers didn't need Jason Voorhees or Michael Myers masks; they just needed to smile.

But, for the killer, smiling was the second-hardest thing to do tonight. They wanted to run out of the train right now and get a room in a hotel. They'd order room service, a burger and chips, and run a hot bath, then they'd turn on the telly and watch anything other than reality TV. They'd nibble the chocolate on their pillow and forget about killing.

But they knew that would never happen. The victim was in their blood, and there was more at stake than their vendetta.

Placing their cheek against the cold window, they peered down the platform and counted the people who had been brave enough to hurry off the train. Ten in all, including the cute couple who shared a clootie and the man in the green suit. The killer watched them trudge through thick snow, buffeted by the wind, holding woolly hats onto their heads. Maybe they were going to spend the night at a hotel or in the waiting room, try their luck with other trains tomorrow.

Whatever they were doing, they'd made the right choice. Those that stayed on the train were one click closer to death.

They just didn't know it yet.

Chapter Eighteen

Roz lies on the gurney, hospital gown open. Behind the blue screen, someone is shaving her pubic hair. Scrape, scrape, scrape. The radio plays "It Only Takes a Minute" by Take That, and she knows she'll always hate this song from now on. No one looks at her. They move her legs because she can't. She can't do anything.

The blood-pressure machine gives a warning screech. They are cutting her. She can feel it, but it doesn't hurt, not exactly. It still makes her want to scream. The room smells of detergent and ash. The doctor is rummaging inside her as if searching in a handbag, pulling out intestines like handkerchiefs and removing the baby as if she were a purse.

After a labor that turned out to be useless, this woman can do nothing but wait. An endless wait for a baby's cry.

✔✔✔✔

Roz started, waking herself up. She jerked upright, her heart pounding. Sweat covered her chest, and her hands were cramped from grabbing the sheets in her sleep. She held her stomach, traced the lilac C-section scar that still felt numb to the touch all these years later.

Something was different. The train wasn't moving. They must be at a station. She looked at her phone. It was half two. Only thirty minutes to the operation. Roz didn't know if Heather would be allowed her phone, but she sent a message anyway. A message as full of love and reassurance as words could carry.

The train jolted as other railcars were joined or cast off. And then again, as if trying to shake away the nightmares she thought she'd stopped having. It made sense that the night terrors were back. As Heather went through her birth trauma, Roz was reliving hers. She couldn't decouple them forever.

Kneeling on the bed, she leaned to look out of her little window. They were at Edinburgh Waverley station, recognizable even through the snow that covered everything in sight. The cabin jolted as railcars were added or shed. The train must be getting ready for its next stint. Even for her, a born Highlander, it was hard to believe it took as long to get from London to Edinburgh as it did from Edinburgh to Fort William. What was harder to believe was that she'd managed to sleep at all. She had been so worried and cried so much she'd exhausted herself. The train had lulled her, coddled her with its rock-a-bye-baby-ing.

She'd be doing that soon. A new baby, her granddaughter, in her arms. She would have to change the words though, just as she did for Heather. What kind of sicko makes up a lullaby about a cradle and a baby falling from a treetop? Perhaps it was to prepare parents for infant death, at a time when it was so common as to be expected. But there was no need to carry it on now. As far as she was concerned, it now went: "when the bough breaks, the cradle won't fall/Baby is safe now, in my cuddle."

She pushed away thoughts of Heather's baby not making it through and focused instead on not knowing how to be a grandmother. Heather had, of course, sent her a book on the subject. It was in her rucksack, its spine uncracked. She had read the first patronizing section and then closed it. Not a great start to grandparenthood.

Rather than saccharine platitudes, she needed someone to tell her what being a grandmother was really like. The truth. Her mum had been the one to talk to her about motherhood. How mastitis was possibly the worst pain known to humankind, red-hot-poker-inside-the-tits kind of pain, made even worse when breastfeeding. How people told you to relish every precious moment because "time runs quickly," but time quickly became constipated at four in the morning when a baby had been crying for hours. How some held their baby and felt mild curiosity, shock, or horror rather than overwhelming love.

If only her mum had lived a few more months, she'd have met her great-grandchild. If there were an afterlife, her mum would be really pissed off. She had hated missing out on things; was always the first to arrive and the last to leave. She practically invented FOMO.

Roz got off the bed and opened her suitcase. Her mum's recipe book was tucked into the zip-up pocket, visible through the mesh. Taking it out, she sat with the wrapped book on her lap, her hands on top as if she could absorb the wisdom through the brown paper, soak it up like it was vinegar. Roz unpicked the knots in the string that her mum had tied. Peeled the brown paper like onion skin.

And there it was. Mum's recipe book. Bible-thick and full of Mum's knowledge and thoughts. Maybe it would give Roz the ingredients for being a good grandma.

Taking a deep breath, she opened the book. On the inside cover, sellotaped to the cardboard, was a note addressed to Roz, written on her mum's blue notepaper. The handwriting, though, was not Liz's elegant, at times unreadable, spikes, but rounded and clear.

Dearest Roz,

Vianda, my hospice nurse, is writing this down for me as my poor fingers are struggling to hold a pen. And as Vianda's a lovely woman, she's not going to like saying this, she'll say I'm waking the witch in me and you, but say it I'm gonna. I'm pissed off with you, Rosalind. Really fucking livid. I'm a crone with days to go, my insides eaten by a bastard canker and my heart torn by a daughter who—

Roz closed the book. Now was not the time. She felt bad enough about herself as it was.

Moving to the sink, she splashed water on her face. If she were at home, she'd go out for a walk, let the dark absorb her thoughts. But it was not wise to get off the train here. She'd probably get distracted by something and end up stranded in Edinburgh in a snowstorm. If the bar was still open, she'd get a coffee, something to keep her awake while she waited for news.

Once more she could do nothing but wait till the baby cried.

Chapter Nineteen

Despite the coke, sadness settled on Meg as the train departed Edinburgh Waverley. Grant wasn't in the club car, and she felt his absence like a phantom limb. She knew that wasn't a healthy feeling, that they were in a poisoned relationship. For a moment, she'd thought of jumping out and joining those who'd bailed, leaving everything, including Grant, behind on the train. Just the thought of it had felt freeing, and she'd wondered if the man in the seated railcar was right and she should leave. She had peered into the snow but found no answers. And then the train had moved her on.

She looked in her bag, just for something to do. Applied even more makeup. "Has anyone seen my scissors?" she asked out loud. But nobody replied.

The train flew past the other Edinburgh stations. Trees scraped at the windows. Dark houses loomed then turned away. No friendly lights on in windows, no sense that there was refuge anywhere.

Grant slipped back into the club car after, she presumed, another vape break, and slid across the booth next to Meg, snuggling up close. She felt a spike of joy. Out of all the fun people in this room, he had come to dock with her. She was his harbor.

He kissed the top of her head and drew her to him. "You all right?"

She nodded. And she was, now he was here. The sadness had lifted. Grant often said her moods shifted as many times a day as the weather in the Highlands, and this proved him right. "You having a good time?" she asked.

He shrugged. "Rather be in bed with you, but it's a laugh."

"We could just go, you know. To bed. Right now."

He leaned in, smiling. She could smell the sour booze on his breath, the cheese and onion crisps. His pores seemed to open and close. His pupils seemed to contract and dilate in time with his breathing. A wave of nausea rose up, and she pulled away. And then he wasn't smiling anymore.

Chapter Twenty

Quite a few quizzers remained in the brightly lit club car when Roz reentered. They seemed to be taking a break before the next round of answers. All four Quizlings were there, though their teams had dwindled. Sally was present too, although she probably wasn't much help answering questions, as she'd fallen asleep on her son's shoulder. Aidan looked even more mortified than teenagers usually were by their parents.

Meg and Grant were sitting in a booth, in the middle of an intense conversation. Blake and Sam were chatting about *Doctor Who*, Craig sat alone at a table, staring into space, muddling sugar into a whisky. Someone's phone was playing the usual list of Christmas hits.

Across the triangular tables was a cobbled-together buffet: a tin of Heroes, chocolate-coated Brazil nuts, mint Matchmakers, an oval box of Eat Me dates with their tiny spear, a Terry's Chocolate Orange splayed into segments, and an untouched box of cherry liqueur chocolates. There was also a gift basket with only a chorizo sausage and a Christmas pudding left in the straw, like the strangest of nativity scenes.

Facedown on a seat was the book Nick, the man in the green suit, had been reading. Picking it up, Roz saw it was open at the poem, "A Visit from St. Nicholas" which, she realized when she read the first lines, was better known as "The Night Before Christmas." Things were definitely stirring in the club car before Christmas.

Ayana was reading a quiz book. Ember was leaning back against the bar, taking everything in as she stood in what seemed to be companionable silence with Liv. Roz could tell that Ember was an observer. In another life, she'd have made a great police officer. But you need a certain amount of oomph to wield the law. The belligerence and belief in yourself needed to stride into danger was necessary in a police officer, even though it was what also caused so many problems in the Met.

"Roz!" Ember said when Roz approached. She was clutching her glass tightly, with one palm on top, as if stopping herself from drinking any more. Or perhaps a habit she'd picked up, as Roz had, to prevent people spiking her drink. "I've been worried about you. Are you okay?"

"Not really." Roz looked into Ember's open, concerned face and decided to tell her. "My daughter's having an emergency C-section. The baby's premature, and Heather's ill."

"Oh God." Ember held on to Roz's hand. "That must be terrifying."

"Just a bit. I'm a bawhair's breadth away from bawling."

Ember drew Roz into a hug that almost tipped Roz over into sobs. Over Ember's shoulder, Liv looked at Roz with sadness.

Craig came over, concern clouding his face. "I'm so sorry. I overheard what happened." He placed a tentative, gentle hand on her arm, then pulled it away again. Roz felt an immediate sense of loss.

"Did you know," Blake said, "that the first cesarean undertaken in antiseptic conditions was here in Scotland, in Glasgow to be precise, by Murdoch Cameron, in 1888? He had worked with Joseph Lister, you see, who revolutionized surgery through sterile conditions."

Roz stared at him. "Knowing that helps me or my daughter how, exactly?"

Blake shrank in his seat. "Just that Scotland's a good place to have a C-section." His face crumpled.

"Sorry," Roz said. "That was unnecessary."

"No, my fault," Blake replied. "I tend to spout facts when I don't know what else to say."

"You're not alone. Twenty-nine-point-three percent of people do the same," Roz replied.

"Really?" Blake said, sitting bolt upright.

"No."

Blake's face fell again. "Ah. I see."

Roz thought she should try and find coffee before causing any more problems. Oli had gone, but Beefy was sitting on a stool behind the bar. His eyes were closed, his arms folded.

"I know the bar is closed, but could I get some coffee?" Roz asked him.

Beefy opened his eyes slowly. "Is it for this lot?" he asked. "Because no amount of coffee is going to sort them out." He glanced over at Meg, though, with something—if she were giving him the benefit of the doubt—like paternal concern on his face.

"It's for me. I need to stay awake tonight."

Something in Roz's expression must have got through to Beefy. He swiftly got off his stool and started making the drink.

"I hope everything goes well for your daughter," Craig said. His voice was low and intimate.

"Thanks." She didn't know what else to say, so tried to change the subject. "Have you got kids?"

"Three," he said. "The younger two are with their mum, and I'm spending Christmas with my eldest."

"So you and their mum are not..." She left the sentence baited.

"We split a few years ago. All very amicable, no drama. But then we were never full-on fireworks, more a sparkler that fizzled out before we'd had a chance to write our names in the air."

Roz watched him gaze out of the window as a small station whipped by. "That's so sad."

"What about you? Do you have a husband or wife or both tucked away at home?" He avoided her gaze as if he didn't want to know the answer.

"Nope."

"That was short and sweet."

"Like me. Only I'm not sweet."

"Oh, I don't know. I bet you'll make a brilliant grandmother. Are you excited?"

So much for getting the conversation away from the baby. "I'm excited and terrified at the same time. They're the same emotion." Roz reached into her handbag, took out the silver cube, and held it up, twisting as she talked. "Just on different sides of the same cube."

"Roz, can I ask you something?" Craig was about to continue speaking when Grant, now standing on a banquette, drastically increased his volume.

"Sing with me!" he bellowed, swaying back and forth. His singing voice was deep and rich and only slightly out of tune as he crooned "Blue Christmas" to Meg. Meg smiled at him but didn't join in. He then jumped down and tried to pull Liv over to accompany him in singing along to "Baby, it's Cold Outside." Liv half smiled while backing away, then carried on talking with Ember.

"I'll sing with you," Aidan said, looking up at Grant with adoration. He stood next to him, and seemed to swell with pride as Grant's arm went around him.

As all parents knew from experience, this was all going to end in tears.

"I'm heading back to my room," Roz said, picking up her mug of coffee. "Going to wait for more news. I can't bear to watch things get out of control. I'm not paid to do that anymore."

"Part of me wants to convince you to stay," Craig said. Part of her wanted him to convince her too. Another part of her wanted to take him to her room. She didn't like being partitioned. His eyes locked on to hers. "But you're doing the right thing. This is all going to end in tears."

"That was just what I was thinking."

Craig nodded slowly, turning toward Grant. "I'll stay here, keep an eye on this lot."

"Are you sure you're in the CPS and not the police?"

"Very sure. I'm a lawyer. I'm trained to argue, not enforce."

"Where did you train?" Roz wondered if she knew him from the University of Glasgow, not that she remembered much from her university days. They were a haze of hash smoke chased by trauma.

"King's College, University of London. I still lecture there, occasionally. Do my bit for the new generation."

"Everybody up!" Grant was now trying to get everyone to join him in a conga. Time to go.

She said a reluctant goodnight to Craig, with a half promise of a shared breakfast in the morning, then walked back to Ember. "Having fun?"

Ember shrugged. Her face was flushed, but then she must be hot. Even though she'd unzipped her parka, she still had it on.

"Do you want to walk back with me?" Roz asked.

Ember shook her head. "You go. I'll stay. I'll be here if you need company later."

Roz nodded. If Ember wasn't having fun, why was she staying in the club car? Her instinct told her something else was going on. "I'm in room nine, if you need anything."

Ember nodded, but her attention was already elsewhere. Maybe it was just that Ember fancied someone in the room and didn't want to let that go.

As Roz passed Meg's booth, Grant climbed back onto the seat and grabbed Meg's shoulders. Roz saw his knuckles whiten as he gripped Meg harder and remembered the bruise on her flesh. "We're going to do the fucking conga," he said. "We're going to have fucking fun. What is it with all you fun-suckers? Does no one know how to have a good time anymore?"

"Please, don't, Grant," Meg said. "I don't feel well. Everything's gone weird." She was holding her hand out in front of her, waving it slowly, as if it were making vapor trails.

"Let her be, would you?" Roz said to him. "She's told you she doesn't want to play, and I don't blame her."

"It's okay," Meg said, her eyes cast down to the floor. "Don't worry about me."

"But I do, love," Roz replied. She sat down next to Meg on the banquette.

"Fuck off, we're having a moment here," Grant said.

Roz ignored him. She leaned close to Meg and whispered, "You don't have to put up with this. Say the word and I can help."

Meg's large pupils were like shiny black berries. "You're making it worse," she whispered. "You don't know."

"But I do. I promise."

Roz's phone bleeped with a new WhatsApp from Ellie: Going into the operating theatre now.

"You should go," Meg told her. "Grant is no angel, but you don't understand what we have."

"I think I do," Roz said. She had seen enough relationships that veered between obsessive love and anger that killed.

"I heard you talking about your daughter. Concentrate on her, not me."

Roz held her gaze, trying to divine whether that was what Meg really wanted. But she could only go by her words.

"You heard her." Grant pointed to the door, a smirk sliding up his face.

"I'm watching you," Roz said to him.

He laughed at that, a gleeful bark of victory that reminded her of another man. Roz turned to the door, hardly able to see between the tears and the memories.

Chapter Twenty-One

Meg stared at Grant as he watched Roz leave, his fingers tapping on the table. This was going to be bad, she knew it. Either he was going to follow Roz and hurt her, or he'd hurt Meg. Or someone else. Other people, like Meg, turned their rage inwards on themselves, but not Grant. His anger was always directed outward, usually at her.

She held on to his arm in the way he liked, showing she couldn't get her hand anywhere near around his bicep. "Ignore her, baby. She's under stress. Her daughter's in the hospital."

"I don't give a fuck. Given me nothing but grief since she first saw me."

"I know. It's not right. I'm sorry." She kept her tone soft and melty. Do nothing to antagonize.

He then pointed at Beck. "And that bitch over there is no better. Trying to shut me up or make me stop vaping."

Beck looked over, chewing her lip.

"How about we go to bed, like you said?" She stroked the side of his face. Stubble was beginning to spike through the skin.

He then turned and focused on her face. "You pushed me away. After you said we should cuddle in bed." His mouth smiled but his eyes flashed.

"I was just feeling sick, that's all."

He grabbed her chin and held it hard. He squeezed just above her jawbone until her eyes filled with tears. "You don't pull away from me," he said, softly. Anyone looking over would just see him holding her face as if he loved her, but his fingers pressed into skin and bone. "Do you understand?"

She tried to nod, but he was holding her too tight. He then sighed and placed his forehead against hers. He'd seen heroes do that on a Netflix show about Vikings and had been doing it ever since. Thought it connected him with what he claimed were his Nordic ancestors. She hoped the inspiration would stop there. He had once threatened to "blood eagle" her when she hadn't replied to a text one night. She'd had to look up what it was and had started shaking. Just his head touching hers though, made her lean into him, wanting more.

"We'll go to bed when I say so," he said. "Got to give them their money's worth." He then reared back, letting her go so abruptly that she tipped forward and banged her head against the table. "Be more careful," he said, then turned back to the partying.

Blake cheered, coming toward him. "Grant!" he said, handing him a full glass of whisky. "We're comparing specialist subjects. Mine's 'The Life and Works of Douglas Adams.' What's yours?"

"Women," Grant said and raised his glass. People laughed.

Meg felt the fog descend again. She wished she wasn't so dependent on him, but maybe that's what love was. Mum had called her relationship with Dad "a roller coaster of emotions, sweetheart," but, to Meg, a roller coaster was too safe a comparison. Even if your feet weren't touching anything, you were always strapped in on a ride. And unless you were in the wrong place and the wrong time, a roller coaster wouldn't kill you. Love, though, quickly had its hand around your throat and wouldn't stop squeezing until one of you called time.

Chapter Twenty-Two

The blue hospital curtains screech apart. Roz tries to count the ceiling tiles, but now they're moving too fast. The porter stares down at her as he pushes the trolley. Corridors close in. Roz has never known tiredness like this. A heavy caul lies over her. She wants to curl up under it and never surface.

Machines beep and blare. "Baby's heart rate is slowing. Mum's is racing," someone says. "We need to get her out, now." Her heart is already pulling away from Heather's; it can't take its own beats.

Her mum runs next to her. "It's going to be okay," she says. But Roz can't see how anything will be okay again.

❦

Roz sat on her bed, trying to click away the memories. The mirrored cube multiplied the ceiling light and flashed it around the cabin. "I'm here right now. I'm safe and okay."

Once the past had slunk back to its place behind the present, Roz took out her phone. She didn't have God to turn to, all she had was Google. How long do cesareans take? she asked it. Other potential queries included consequences of preeclampsia? and chances of baby surviving birth six weeks early? Google, as ever, provided many conflicting answers. That was why people liked deities—at least they gave you definitives.

She was aware, though, that she was using the rhythm of the train as a kind of rosary, saying "Please let them live," over and over, in time to it. Her own grandmother's Catholicism coming through at a moment of crisis.

She held her phone in her hand, willing it to ring. When it did, she reacted so quickly that she fumbled the device. She could hear Ellie's voice, low to the ground.

"Ellie?" she said, on the floor herself now. She gripped the phone, lifting it up. She wasn't going to let go again.

"Heather's out of surgery," Ellie said. "They're taking her to the Maternity Emergency Unit. She's having seizures."

Roz had read enough in the last hour to know this could lead to a stroke. "They're going to give her magnesium, right?"

"Yes, straight away."

Roz made herself say it: "What about the baby?"

"She's not breathing well." Roz could hear Ellie walking quickly along an echoing hospital corridor. Something on wheels rolled nearby. "I'm going with her to the neonatal ward, where they'll put her in an incubator with oxygen." Ellie paused. It sounded like she was the one fighting for breath. "She's so small, Roz. Barely four pounds, and they said she'll lose more weight. I can't bear it." Her voice was full of tears, as if they'd all gathered in her throat.

"Bearing it doesn't mean not feeling pain. It means getting beyond it, in time. Adrenaline and love will see you through for now."

"But if I go with the little one, I can't be with Heather."

"What did Heather say?" Roz said, knowing the answer.

"She said I should be with the baby."

"Then you're doing the right thing. And you're all in the right place," Roz said, feeling like one of those platitudinous baby books herself. She had to do better. "Look, love, this is going to be hard for you, I know. Incredibly. You now have two people to love. But hearts are like mozzarella: warm them up and they'll stretch as far as they're needed."

Ellie laughed through the tears. "Trust you to use a cheese simile."

"What can I say, I Camembert to be without one." Roz heard the tears in her own voice now, could taste the salt running down her throat.

"We're at the unit," Ellie said. The wheels stopped and a door opened. "I have to go. I'll send you the photos the midwife took."

"Ellie," Roz said, not wanting to let her go. "I just wanted to say, congratulations. You're a mum. May you be a better one than me."

Ellie ended the call. Roz called Heather's phone but got the answerphone. "Ellie just called," she said after the beep. "You, my wonderful daughter, have a daughter! You're incredibly brave. Rest well and know that I love you. And get some of the hospital toast—the cliché that toast eaten post-childbirth is the best you'll ever have is absolutely true."

Roz was still on the floor, her back against the toilet door. There was nothing to do now but wait and repeat the prayer of the train: "Please let them live, please let them live, please let them live."

Chapter Twenty-Three

Meg had lost track of time. And Grant. He had slipped out for yet another vape break and not returned, but that must have been a while ago. Or was it? The club car was almost empty for the first time since they'd entered. Only she, Ember, and Liv remained. They were in the corner, sharing a packet of crisps.

"Where's everyone gone?" Meg asked them.

Ember looked over to her. "Grant led the conga out, saying that there wasn't enough room in here. Though the corridors are even smaller in the sleeping cars."

"He's probably knocking on doors, waking people up," Meg replied. At the beginning of their relationship, she would have found this kind of behavior exciting, arousing even. She'd loved his spontaneity and cheek. She knew now that it wasn't about "having a bit of fun" as he'd insisted. It was about Grant having an impact on people, for good and bad.

Meg felt so strange, as if her head were too big. The lights were too bright. The room wouldn't stay still, even though she knew it wasn't moving. But then she'd hit her head on the table when Grant let her go. Either that or she drank too much with too little in her stomach. She needed to pull herself together quickly, as she had to do another live stream soon. The fans were getting restless, demanding more. She had played for time by inviting an AMA—Ask Me Anything—and was trying to reply, but one question had left her unable to answer.

What would be your biggest achievement in life?

And she didn't know. She didn't even know what she wanted. At least now she wanted to know what she wanted.

Meg heard laughter and the raucous singing of "All I Want for Christmas Is You" in the next railcar. Grant's voice was the loudest. She wondered who he was talking about…or singing to.

Beefy charged through the club-car doors. He stared back up the corridor toward the singing. "Back in here, everyone, and I'll thank you to be quiet. This is a train for sleeping on, you know. You might consider doing that." He then slumped into a booth and folded his arms, as the conga line returned to the club car.

Beck was at the front of the line, with Grant behind her, then Ayana. Aidan was next, looking as if he was having the time of his life, followed by a stumbling Sally, her eyes barely open, then Blake and Sam. The conga line's movements blurred into one, a millipede of mullered people. Maybe she could get everyone to do a Christmas dance for TikTok, because this conga line would not make good viewing.

Beefy stared at Grant as if he wanted to throw him from the train. Meg didn't blame him. Grant's long legs kicked out of time, his singing was out of tune, and his arms were wrapped around Beck's waist. Earlier, they'd seemed to loathe each other, but now she wouldn't have been able to slip a piece of paper between them.

Meg felt the prickly heat of jealousy.

Ember and Liv walked over to Meg, dodging the weaving dancers, stepping over or around the raised legs.

Liv yawned and rubbed her eyes. She looked exhausted, her eyes shadowed, and younger, as if tiredness had stripped away a few years.

"I'm off to bed," she said.

Ember gave Liv a little hug and watched as she exited the car. Meg felt another stab of envy, this time at how Ember and Liv had managed to become friends in such a short time. Meg hadn't made real friends since leaving the sixth form. Fame brought fake friends.

"Shall we join in?" Ember asked her. She was holding out a hand and watching Meg carefully.

"Not sure I'm not in the mood," Meg replied. Part of her yearned to join in, and she loved feeling wanted.

"You'd be doing me a favor. I don't have the confidence to do it by myself."

Meg sighed and nodded. She'd already had too much to drink, and not nearly enough to eat, but she swallowed the last of Ayana's drink anyway. As she took Ember's outstretched hand, she saw that the bruise on her own wrist was showing through the makeup.

Ember didn't say anything, so she may not have seen it. Although she did give Meg's hand a gentle squeeze. "Come on," she said, as the conga reached the bar. The line broke for a moment, as it awkwardly turned to go back the other way, far too many people in a narrow space.

Tapping Beck on the shoulder, Ember said, "May I cut in?" As Beck looked around, confused, Ember took over at the front of the line, with Meg, then Grant behind her. Beck stood, glowering, as the conga took off again without her.

"Decided to join us, have you?" Grant leaned down and whispered. His breath was sour.

She nodded. "I wanted to be with you."

"Glad to hear it," he said, putting his arms fully around her waist and squeezing so tightly she could hardly breathe. She'd once dreamed about being held by him. The first thing she'd noticed about him was his arms. The carved-out chunk of them emerging from his sleeves. Their first date had been to a bowling alley. He'd got strike after strike, the pins not standing a chance. He'd then scooped her up in celebration at the end, making her feel small, light, and safe. Now she just felt small.

"Keep it to a dull roar, would you?" Beefy the steward said as he walked out of the club car. His face seemed to pulse and glow, like Christmas tree lights stuck on an annoying setting.

Grant let go of her and stepped out of the line, looking around. He then grinned at Ember and slipped back into the conga behind her.

Meg looked at her hands. They were gripped tightly together, nails pressing into her flesh. She let go, her fingers cramping. What was she doing? Perhaps Grant was right, and her jealousy was out of control. He thought it a symptom of her relationship with her dad. "You're projecting his rejection of you onto me, darling," he'd said to her after he'd been on the reality show *Celebrity Therapy*. Meg and Grant each went on several of those C-list celeb programs a year, from interior design to cooking to deep-sea diving. They helped to, as Grant put it, "build the brand and grow the cash stash." Usually they forgot everything they'd picked up within a week, but Grant had actually learned a lot from that therapy show. He was really sweet for a while afterward but was still able to point out that she was invading his boundaries when she asked where he had been all night.

She should have been grateful for Grant and everything else she had—she'd learned that on *Celebrity Ashram*. She moved out of the conga line, hoping to make things up with him, to him. Then she saw Grant turn and bend his head close to Ember's shoulder. He whispered in her ear and kissed her on the neck. He then placed his hand on her shoulder. Ember froze as if never wanting the moment to end. Of course she did. Why wouldn't she? He's Charming Grant! It would always be like this. He would never be happy with just Meg. She could see that now.

Meg felt as if she was rotting inside. The conga carried on, circling her. An unending train of faces laughing, gurning, turning toward her and away. Faces coupling and decoupling. She didn't know what was real or unreal anymore.

She lurched forward as Grant passed her, grabbing his arm. He shook her away. She put her arms around his neck, and he just lifted her up and stood her on one of the triangular tables. She was small, but her head still touched the ceiling. Stooping, she placed a palm onto the window to steady herself. It felt cool under her hot fingertips, and she wanted to press herself naked against the glass.

The conga had broken into clumps of people, all dancing. They seemed far below her, undulating. Meg scanned the club car. Maybe she could go to Beefy for help. He seemed kind. But she couldn't see him anywhere.

Meg felt the scream come out of her throat but didn't hear it. Others seemed to though. They stopped undulating and stared at her. The scream kept coming, like a magician's handkerchief. She didn't know where it all came from. She felt frozen in place, a brittle figure on a wedding cake.

Grant approached her. He was a cartoon version of himself, his movements and speech coming out slowly. His face morphed in micro-moments between laughter, surprise, embarrassment, and rage. She knew she was humiliating him. The most dangerous thing she could do. Meg put a hand to her face to stop herself from laughing and found instead she was being sick. It poured through her spread fingers onto her shoes, the table, and the floor.

"You're disgusting," Grant whispered. Spittle glistened from his capped tooth to his filled lip.

Meg twisted away and placed her forehead against the cool window, bent over with shame. She stared at her reflection. Her reflection tried to smile back.

"Don't you turn away from me." He grabbed her hips and swiveled her around to face him, as if she were a broken ballerina in a music box. Everything whirled around her as she tried to get her balance. "You're a joke. A fucking embarrassment." His voice was so quiet she could hardly hear it, and he kept a loving smile on his face. Always performing for other people. Always hiding what he was in plain sight.

Something clicked inside her. She broke away from him, lurching off the table into Craig, who helped her down. "What were you doing, with her?" she said to Grant, pointing at Ember. "I saw you kiss her."

Grant's upper lip curled into a sneer. "You're crazy. Now everyone will know it."

Ember held up a hand, shaking her head. "He just said I looked and smelled nice." She shrugged as if to say that was hardly a crime, and, hey, she *did* look and smell nice. "It's not what you're thinking. I promise."

Meg laughed. She knew she sounded unhinged but found she didn't care. "That's the biggest cliché. Because if you know what I'm thinking, it's probably true."

"You're drunk," Grant said, "and God knows what else. You need to go away before you say or do something you regret."

"Sounds a bit like a threat, mate," Craig said, his accent thickening. "I'd back off if I were you."

"Fuck off," Grant said, pushing Craig away. "Don't 'mate' me. I don't even know you. You're just an ugly old fucker trying to party with young people. What are you, some kind of pervert?"

"Why is everyone shouting?" Sally bellowed from her booth.

"You keep out of it too," Grant snapped at her. "Think you can lecture me? Do your children usually see you off your face? 'Cos sure looks like they're used to it. And if you think your husband has been faithful to you, you're as stupid as your children."

Aidan blinked, confused and hurt.

Meg knew how he felt. The world was tipping and it was all her fault. "Please, stop," she screamed. "I can't take it. I'll go, then it'll all be okay again."

"Meg," Ember was calling to her, but her voice sounded strange, as if she were underwater. "I can help you!" It was this that made the tears form, that someone wanted to rescue her. But Grant would think he had caused them, that he had won. Again.

Meg wouldn't let him see her cry, not this time. She ran out of the club car, aware of the phone cameras turning her way. Her eyes stung as she stumbled down the corridor to their cabin. The train itself seemed to whisper to her: *he doesn't love you, he doesn't love you, he never loved you.*

Chapter Twenty-Four

Roz lay on her bed trying to read, but the words slipped through her head without her registering them. Minutes clicked by. The last message from Ellie was a while ago. Heather was being given magnesium sulphate for the seizures, and tablets to try to bring her blood pressure down. The baby, not yet named, was being fed formula through her nose and into her stomach.

Roz scrolled through her photos to the last one Ellie had sent. Her granddaughter, eyes yet to open, was bundled in blankets in an incubator. She looked so small, so unheld. Roz had to twist the mirrored cube to stay in the present, and not tumble into her past. She turned it along with her thoughts, feeling her own blood pressure decrease with each click. A plan formed as the room lights bounced off the reflected surfaces. She would go straight to the hospital and form a tag team with Ellie—one of them with the baby, the other with Heather, then switch. At night, she'd go to their flat, and cook protein-rich food—important, according to her recent, frantic research into severe preeclampsia—and bring it to Heather's bed. Roz would be there to do skin-to-skin with the baby, again important for preemies (how she wished she didn't know that was the name for premature babies), when Ellie was by Heather's side.

If skin-to-skin had been more of a thing when Heather was born, then maybe they'd have bonded. Roz had never admitted this, but she hadn't wanted to hold Heather at all at first. She was in such shock that all she could do was eat strawberry jelly from the little plastic tubs the nurses gave out. Maybe if five-pound Heather and her little spider monkey arms had been placed on Roz's chest then, they'd get on better now.

She checked her watch. It was half-past seven. Roz opened the curtains, but there was nothing to see yet; the dark was keeping the Highlands to itself. Soon the sun would take over, and Roz would be able to distract herself by staring out of the window instead of at her phone. Seeing the stunning landscape pass would help her feel that she was really on her way home. She opened the window slightly, and felt the ice in the slice of air that cut into the cabin. Snow fell at a slant.

In the corridor outside, she heard the main door into the sleeping railcar open. Light footsteps ran past, accompanied by the sound of a woman sobbing. A cabin door opened, then closed.

It could be Ember, her tears returning, now that the party was dying. Roz wondered if she should go and comfort her; after all, she would be able to hear which cabin she was in. But, then, Roz had given Ember her room number. If she'd wanted to knock, she would have. And Roz knew that she was trying to make up for not being with Heather. She'd found another woman, not much older than her daughter, to mother and bother.

But, if she was really honest, she wanted to talk to someone. She had no friends who would welcome a call at this time in the morning. Hardly any friends at all outside of the station. Was this all she had to show for five decades on the planet—no one to lean on when crises hit? Roz again wished that her mum was still around. Then she remembered the letter in the recipe book.

She picked up a piece of her whisky tablet and nibbled around its edges. She would leave a piece out for Santa tonight. It would be as if Mum was there. In a way, she was—in her recipe book. If only Roz wasn't such a coward and was able to open it again. She could run after armed robbers but couldn't read a recipe book.

When her mum had been in the hospital after her first stroke, three years ago, Liz had somehow found the energy to send the recipe for her much-prized, and previously highly secret, recipe for spiced shortbread ("*the secret is in the semolina*")—and written on the back, in her own, jagged writing, was the following:

> *Darling Roz,*
>
> *Hospital beds are strangely squishy, as is the food. I can attest to this as I'm in a hospital bed and eating hospital food as I write. If you can avoid both of these occurrences, Rosalind, I recommend it. Sometimes, however, one has no choice and, if in this situation, all I can suggest is that you bring with you an array of condiments and keep them in your handbag or cabinet. A dash of Tabasco can do wonders to—*

The train screamed right then, as if in pain.

Roz's whole cabin seemed to lunge to one side. The recipe book fell, and the toilet door flew open. Her bags slid. Roz was rolled across the bed onto the floor. The cabin then switched and teetered back the other way, shunting everything once again. Roz grabbed the recipe book and held herself in the brace position while the room settled around her.

Screeching, wrenching brakes. The smell of scorched metal. Shouts and screams from everywhere, including nearby cabins. And then stillness and a strange, weighted silence. The train had stopped.

Footsteps ran down the corridor. "Everyone stay where you are," Beefy shouted, out of breath, fear clear in his voice, "while we work out what's happened."

Voices came from outwith. Crunching snow. Swearing. She used the sink to pull herself slowly up to standing.

Looking out the window, she saw that the sun had yet to reclaim the sky. The stars were visible in the dark sky, looking down on a wounded train. This wasn't the Christmas Eve morning she had been hoping for.

Beefy and a woman in a uniform—possibly Bella, the train driver—were sidling along the tracks, clomping through deep snow. They shone far reaching flashlights onto the tracks. "The cab and seating railcars have come off the rails," the woman shouted. She was pointing to farther down the train, beyond where Roz could see.

Roz thought immediately of Tony and Mary, hoping they were both safe in their seats.

Beefy, a bit ahead, shouted something back that Roz couldn't hear. Whatever he said though, couldn't have been good news, as the woman kicked at the snow. She turned and swept the torch around in a circle. The train track curved around the base of a mountain. Should anyone be silly enough to climb it, there was clear, if snow-covered, access to the slopes, although, when the light hit it right, Roz saw a flash of dark ravine ahead.

"Oli can carry on sorting breakfast. Beefy, check if anyone's hurt," the woman said, walking toward a door. "I've got a signal at least. I'll make some calls. See how long it's going to take for the engineers to arrive and get us moving again."

She shone the torch at the train, making Roz blink. "You okay?" the woman shouted to her.

"Fine," Roz replied. "Anything I can do? I've just retired from the police, so I can boss people around."

The woman laughed and approached Roz's window, carefully wading through the snow. She was in her late thirties, with hair as dark as Roz's once was, and was shivering, her lips beginning to go blue. She gazed intently at Roz as if checking out her capacity to lead.

"If you're at all unsure, you can check my credentials." Roz grabbed her wallet from her coat pocket and showed her expired card. "I'm Roz. Formerly DI Rosalind Parker, CID, Lewisham. Specialist in obtaining confessions and fucking people off so much, they fuck up so I can catch them."

"Then I'm very pleased you're on my side. I'm Bella, the driver. And you'd better get going and help me, otherwise I'll confess something. The club car stayed on the tracks so if you could get everyone in there it should be safer, and we can make sure everyone's fine."

"How did this happen?"

"A huge tree fell on the tracks, but I only saw it when we rounded the bend, so I had to put on the brakes. I thought we were going to topple into the ravine."

"We couldn't still, could we?" Roz asked. She realized she was gripping the windowsill as if that could stop them from falling.

"No, I don't think so. Although I'll be happier when we've got everyone into the club car and can decouple the seated railcars. Safety first and all that."

Knock, knock, knock at her door. "Is that you, Roz?" Tony's shaken voice came from the corridor.

"You answer that and get started," Bella said, already beginning to move away. "I'll join you soon as I can."

Roz closed the window and opened her cabin door. Tony was holding Mary up. Both looked shaken, and blood was trickling down Mary's face.

"You're hurt," Roz said, pointing toward the cut. "Did you fall?"

Mary touched the side of her head and looked with confusion at the blood on her fingers. "Must have been poor Mousetache, giving me a scratch. He scrabbled in my lap when the train tilted and tried to climb up on my head. He didn't mean to hurt me."

Of all the times at work that Roz had heard the phrase "they didn't mean to hurt me" said of a loved one, this was the only time she'd believed it.

"Where's Mousetache now?" Roz asked, not seeing the cat backpack.

"We don't know," Tony said. Tears made his eyes shine. "He must be hiding in the railcar somewhere, but won't come out. He might be hurt or—" He placed his hands over his face.

Then Roz realized she'd been mistaken, and Mary was the one holding Tony up.

"Mousetache will be just fine," Mary said. "We're on the way to find some nice cheese and make a little trail for him into the backpack."

"Right now," Roz said, "I need you to go to the club car, and stay there. Your railcar came off the tracks."

"Well, clearly," Mary said. "It was like walking on a funhouse floor. Without the fun."

"More like a ghost train, especially when the lights kept flickering," Tony said.

"Either way, it's a fairground ride, and probably best you're not in there." Roz saw Tony open his mouth to object. "Don't worry, we'll find Mousetache. Was there anyone else in the seated railcar with you?"

"Only your man with his coat over his head," Tony said.

"You might need to be more specific."

"Man in his forties, maybe. Looked like he'd been sleeping rough, or at least had had it tough lately."

The stowaway man. Roz worried that she hadn't done him a favor after all by turning a blind eye. "I think I know who you mean."

"I wouldn't have noticed him other than that I nearly came to blows with him."

"In what way?"

"He was haranguing the poor, skinny, famous lass with the hair," Tony said.

"Meg?"

"That's it. She came into the railcar, and he told her to get off the train."

"He backed off when Tony spoke to him," Mary said, her pride obvious.

"Didn't hear a peep from him after. Slunk away for a while as well. And then he wasn't in his seat when I woke up, which was not long before we crashed." Tony turned to Mary. "You were up earlier, Mum. Did you see him?"

Mary shook her head. "No. Although his coat's still there."

"Okay, so he probably didn't leave," Roz said. "Unless he wanted to freeze. I'll look into where he is. For now, hunker down in the club car and we'll go from there."

A cabin door at the end of the railcar opened and a very sleepy-looking Phil emerged, baby in the crook of his arm. The baby was guzzling milk, and Robert the toddler was tugging at Phil's pajama leg. "What's going on?" Phil asked through a yawn. "Why have we stopped?"

"The train derailed, so we're making sure everyone's safe."

His jaw dropped, making his long face longer. "We slept through it. Is Sally okay? What about Aidan and Liv? They're not in their room. Tell me they're all right?"

"I haven't seen them yet," Roz replied. "I've only just come out."

"And Meg, is she safe?" He pointed at the door two along from him and two down from Roz's cabin.

"I don't know. Why do you ask?"

Roz's inner raised eyebrow must have shown on the outside, as he then flushed and said, "Once someone's teacher, always their teacher. I'm worried about the students too."

"Of course." An interesting silence swung between them.

"I'll throw some clothes on and meet you in the club car," Phil said, hoisting up the toddler and slipping back into his cabin.

Roz started knocking on all the cabin doors, calling out, "Time to get up, everyone. Get to the club car." There was no reply from Meg and Grant, but maybe they were still in the club car. Roz began working on a mental to-do list:

1. Find out how many people got off the train at Edinburgh and other stations.
2. Roll call of remaining passengers.
3. See to any necessary first aid, including for shock.

She stopped then, remembering that she had the very best thing for shock. Roz dashed back down the corridor. It was odd to no longer feel the rumble and hear the muttering of the train. It felt lonelier. And that her prayers would no longer be amplified.

In her cabin, Roz grabbed one of the bags of tablet and the tin of shortbread she'd made. She could make more later; right now there were people who needed sugar. She remembered something her mum had said, when they last made apple cake together in the summer before Mum's fall: "The best cake for a crisis is any cake. And the best person for an emergency is you, darling. You've always had a clear voice and a level head when things go wrong. You come alive when the stakes are high.

Remember that when you retire. You're going to need something else to feed that part of you."

It was true. One sign of an emergency and she had a sense of focus and purpose. She needed that, she realized. She was no longer a police officer. Other than being a mother and grandmother, what was going to feed her now?

Chapter Twenty-Five

In the corridor, Roz ran into an agitated and out-of-breath Aidan.

"Are you coming to check on your dad?" she asked.

"And the little ones," he replied, gripping a brown inhaler in his hand.

"I've just seen them. They're all well. It didn't even wake them up, the noise in the corridor did."

Aidan's laugh was accompanied by a wheeze. The little red spots on his cheeks began to lessen.

"Your dad is just getting dressed, and he'll be coming to the club car in a few minutes. I bet he'd appreciate you getting him a coffee."

Aidan nodded, looking like an eager little boy. He turned and walked quickly away. Roz was sure she saw him skip.

Mary, Tony, and Ember were settled in the club car when she entered, in a booth of their own. In the adjacent one, Liv was curled up in a corner next to Sally, who was slumped in a corner, drool crust on her chin, presumably having slept there right through the crash. Grant lay on a banquette, holding a rolled-up tea towel to his temple. Craig sat at one of the triangular tables, looking out into the snow. He looked across to her, and his smile calmed her.

Aidan was dutifully getting coffee at the bar and Sam, Blake, and

Ayana were in another booth, heads leaning into the middle of the table, their faces lit up. They were talking about having a snowball fight and what they would tell their friends when they got home. To Roz, being stuck was a terrible inconvenience; to them it was the best adventure.

"Where's Beck?" Roz asked.

"She went to bed a while ago. She's still sleeping, probably."

Behind the bar area, Oli was busy sorting breakfast trays and making hot drinks. Roz went up to him, the smell of coffee making her mouth water.

"Where are we?" she asked, looking out of the window. The edges of a dark mountain range were outlined in orange. Snow fell as if it was never going to stop.

"In the Grampians, so south Highlands. That's Ben Doran," Oli said, pointing to the pyramid peak. "Also known as Beinn Dòrain."

"In the middle of nowhere, then."

"Aye. And not far away there's a hanged martyr's hill. Not the most hospitable of places to stop." He sighed, then poured her a cup of coffee. "Still, at least we've got booze, food, coffee, and tea."

Roz took the cup with thanks and allowed herself a moment to savor it.

"There's a poem about this place," Sam was saying. They pointed to the mountain. "By Duncan Ban MacIntyre. It's called 'Moladh Beinn Dòbhrain.'"

"In praise of Beinn Dòrain," Roz said. She was once again amazed that her long-untested linguistic prowess had risen up to the surface.

"That's right!" Sam said, eyes bright, more animated than Roz had ever seen them. They stood up and started walking up and down the railcar, reciting:

> An t-urram thar gach beinn
> Aig Beinn Dòbhrain;
> De na chunnaic mi fon ghrèin,
> "S i bu bhòidhche leam..."

Sam's voice resonated around the railcar and seemed to carry to Beinn Dòrain itself.

Silence then lay over the club car.

"I'd recite the rest," Sam said, looking a bit freaked out by everybody else's lack of response. "But I don't like the sound of my voice that much."

"Well, I do," Blake said. "How many verses are there?"

"Eight." Sam started to blush.

"You can recite them to me later," Blake said, moving to stand by Sam.

"What does the poem mean?" asked Ayana.

"That goes beyond my translation abilities I'm afraid," Roz said.

Sam placed their hands together. "Basically, it's a love song to the mountain. MacIntyre was a gamekeeper in the area. He loved this place."

"I think it's magnificent," Craig said. "Both the mountain and the poem, which I just about followed in Gaelic."

"What I love," Blake said, going up to Sam and kissing them, "is that I don't know any Gaelic, but I can feel the hills and mountains in the syllables. The crags and valleys are there in the rise and fall of the meter, the terrain inhabits the consonants." He looked at Sam with lust. "I didn't know you could roll your 'r's like that." Seemed like Sam wasn't the only sapiosexual in the group.

Roz understood being aroused by wisdom. Well, she thought she did, anyway. There was something extremely attractive about someone imparting knowledge. Craig knowing Gaelic, for example, sharpened her attraction to him in a manner that she wished would go away.

She looked away from him and out of the window. The snow was getting thicker. The sun was beginning to hike up the sky though, giving the landscape an unreal glow, the snowflakes looking almost like pixelation. She placed her face close to the glass. The external lights on the train showed a set of deep footprints leading away from the train.

Pointing to the prints, she asked Oli, "Did you see Beefy or Bella walking on that side of the tracks?"

"No," he said, peering out. "Haven't seen anyone over there." Oli shivered in sympathy. "Can't be much fun in this cold."

Roz thought of the stowaway, without his coat. "I know this is a funny request, but when you've finished serving breakfast, would you mind following those footprints? I'm worried someone's out there, lost. And in this weather…"

"No problem," Oli replied. "In fact, I'd like to get out and about. It'll be pure dead beautiful once the sun's overhead."

"Be really careful. You won't know what's underneath the snow. Go slowly, and follow the prints exactly, so you'll know how deep it goes."

Oli rubbed his hands together and grinned. He was loving this. Being stranded on a derailed train in the snow was high adventure to him. Roz wondered for a moment what it would be like to be in her twenties again. Then shuddered. She'd rather be forty-nine and give as many fucks as she'd had in the last year. Which was none.

"Do you know how many passengers remain on the train?" she asked.

Oli took a form out from underneath the bar. "Beefy filled this in last night—hard to be sure but some got off at Edinburgh, a few more at Glasgow, so we think that leaves seventeen passengers." So, Roz thought, eighteen with the stowaway.

"Only three members of staff?"

"There'd usually be more, but with the cancellations, it was only us willing to be in Fort William if we can't get back tomorrow. Beefy would much rather be in London, but he has some family up here, and Bella's are in Tulloch. I'll be stranded though."

"There are worse places to be stranded," Roz said and was surprised to find she meant it.

Bella strode into the club car, rubbing her hands and stomping her feet. Snow fell from her boots onto the carpet. "Hi everyone. I'm Bella, your driver. Or was. I'd like to apologize right now for us being stationary. None of us wants to be in this situation. I've contacted the engineers and they'll be here when they can, but it's going to take a while, I'm afraid. I've had word that our rescue will be delayed as we are currently unreachable by road and there's a tree on the line near Tulloch. I've told them we're a priority, as there are children and older people on the train—"

"Don't stir yourself on my account," Mary called out. "I'm having the best time." She pointed to the bottle of port on their table. "Tony raided our suitcase. We were keeping this for the family Christmas, but I dare say we can find another when we eventually get home."

Roz's heart was thumping as she thought of Heather, Ellie, and the baby. "Is there no way we can get them here any quicker? Get us to the front of the queue?"

"I also said we had celebrities on board, so that should expedite our rescue. If you also tweet about us being stuck, I'm sure train wheels will turn quicker. But you didn't hear that from me." She placed her finger over her lips. "While they last, food and soft drinks are complimentary. So drink up, sit tight, and stay away from the front of the train." She moved toward the door, stopping as she exited to say, "And enjoy the view!" She hurried out before anyone could stop and ask awkward questions.

Roz looked around the cabin and clapped her hands. The excited chatter faded and people looked her way. "Is anyone hurt?" she asked.

"I bashed my head," Grant said.

"Have you put ice on it?"

Grant jabbed a finger over to Oli. "He's run out of ice, so I had to go out and get some snow and pack it in here." He placed the now-wet tea towel back on his head and winced.

"Did you black out at any point?" Roz asked.

Grant carefully shook his head. "No."

"And do you have a headache?"

"I hit my head," he snapped. "'Course I have a headache." He took a swig from a half-empty beer bottle and grimaced.

"Roz is just trying to see if you have a concussion, lad," Mary said. Her voice was sharp.

"And it could well be," Roz said, standing up again. "As you were drinking before and, apparently, after you banged your head, usually I'd be sending you straight to A&E. Alcohol is a bad plan if you have a brain injury. But seeing as we've no idea when we'll get going again, let alone to a hospital, you should rest, stay awake, and lay off the booze."

Grant's laugh was sardonic.

Reminded by the mention of the hospital, Roz got out her phone, but there were no new messages from Ellie, and no word at all from

Heather. What if the situation had gotten worse? She remembered what her Googling had uncovered: that eclampsia could lead to coma. She felt adrenaline and panic at the last conversation she'd had with Heather. What if it really was their last, and that was how they'd left it?

She had to stay busy. It was the only way she'd get through this.

She spotted the dried vomit on Grant's shirt. "Were you sick?"

"That's not mine," Grant said with disgust.

"Often go around with someone else's vomit on you, do you?"

"Meg wasn't feeling good," Aidan said. "She was sick, a bit. A bit got on me. Not long before the crash."

"Where is she now?" Roz asked.

Grant shrugged and did not meet her eyes. From the guilty looks on his and other faces, something had happened earlier.

"Did it not occur to you to go and find her after the crash?" she asked him. "Or even right now?"

"Thought you said I should rest."

"Fine. I'll go. I'll make sure Beck is okay as well, but I'll need your key cards in case they're asleep or injured."

Ayana gave her the card for her and Beck's room, while Grant plucked his from his pocket. "You're welcome to her," he said. He then lay back down on the banquette. Not the ideal way to stop himself going to sleep, but Roz didn't feel like telling him again.

Roz plonked the homemade goodies she'd retrieved from her cabin on a triangular table and said, "Help yourself—handmade whisky and raisin tablet, and spiced shortbread. Keep you going till breakfast."

Chapter Twenty-Six

Roz knocked on Beck's door. "We need you up and about, Beck." She tried to keep her voice light and airy, with just a bite of cold.

"Go away." Beck's voice was muffled.

"Can't do that, I'm afraid. We need everyone in the club car."

"You can't make me."

"True." Roz thought for a moment. "But I can make it really annoying for you to stay." She then started singing "Mull of Kintyre" at great volume and with little attention paid to the right lyrics or being in tune. "Join in, why don't you?"

It took less than a minute for Beck to open the door. Her hair was all over the place, her cardigan buttons in the wrong holes. "You could've just let me sleep. I wasn't hurt. The side of the bunk kept me in place."

"But then you wouldn't be able to see the sunrise."

Beck looked out of the window into the dark. "Yeah. Nice." She then trudged away.

"Did you win, by the way?" Roz called after her.

"Of course, I did," she said without turning back.

Roz was about to knock on Meg's door when Phil and the kids came past. He somehow seemed more worried than he had been ten minutes before. "Sally's not angry with me, is she?"

"Why would she be?"

"Just checking," he said, then hurried toward his hungover wife. More than railcars needed decoupling on this train.

She knocked softly at first. "Are you all right, Meg?"

No sound from inside. She knocked again, louder this time. "Are you in there? It's Roz, the one who suggested the quiz yesterday. I'm checking everyone's all right. Can I come in?"

No answer.

Roz placed the key near the handle but it didn't open. It must be locked from the inside.

"Everything okay, madam?" Beefy said, coming down the corridor toward her. He was so big, he blocked out most of the light.

"It's ma'am," Roz said automatically, used to telling new recruits how to address her.

"Sorry, ma'am," Beefy said, confusion and contrition crossing his face.

"No, I…oh, never mind. That was from my days in the police. I'm just a civilian now but haven't gotten used to it yet."

"Bella said you were in CID. Big respect." He did a kind of salute, large hand held parallel to his face.

"Thanks, although wait to see if I deserve respect first. It isn't automatically due to everyone. Anyway, to answer your question, no." She pointed into the cabin. "Meg isn't answering, and it's locked from the inside."

"Hello?" Beefy said, standing close to the door. "Miss Meg?"

More silence.

Roz felt a familiar freezing fear. The intuition that something was very wrong behind a closed door. She turned to Beefy. "Is there some kind of override to lift the latch?"

"Normally there would be," Beefy said. "But some of the train's electrical systems are out because of the crash. Bella's trying to sort them."

"Can you break through the lock to get in?"

"Do you really think that's necessary?"

When Roz nodded, Beefy sized up the door. "I'll give it a go." He breathed in, chest expanding, then barged at the door. It gave a little, but didn't open. Beefy rubbed his shoulder. "Tricky without a run up. Do you really think she's in there?"

"I hope not, as she's not answering. But it's locked from the inside and no one else has seen her."

Beefy nodded, his worry lines deepening. He then threw his full bulk at the door, crashing through into the room and steadying himself with a hand on the bathroom wall. Roz couldn't see past him, but his gasp then the keening sound he made told her everything.

"You'd better step out, Beefy." Roz placed her hand gently on his outstretched arm. He was trembling.

"I don't understand," he said, stumbling back into the corridor. He turned to Roz, as if she could explain and make everything okay.

But she couldn't.

Meg was lying on the floor, body twisted. Blood congealed under her head. Roz could only see one eye from where she stood, but it was swollen and open, unblinking. Roz didn't need to fully enter the room to know that Meg was dead.

She had to check though. It was protocol, in case a life could be saved, but it was also human, a need to make sure nothing else could be done. Taking a large, careful step, Roz stood on the one bit of floor that wasn't covered in clothes or cosmetics. She crouched, very slowly, and reached for Meg's nearest hand. The skin still had warmth to it. And no matter how long Roz waited with her fingertips pressed against Meg's inner wrist, she was never going to feel a pulse. She went to check the carotid artery, then stopped. Meg's throat was red with what looked like multiple scratch marks around her neck, as if she'd been trying to pry someone's hands away. Someone had tried to hurt her. And they had succeeded.

A wave of grief crashed through Roz. The poor girl had lived for other people's likes and had never found a way to live for herself. Roz thought, then, of Grant, and how he had treated Meg. Grief shifted into anger, making bile rise and her heart burn. Even if he hadn't been the one to kill her, she knew in her gut he'd tried to, if only her spirit.

Beefy was sobbing silently next to her. "She's dead, isn't she?" Even now there was hope in his voice that she'd contradict him.

Roz nodded.

"But, how?" He looked from Roz to Meg and back again. "The derailment couldn't have killed her, could it? It wasn't that bad."

"I don't know." But she could guess.

"You'll find out, won't you?" Beefy put his big hands together in the prayer position. Tears tobogganed down his face.

"It's not my job anymore." This was a clear case of not her circus. She could walk away from this and leave it to coppers who were still being paid.

"But if it wasn't the crash, do you think she was murdered?" He nodded toward the body but couldn't look at Meg without crying.

"It's a possibility that can't be discounted," Roz said. She got straight back into her patter like a comfy old coat.

His hand went into a fist. "I bet it was him. That cocky twat, Grant."

"Speculating isn't going to help." Although he was probably right. If it wasn't an accident—and it didn't look like one with these marks on her neck—then Grant was the most likely suspect.

"Please help her." Beefy's voice had grown as small as his body was big.

"It's not my place anymore, Beefy."

"But you've been trained, and you're here right now. And you were watching her last night. I saw you."

If Beefy had been watching her, he'd have been keeping an eye on Grant too. He may know something that could help the investigation.

But it wasn't her case. "All I can advise you to do is seal off this cabin so evidence isn't compromised, and put Grant in another cabin, if you can. It's not likely he'll run off, probably catch hypothermia if he did, but we need to make sure he's here, ready to be questioned, when the police arrive."

"But that could be ages. I was once stuck on a train in the Highlands for thirty-four hours. And that was without there being a crime on board. Then once they get here, everywhere will be searched, and we'll be taken back for questioning. It could take days."

Panic seared through Roz. She couldn't be that long. Heather needed her. She couldn't spend Christmas Eve and possibly Christmas Day on the night train. She took out her phone. The signal was low, one bar, but still there. But there was no update on Heather or the baby's condition. The doctors must have done their morning rounds by now, surely?

"Besides," Beefy continued. "If it wasn't Grant, then the killer is someone else on the train. And I'd rather you found them before anything else happened."

He was right. The killer needed to be identified and detained. And maybe, if she had sufficient evidence, the police wouldn't keep the passengers too long. It was a long shot, but what else was she going to do? Have flashback after flashback? There was only so much pacing she could do in a tiny cabin, and she only had two hands to wring. She had no choice but to find out what happened to Meg.

Roz switched into professional mode. It was easier than letting herself feel, and far more productive, although rage often fueled her investigations. Gave her energy to do what she had to do. "Dial 999," she told Beefy. "We need an ambulance and investigative team for a probable crime scene. Ask them how we can place Grant under temporary cabin arrest without being charged with kidnap. I also need hygienic gloves, shoe covers used for cleaning or in the galley, and ziplock bags if you have them." Roz thought of the possible problems with investigating, how it could compromise the case. "Order everyone apart from Grant to stay in the club car." In a normal investigation, she'd have help. Someone with a knowledge of the law and an eye for detail that she could team up with. "And could you ask Craig to come here, please?"

Beefy nodded, his eyes glazed with shock. He hurried down the corridor, sniffing.

Standing in the entrance, she scanned the room. In her time in CID, she'd developed her own technique for examining crime scenes, in person or in photos. She looked at each part of the cabin as if it were a jigsaw puzzle that she had to solve. She was glad to use that method now. It added another layer between her and the horror.

Meg's handmade decorations were strewn across the room. A sad, broken paper doll lay on her twisted torso. A piece of mistletoe was stuck behind the picture on the wall, and the rest was near the body. There was blood on the edge of the sink, possibly where Meg had hit her head.

Clothes and cosmetics were thrown everywhere, on the bed, on the floor, in the sink, in the shower area. The train derailment could have done that, she supposed, but the room was in such a mess that it could have been trashed during an attack. Or perhaps someone searched the room after Meg died.

Various pots had fallen onto the floor. It was a roll call of fancy creams that Roz had heard of—Crème de la Mer, Dr. Barbara Sturm, Augustinus Bader, Estée Lauder, Chanel—and more that she hadn't, including Advanced Snail 92, Atropa eye drops, Anese Calm Your Tits Boob Mask, and Le Tush Clarifying Butt Mask. A tub of Lush's Silky Underwear talcum had spilled on the floor, making the room smell of jasmine and vanilla. The edge of the powder had a mark—a curve and several lines. Not enough to suggest a clear footprint. A compact mirror had broken. She then counted the mirror shards scattered like stars across a sky of fallen clothes.

Roz centered her attention on Meg's body. She was still fully clothed, and Roz felt an instinctive relief at that. As well as the marks on her neck, the purple bruising on her upper arm and the yellow band around her wrist, there was slight discoloration on Meg's jaw that hadn't been there earlier. Roz knew she should never assume, and she'd never have said so out loud when on the force, but she'd put money on there being other signs of violence on her body.

She took out her camera and started taking pictures. First of the room and close-ups of every item in it, then the door and window. Finally, she took photos of Meg: full-length photos of her body, crops of her bruises and injuries. Strangely, the one image that made her want to cry was one of Meg's hand and curled fingers almost touching her cracked phone, as if trying to use it even after death. One evening in her near company— not even that—five minutes of eavesdropping and mild cyberstalking had showed Roz that Meg lived her life through a screen, and that was what she still reached for in death. Or maybe there was something on the phone that could help the investigation.

Roz turned then to possible cause of death. She obviously couldn't determine exactly, but she took photos of signs that Meg had died of asphyxia or respiratory failure, with possible sudden cardiac death. The whites of her eyes were dashed with petechiae. Blood trailed from her right nostril. She showed cyanosis, her lips and nails tinged hospital-curtain blue.

A postmortem would be able to tell, hopefully, if she had been smothered or strangled, or—the other option with asphyxiation—poisoned. They'd look for abrasions to the skin, material fragments in the mouth and lungs, contusions on the inner walls of the respiratory tract, hemorrhagic infiltration into neck muscles, injury to the hyoid bone, chest compression and rib fracture, toxicity in the blood and tissues... If Grant or anyone else had killed her, then Meg had to be sliced open, violated again, to find out.

The other question was, how was she murdered in a locked room? The switch lock had been manually turned from within the cabin. The locked window showed no sign of forced entry. Meg was killed in her room, yet she had been the only one inside.

"Beefy told me you could do with some support," Craig said, coming through the sliding doors at the end of the corridor. He was standing straighter, looking less shabby. In lawyer mode. Roz was surprised by the upwelling of gratitude and relief she felt. He handed her boxes of blue plastic gloves, shoe slippers, and ziplock bags.

Craig took a startled breath as he stood beside her and covered his mouth with his hand. They both then looked at the scene in silence. It felt to Roz like crime scenes had their own gravity, as if the air were heavier upon them.

Roz slipped on the gloves and plastic shoe coverings. "I checked for sign of life earlier, but a witness of me collecting evidence would be good." Choosing the only clear piece of carpet, she stepped once again into the room. Bending down, she picked up Meg's phone between her covered thumb and forefinger, and dropped it into a makeshift evidence bag, zipping it closed.

Craig held out his hand, and she took it as he helped her back into the hallway.

"Could it have been an accident?" Hope held up Craig's voice. "Hard to tell if there was a fight or if all the mess was the derailment. Maybe she fell and hit her head?" He pointed to the blood on the side of the sink area.

"That wouldn't explain the marks on her throat or the signs of asphyxiation."

Silence held them together again. "I should've done more last night, when they were arguing," he said. "Or gone after her when she ran out before the crash. I thought about it."

"Then decided it wasn't your business?"

He nodded.

"We all should have done more, but none of us could have. Not without her consent." Roz hoped she was speaking the truth. Because she could have done more, but only if she had dragged Meg away from Grant, Meg's will again being ignored. "Some people who have been abused feel they don't deserve to get help."

He turned his head sharply to look at her. "You sound like you're talking from personal experience." Something in her tone must have given her away. She remembered Mum asking her, again and again, what had happened when she'd turned up at the family house at 7:00 a.m., the morning after the rape. Roz had sat in the bath, shaking and broken. Too ashamed to tell Liz. "I just meant it's hard for victims to speak up, for many reasons. You must see it in the CPS all the time. God knows there's been enough times when the CPS decided that one of my sexual assault cases didn't have enough evidence. Victims go through all the trauma of coming forward for nothing."

Craig didn't reply to that. Instead he continued to look at her, seeming to search her face for hidden things. Roz turned away. "What's your plan?" he asked in the end. "And how can I help?"

"I need to talk with everyone on the train. It'd be useful to have a CPS lawyer on my side for once. Last thing I want is to prejudice a case." She looked over at the window, wondering if maybe they should look for signs of entry from the other side. "And it'd be great if you checked outside, in case the killer somehow got in through the window. Take pictures of the ground before snow covers any evidence up completely."

"No problem. I'll be glad of something to do."

"Me too." A familiar and welcome calm clicked into place. She could actually do something. Help one more woman before she really retired.

Chapter Twenty-Seven

"Why are we in here?" Grant asked as Beefy showed him into a cabin vacated by one of the guests who left at Edinburgh. "You said you had something to show me before the press found out."

"Something to tell you, at least," Roz said.

Craig entered the cabin. His face was pink from being outside, his ears an endearing bright red. Snow sat on his salted hair.

"Any luck?" she asked him quietly as he stood in the doorway. Although luck may have been the wrong word.

"Difficult to say. Possibility of boot prints walking to the window, but the snow's too heavy to be sure."

"Can we get on with it, whatever it is?" Grant said. "I want my breakfast."

"I'll wait outside, ma'am," Beefy said, moving into the corridor and shutting them inside the cabin.

"You might want to sit down," Roz said. She heard her voice in its "delivering bad news" mode, a combination of soft, respectful, and firm.

"I'll stand, thanks." Grant took out his vape cigar and started puffing on it. Vapor filled the room. "Has this got something to do with what happened last night?"

"What happened, exactly?" Roz asked.

"Don't play coy. Just tell me how much you and the big man in the hallway want, then we can make all this go away and I can eat a bacon sandwich. Okay?" He took another big inhale.

"Just so I'm clear, are you trying to bribe us?" Roz asked.

Grant looked from Roz to Craig, eyes narrowing, assessing. "Why am I here again?"

"We've got some bad news for you, I'm afraid." Roz gestured again to the bed. "Meg has died."

"I don't understand. What do you mean, 'died'?"

"I'm afraid your girlfriend has passed away," Craig said. His tone was full of sympathy.

Grant lowered himself onto the bed, gripping its edges as if that could steady his mind and shaking body. He was getting paler by the second. His mouth moved but no words came out. He didn't even inhale his vape.

His shock didn't mean he was innocent though. Roz had witnessed people being somehow surprised that the person they'd murdered had died. Especially where there was domestic violence. Cases like this used to be called crimes of passion, and still were in some countries. People thought it happened in a daze of rage: the mist descending, the developed frontal cortex left pondering in a corner while the animal amygdala took over. When the frontal cortex got back in the cab, it couldn't comprehend what had happened.

"She can't be gone." He looked out of the window as if Beinn Dòrain could provide the answers Roz could not.

"I'm afraid she is," Roz replied. "I found her."

"She's in the cabin?" He was blinking as if trying to picture their room with Meg dead inside. When Roz nodded, he said, "I've got to see her." He made a move toward the door, and Roz stepped in front of him.

"I'm afraid no one can enter your cabin until Meg can be taken away. It's protocol in this situation." Roz grimaced as if conveying to Grant that she didn't make the rules and that she was on his side. At least, while it was convenient to be so. "You can have this cabin for the rest of the journey."

"But how did she die?" Grant asked, sitting down again. He shifted into the far corner and held a pillow in his lap. He looked like a little boy again, sucking on his vape like a lollipop.

"That's what we need to find out. And you can help us." Roz took out her phone. "If you don't mind, I'd like to tape our chat, just so we all have a record of it. Okay?"

"What can it be used for?" Grant asked. "Like, can it be used for evidence?"

Roz hoped her face was more composed and noncommittal than she felt. "I'm making sure that we can't say you said anything you didn't, if you get my drift."

"You should know," Craig said, "that lawful and valid recordings can be used in court, although Rule 32.1 of the Civil Procedure Rules permits the court to exclude it as evidence if necessary."

"Yes, that's correct, thank you, Mr. CPS," said Roz. "So, are you okay with me to record or not?" When Grant reluctantly nodded, she continued, "Let's start with anything you can tell me that would help us determine the cause of Meg's death."

"Like what?"

Like whether you killed her, you bastard.

"Any information we could use to work out what happened?" Roz deliberately used language that reflected what he said when they first entered the cabin. See if he noticed.

"What are you getting at?" He had noticed. "She went off on one, then ran out."

"In what way did she go 'off on one'?"

"She got it in her head that I was flirting. Started screaming at me."

"And were you?"

"Flirting? No more than anyone else would."

"And who did Meg think you were flirting with?"

"One of the students, Ayana. The pretty one. God knows why. Meg was mad, that was clear."

"And did Ayana respond to Meg's accusations?"

"Yeah, she denied it, of course. 'Cos it didn't happen. She said Meg had gotten it all wrong. Same thing *I* told Meg."

"So why would she suspect you were flirting?"

Grant exhaled, adding another layer of vapor to the cinnamon-scented air. "She's paranoid. Always checking my phone, asking where I am."

"And then she ran out?"

"Yeah, stumbled out of the railcar."

"But you didn't follow her? To see if she'd be okay?"

Grant shrugged. "She was being insane. There's no talking to her when she's in that mood. I told her to go to bed and thought she had. Assumed we'd talk in the morning, like we always do after an argument." He then went paler as if realizing that Meg would have no more mornings.

"It's difficult, isn't it?" Roz said, making her tone soft. "Each time you remember that they've died." The early stages of grief, she knew, were like a bad can opener. Its teeth weren't sharp enough to cut through tin hearts in one go. It chewed through a little but not enough to see what's really inside, then stopped. After a while, it started again. One painful millimeter at a time. Roz hadn't even begun to open the tin of her mum's death.

"Did you often argue?" Craig asked. Roz wondered if he had noticed her reaction and was giving her time.

"No more than other couples." Grant's voice took on a defensive edge.

"Your disagreements get reported more than most people's though," Craig said.

"Yeah, but we're famous, so the press write about it. Everyone rows. We're just a normal, passionate couple." He paused. Closed his eyes. "*Were* a normal couple."

"Did your arguments ever turn violent?" Roz asked. Grant's fingers twitched, as if daring Roz to state what she was implying. "I'm covering all the bases, that's all. Trying to get a clear picture."

"I never hit her, if that's what you're saying." Grant was the picture of innocence. "I would never hurt my Meggie."

"You never laid a finger on her? Never caused her to bruise, even accidentally?"

Grant blanched enough to see him pale further beneath the spray tan. "She bruised easily. She was very sensitive."

Ah yes. The "too sensitive" defense, used about skin and people by those who broke them.

"Well," he said, eyes shifting to the right. "I've had to grab hold of her shoulders or arms at times, if I thought she was going to hurt herself." Another line she'd heard many times.

"And was that what caused the bruise on her inner arm and the one around her wrist?"

"I can't remember," Grant said. "Maybe." His eyes were going from left to right. Roz had seen the same thing on many suspects who were trying to invent what had happened while offering a slice of truth. "I remember her being drunk coming out of a club a week or so ago, and I stopped her from falling."

"And there is no time when you could have accidentally hurt her throat?"

"That's personal. Intimate stuff. Consensual stuff between Meg and me. You don't know what goes on behind closed doors."

Roz's simmering anger boiled over. Abusers were increasingly using the defense of agreed BDSM practices to account for "accidental" death, when those communities usually had more safety rules than the so-called "vanilla" majority. Roz opened her phone and scrolled to the close-up photo she'd taken of Meg's scratched neck.

Grant went even paler. Not even a Claudia Winkelmann fake tan would cover that. "It wasn't like that when I last saw her. That wasn't me."

"Any idea who would want to hurt her?" Craig asked.

"She had loads of trolls, the odd stalker. She got some messages, threatening stuff. But they don't mean it. They're just sad, lonely fuckers shouting into the void."

"What kind of threats?" Craig asked. "Physical violence? Sexual?"

"Said they'd kill her, rape her. All of that." He said this so casually. "Usual thing for the famous."

"You get a lot of the same thing, do you?" Roz asked, knowing the answer. Straight men rarely got those threats.

"God, no. They wouldn't dare."

"Did anyone specifically threaten to strangle or suffocate her?" Craig asked.

"Not that she told me. You'll have to look at her phone."

Oh, don't worry, I will, Roz thought. "You mentioned stalkers. Did she know who they were?"

"There was one in particular, with a restraining order out on him." He paused as he thought. "Iain," he said after a while. "That's it, and spelled funny. With two 'i's. Used to comment on her posts all the time, even put photos of us up himself. Came to the flat once or twice and tried to photograph her through the windows."

"Can you describe him?"

"I only saw him from the back, when he was running away from the flat. He wore a bandanna and had straggly hair. Carried a plastic bag. Wore an old brown coat that looked like it came from the reject bin of a charity shop."

Roz felt the hairs on her arm rise. The description matched the appearance of the stowaway, the one she'd let on the train.

"You all right, Roz?" Craig asked.

She realized she was gripping onto the sink by the window and looking out into the dawn. "I'm fine. So you and Meg," she continued, addressing Grant, "haven't actually seen his face, even after you went to the police?"

Grant shrugged as if this wasn't important. "The police were handling it. I just didn't want people getting dodgy pictures and making money off them."

"And you weren't worried that Meg was in danger?"

Grant shrugged again. "He was one of the few trolls who *didn't* make death threats."

"Oh, that's all right, then," Craig said, his sarcasm clear.

She smiled at him, then turned back to Grant. "The only other thing we need to know for now is what you were doing after she left the club car. After all, you started this conversation by offering us money to forget about something that happened."

"I was in the club car most of the time. I popped out for a sneaky vape break every now and again, just to avoid that stuck-up princess snarking at me."

"Beck?"

"Yeah. Stupid cow."

"Is there anyone who can corroborate your 'sneaky vape breaks'?" Craig asked.

"Not really." Grant looked toward the window. He was playing for time, Roz was sure. She waited, letting silence apply pressure on him. "Look, I may have snogged that student, Ayana. That's why I offered you cash. I thought someone might have seen us. If I wanted a photo in the press, I'd organize one."

"Where were you when you both 'snogged'? And when did it take place?"

"After the first round of that stupid quiz. We went out for a smoke and were sticking our heads near the window in the corridor two railcars down from the club car. We leaned in close and, well, you know how it is." He winked at Craig.

"I don't think I do, Grant, no," Craig said.

Roz wanted to hug him. "Did Meg see you kiss?"

"Don't think so." He paused. Then something like revelation passed across his face. He looked up at the light on the ceiling. "You don't think she saw and hanged herself?"

A look crossed Grant's face that Roz couldn't quite read. Maybe he was anticipating a juicy magazine deal—*Grant Reveals All About Tragic Heartbreak*, shortly followed by *Grant Reveals All About Healing from Heartbreak with New Love*.

"We don't know *what* happened yet," Roz said. "That's why I need to ask these questions, hard for you as they clearly are." She paused and applied the face she used to feign sincerity to witnesses who thought they were cleverer than her. "You must have cared for her very much."

"Absolutely. She was my world. Love of my life." Grant put his hand over where his heart should have been. He looked around, as if there could be a camera on him.

"I can see this is such a shock for you. We'll let you rest. Get you a cup of tea and bring you some breakfast."

"In here?" Grant looked around the room.

Roz would have to improvise to get him to stay without force. "Well, we can't have any potential witnesses mingling and getting stories mixed up. And if a stalker killed her, then it's best we keep you safe, with Beefy watching the door."

"Right, yeah. Sure." Grant nodded as if his personal safety was the most important thing. "I'll have bacon, eggs, coffee, toast, and a bottle of champagne."

Roz tried to keep her face snow-smooth. "I'll ask Bella or Beefy to sort that for you. And I have to ask you for your phone, I'm afraid."

Craig held out one of the ziplock bags.

"The police will want to check it for messages and anything that could help," Roz continued. Then she thought of how Meg and Grant lived their lives in front of cameras. "Did anyone film your argument?"

"Probably. There's always someone pointing a phone at us," Grant said.

Chapter Twenty-Eight

Roz needed some air. All that vape smoke had made her feel dizzy. Watching him exhale had also reminded her too much of the man who'd attacked her. Last thing she needed now was another flashback.

Grabbing her coat and scarf from her cabin, she bundled herself up, then opened the train door. Roz knew it'd be cold outside, but when she pressed the button to open the outside door, the wind knocked her backward, cold air slicing at her face. She stepped down into the snow, wishing she had brought her wellies. She was out of practice of living in the Highlands. It had been a very long time since she'd lived in Fort William, and short visits didn't count.

"Don't tell me, you've decided to walk back," Craig joked. He stood in the doorway, looking down on her.

"Aye, the company int up to much, so I'm leaving." She'd meant that as a flirty joke in return, what the weans would call "bantz," but, judging from the hurt on his face, it hadn't landed. She continued, quickly. "I'm actually gonna check on my daughter, then phone an old colleague, ask her to do a search on the threats Meg received, as well as seeing if Grant's got form for domestic violence." She had to shout to stop the wind making off with her words.

"Good plan. And maybe send her over the names of everyone here, see if anything turns up."

"Including you?" she joked.

"Including me. I am, after all, very suspicious." He smiled, and a shiver passed through her. He shifted from foot to foot. He looked like he was going to say something, then changed his mind. "See you in the club car?"

She nodded. As the door closed, Craig waved awkwardly, then walked away.

The wind circled her, threw snow in her face as she attempted to dial. She tried Ellie first, then Heather but still got no answer.

Laz, her friend and former colleague, was a sergeant working on her inspector's exams. Roz had helped her prepare.

"All right, mate," Laz answered. "Missing us already, are we?"

"Haven't even thought of you lot once," Roz replied. It was amazing how quickly she slipped back into the station routine of banter and hectoring.

"What you calling me for, then? Aren't you on your fancy train?" Roz could hear traffic noises wherever Laz was. Someone shouting at someone else. The call of London.

"I *am* on my fancy train, and very fancy it is too. But something's happened, and I'd like you to do some digging for me."

"Oh, I see. You want a favor."

"Well, it is Christmas Eve."

"Which means I'm on a half shift, so whatever you want had better be finished by one o'clock this afternoon. I'm taking the kids to see *Elf* at the digital cinema."

"Then you'd better get researching. Could you please look into any records for Grant McVey and Meg Forth, especially in regard to domestic violence, affray and assault for McVey, and online threats and stalkers in regard to Forth, particularly a man with the first name 'Iain,' spelled with two 'i's.'"

In the background, Laz tapped on her computer, then stopped. "Meg Forth as in 'In No Time'?"

"That's the one."

"Blimey. What's this in connection to?"

"I found her dead in her cabin this morning, after our train derailed in the middle of the Highlands in a snowstorm. So it's been quite a morning."

"Shit." Laz paused, then gave a kind of horrified laugh as it sunk in. "So, your retirement present, that I in part paid for, is being stuck in the middle of nowhere with a famous body?"

"Generous, huh?"

"Merry fucking Christmas, Roz."

"I know."

"If you're looking into McVey, does that mean you think he killed her? Wait, are you in danger?" For once, Laz sounded genuinely concerned.

"No. I don't think so, at least. Anyway, the local constabulary is on its way." Eventually. "I'm just holding the fort while we wait. Giving them a head start."

"You never can keep your nose out." Laz's tone was full of fondness. "Anything else I can do?"

"I'm going to send over details of the passengers still on the train who are possible, if only vaguely, suspects. If you can get anything on them—"

"Then you'll love me forever, I know."

"I already love you, Laz. But I'll send you some tablet."

"And some shortbread?"

"Deal."

Tension and excitement filled the silence that fell as she walked into the center of the club car. Even the snow seemed to stop. Only the wind kept up its patter, whispering and shushing around the train.

The passengers in the club car knew something was up. Grant, Meg, and Oli's absence must have been clocked. There was no Christmas music, no bonhomie. Roz glanced at Ayana on the students' table. An image of her kissing Grant came into Roz's head, making her shudder.

Bella was leaning against the bar, chewing her lip and staring out the window.

Roz went over to her and, leaning in, whispered, "Any sign of Oli and the missing passenger?"

Bella shook her head. "They've got to come back soon. They haven't got the clothes for this weather. Should I go and find them?" Her voice was so small and quiet compared to earlier.

"We can't keep sending people after people. It's not safe. And I need you in here, keeping this lot under control while I talk to them individually. While I've got you, is there any CCTV on the train?"

"Two cameras in the driver's cab, one in each railcar, including the club car."

"That's great. Can you get me copies, especially of footage from the club car and the railcar with Meg's cabin?"

Bella nodded. "Okay. Are you going to tell them about her?" She looked around at the expectant faces in the room, all staring their way. She then turned back to Roz with pleading eyes.

Roz cleared her throat. Her voice now was strong and clear. "It must be clear to you all by now that something more than the derailment is wrong." She licked her lips, as if that would make the words easier to come out. "And you're right. I have awful news."

"Oh, great. The engineers can't reach us today," Sally said. The heel of her hand was pushed against her head, pressing away her hangover. "We'll have to spend Christmas in our cabins."

"Some of us don't have cabins, *Sally*." Mary said the name in such an arch, particular way, that Roz thought it could replace "Karen" as the go-to byword for privileged complaint. Not fair on most Sallys, maybe, but at least Karens got a reprieve. Funny how there wasn't a similar name for men.

"Everyone, listen—" Craig started to say.

"But they have to come get us," Beck said, pouting. "Our holiday rental is from today. Every minute we're here is one we're not spending there."

"That's true," Sam said, "from a physics point of view."

"Oh, shut up," Beck replied.

Everyone started talking about precisely where they had to be and by when. The murmur levels rose, threatening to spill over.

"We've all got somewhere else to be," Craig said. "But this is more important."

The murmurs subsided.

"Meg is dead," Roz said.

Gasps and intakes of breath rippled around the room. The baby started crying, and Phil stood up, gently jiggling and shushing the infant. Robert started sobbing too, in sympathy and solidarity. Sally screwed up her eyes in apparent annoyance or head pain, but picked up the toddler anyway and bounced him on her knee. He started laughing then. The sound made Roz's heart hurt for her grandchild, in an incubator many miles away.

Questions about what had happened filled the club car before Roz put her hand up, signaling for quiet. "We don't know how she died, but obviously we need to gather all the information we can while we remember it. It may be some time before we can be interviewed by the police."

"Police?" Ayana said. She leaned forward, hands clasped together. Others also showed surprise or agitation at the mention of a police investigation. Beck crossed her arms and scowled; Liv, wrapped up now in a coat, tugged at her fringe; Ember bit her lower lip; Tony shuffled in his seat; Beck said something to Ayana that made Ayana put her hand to her throat. None of this meant anything necessarily. The police made even the innocent feel guilty. And sometimes it was the ones who didn't react that you had to watch.

"It's routine in these situations," Roz explained. "No one knows what took place."

"Where's Grant?" Phil said. His tone was flat, his nostrils flaring.

"Grant is, understandably, distraught, and in another cabin," Roz said, carefully. "With Beefy looking after him." By which she meant that Roz had stationed Beefy outside Grant's new cabin door. "Could you make sure he gets some food and drink in his quarters, Bella? He's requested bacon, eggs, toast, coffee, and a bottle of champagne."

"He's devastated by her death, then," Beck said.

"When Oli's back he'll sort Grant's order, though he might need some help." Bella looked around the room for volunteers. Beck turned away, but a few put up their hands. There was such a thing as community after all.

"Do you think Grant killed Meg, then?" Sally asked. Her eyes flashed as if excited at the thought.

"As I said, we don't know."

"But you think someone killed her?" Tony said, his face creasing in worry.

"And it was Grant's room. He was the only one with the key," Phil said. He paced with the baby as if trying to soothe himself as well. His anger was interesting.

"It's not that simple. Meg's door was locked from the inside," Craig said.

Roz shot him a fierce look. He shouldn't be giving that kind of information away.

"Nothing is being ruled out," she said. "It could be an accident."

"Or self-inflicted," Sally added, a look of disapproving prurience on her face.

Bella stepped forward. "As Roz keeps saying, we have no idea. And we're very lucky to have Roz here to gather the facts, so the police will have something to go on. How would you like to do this, Roz?"

"I'd like to talk with Liv first," Roz said, looking toward the teenager.

"*What?*" Sally said. "Why?"

"I believe Liv has photos or footage of Meg on her phone that might be useful. We're basically starting with anything we can use to get a picture of what happened to Meg, including what happened in here just before she left."

"It's all right, Mum," Liv said. She stood and placed a hand on her mother's shoulder. "I shot some stuff last night. Some of it might help."

"What have I told you about filming without asking?" Sally snapped.

Liv blushed but didn't say anything.

"I'm going to ask you some questions in a spare cabin, if that's all right, Liv?" Roz said.

Liv nodded. She pulled at her hair, her eyes widening.

"I should come with you," Sally stood, brushing down her skirt and trying to smooth her flyaway hair.

"Does she have to?" Liv asked Roz.

"You're twenty, right? As you're not a minor or vulnerable, there's no need to have a guardian. But I have no power here. I'm helping the police with initial inquiries, so you are free to have your mum or dad, both or neither."

"Could you come with me, Dad?" Liv asked Phil.

Sally's shoulders fell forward and her chest went back, as if she felt physically punched in the heart. They did that to you, children. Every day. And then they threw their arms around your neck and told you they loved you. Adorable gaslighters, every single one. Sally turned to look out of the window, as if the drifts of snow could freeze the pain.

Not that Roz blamed Liv; she wouldn't want Sally around either. "If this *was* a police interview," she continued, "you'd have the right to a lawyer, if you wanted one."

"I can come too," Craig said to Liv. "While I'm not your lawyer, I can make sure that the interview is fair and nonprejudicial."

"Thank you," Liv said. She was looking shyly down at her boots.

"After chatting with Liv and then Phil, I'll talk to everyone else in turn," Roz said to the group. "Can I ask you not to confer with each other or compare notes about what happened last night? It's important that I get everyone's individual impressions rather than your memories being affected by others."

She saw them shift in their seats, as if thinking they didn't know what else to talk about.

"Natter about anything else. Netflix. What you're going to have to eat when you get home. The next Doctor Who. Anything but your recollections of Meg's actions last night."

They still weren't convinced. They were all looking at each other, dying to discuss it.

"Memories are like a tray full of water," Roz said, trying to explain. "They might seem clear to you, but they're colored by your own ink, your schema, made up of your past experiences, the way you view the world, your own sense of time, cultural identity and values, and so many other factors. If you lay a sheet of paper on top of the tray, then it will be one color, one set of memories. But everyone else's memories are shaded with their own ink, and if two or more of your memories mix, then they marble together and cannot be separated. If you lay a piece of paper on top, a very different image will emerge than the first."

Blake nodded. "I've read about this," he said. "Bartlett's theory of reconstructive memory. No one will give quite the same version of the same event."

"That's the one. It can make police work very difficult, as people can perceive the details of an event differently, yet still be telling the truth."

Sam's nostrils flared as they stared at Blake. Yesterday, Roz would have interpreted it as anger, but after Sam had talked about being sapiosexual, it read very differently. Sam placed their hand on Blake's knee.

Beck made a face at him. "Teacher's pet."

"And talking of pets," Roz said, "would you please all look out for Tony and Mary's cat, Mousetache, who hasn't been seen since the crash?"

"I'll go and have another look in the seated cars," Bella said. "And when I come back, I'll make sure we all stay here and talk about anything other than Meg."

"Thank you, Bella, that's perfect."

As Roz turned to leave, out of the window she saw two figures tramping through the snow toward the train. It was light enough now to see that one of them was Oli, his long arms holding up a slight man with straggly hair. On the ground next to them was a dark shape.

"Who's that with Oli?" Bella said.

"Is it someone coming to help?" Beck asked. The hope in her voice was childlike.

"Don't think so. Looks like Oli is pretty much carrying them," Sam said.

"Mousetache is there too!" Tony shouted, his face close to the glass. "He's trotting next to Oli!"

Mary's face creased into the biggest grin. "He's rounded them up! Told you he's like a sheepdog."

"But who's the man?" Bella asked. "No one's missing from the passenger list."

"Someone was on the train who shouldn't have been," Roz said.

Bella turned to her, frowning. "Who?"

"All I know is they got on the train without a ticket."

"And you didn't stop them?" Bella said, eyebrows skyshot.

"You thought it was none of your business," Craig said quietly.

Roz nodded. "I'm not proud of it now, obviously."

"So you let on a freeloader and possible killer?" Sally's mouth was wide open in exaggerated shock.

"A killer could just as easily have paid full price," Craig said.

"Is that your man who was talking to Meg?" Tony asked.

Roz nodded.

"He was a funny one all right," Mary said. "But you can't judge him for that. Everyone's funny in a way that's normal for them."

"It might not be him with Oli," Roz said. And she hoped that was true. She hoped that Oli had found someone who needed help and brought him to warmth and safety. But as Oli and the man got closer and stepped onto the train, her hope faded. The stowaway, and Meg's possible stalker, had been found.

"Change of plan," Roz said. "I'm going to interview him first."

Chapter Twenty-Nine

Meg was dead. The killer couldn't believe it. They held a glass of Coke but they felt flat inside. All the fizz that had buoyed them before had dispersed. But they still had to finish their job. It was going to be much more difficult. They were being watched. People were on alert. They felt eyes on them, as if everyone could see through their shield to the shame that lay beneath.

The killer would have to put on a performance, hide in plain sight. They could do that. Course they could. They lied every day, covered their tracks. In some ways, killing was the first thing they'd done in a long time that was truly authentic.

And maybe fortune was smiling on the killer. Maybe it believed in what they were doing. After all, if the killer was trapped on the train, so was their victim. All they had to do was wait for the right time to get out of this room.

A snowflake landed on the windowpane. Its white spokes glistened. The killer watched it cling to the glass while other flakes slid down the window. Like Meg, it stood out, shimmering as if sequined in the weak, early sun. And, like poor Meg, it melted away to nothing.

Chapter Thirty

"Everything all right?" Roz asked Beefy as she, Craig, and the stowaway squeezed past his sentry point outside Grant's cabin.

"He's been complaining and chuntering in there, though he calmed down when he got some food. No one's going in or out on my watch." Beefy showed her the cabin's key card and placed it in his trouser pocket. His face was set with such determination that Roz believed him.

Three cabins down, Roz used the key Bella had given her to open the door to the interview cabin. It was the cabin Nick, the man in the green suit, had occupied until Waverley. He'd left smoothed circles of foil covered in mince-pie crumbs, a shot glass containing whispers of whisky, and a scattering of oats on the floor.

"I'm Roz. I used to be in the police, and I'd like to ask you a few questions. This is Craig from the Crown Prosecution Service, but don't hold that against him. He's all right, really."

"Nice to meet you." The man looked around in confusion. "Where should I sit?"

"On the bed or on the floor?" Roz said. "Wherever you feel comfiest."

He clambered onto the bed, a strong smell of old sweat pervading the cabin. His face was gray and shadowed, lines creating tree-trunk rings around his face. He sat with his legs out in front of him and rocked back and forth.

Roz sat cross-legged on the floor to be nearer his level. "Do you mind if I record our conversation, in case it's useful in the future? You will of course receive a copy." He nodded, as if that was the least important thing in the world. After pressing "record," Roz started her questioning. "Can I ask your full name and where you live?"

"Iain Curran," he said. His fingers fidgeted as if they had an invisible Rubik's Cube between them. "I live in Bexleyheath."

"And how old are you?"

"Thirty-nine."

"Why do you think we've asked to talk with you today?"

Iain looked down. "I shouldn't have run away."

"And why did you run?" Craig asked.

Silent tears flowed down Iain's cheeks. "I saw her."

Roz and Craig exchanged a look. "Who?" she asked.

"Meg." Just saying her name seemed to break Iain. His shoulders shook with racking sobs.

Roz waited until his cries subsided. "You saw her where?"

"In her cabin." He flushed. "I looked through the window. From outside. I used someone's suitcase from the seating car to stand on."

"And what did you see when you looked through the window?"

"She was lying funny, contorted. She wasn't moving." His swallowed a few times before saying. "There was blood."

"Why not stay and try to help her?" Roz asked.

"I knew she'd gone. Passed over. I could feel it." Iain thumped a fist on his chest as if trying to restart his heart.

"You could have let someone know," Craig suggested, gently.

Iain lowered his head even further. "I know. I'm so ashamed. I put the case back and was going to tell someone, but then I thought I'd have to explain why I was looking, and then I knew they'd find out who I was. So I panicked and ran around the tracks, past the ravine, and thought of throwing myself into it. But my legs kept going, so I went with them till they collapsed under me. I just lay there, letting snow fall on me, looking up at the mountain. I don't know how long I was there before I heard the cat call to me."

"Mousetache called to you?"

"He did this 'McNow' sound, then came and sat on my chest. I think it was to keep me warm. Or him warm. Or both. That's how he found us, the young man."

"Oli."

"That's right. Oli." Iain was quiet for a moment. "It's true though, isn't it? I was right? She's dead?"

"Aye," Roz said. "Meg is dead."

Iain held his head and started pulling on his hair. He jerked at it in time with his cries.

"May I ask why you're so upset by her death?" Craig asked.

Iain looked up, surprised for the first time in the interview. "I love her. I thought that was obvious."

From Grant's cabin down the corridor came the sound of hammering on the door. "I asked for champagne! I'm not staying here without booze."

"That's him," Iain said, eyes wide. He wrapped his arms around himself. "He did it. He killed her."

"Try to ignore him. Concentrate on Meg. She deserves that much. In what way did you love her?" Craig asked, trying to keep the questioning on track.

Iain glanced nervously at the door as if afraid of Grant bursting through. "Not 'did,'" he said finally, "'do.' I loved her when she was alive, and I love her now she's dead too. That's called true devotion."

"Some might call it stalking," Roz said.

"That was a misunderstanding," Iain said, blushing. "I just wanted to be near her. Protect her. Especially after I saw him hit her the first time."

In her peripheral vision, Roz saw Craig freeze. She tried to remain casual as she asked, "Can you tell us a bit more about that, Iain?"

"I'd be glad to. I told the police before, but they wouldn't hear a word of it. He had her under his spell, you see, that bully. Wouldn't let her speak up for herself."

"Take us through what you saw."

"I had followed them home as usual, and I know that sounds bad but it's not, I promise. I used to stand on the green that's in the center of the court they live on, looking up at their windows. I used binoculars, especially after I saw him push her. I wanted to be sure. And that night, I saw him hit her in the ribs."

"Did you see what happened after?"

Iain scowled. "*He* closed the curtains."

Roz tried to keep her face neutral as he casually confessed to stalking offenses.

"And was that why you got on the train without a ticket? To follow her and protect her while she was in Scotland?" Craig asked. Roz thought that more of a leading question than she'd like, but that was lawyers for you. Even ones she was unnervingly attracted to.

"That's right. And I failed." Iain looked straight at Roz. His eyes carried more baggage than Grant and Meg put together.

"I've been told that you had an altercation with Meg, not long before she died. You warned her that she should get off the train at Edinburgh. What did you mean by that?"

"I told her to run from him. Get away. Anyone who's seen them together would know why."

"How do you think it appears that, not long after your warning, Meg died?"

"If I cared what people thought, do you think I'd look like this?" He pulled again at his hair.

"Can you tell us what happened before you saw Meg lying in her room?"

"I couldn't sleep, you see. Never can on trains. So, I strolled around the railcars When it derailed, I heard Meg scream. I went to her room, and McVey was disappearing away down the corridor, back to the bar to get even more pissed, I supposed."

"And did you see Meg?"

"No, her door was locked from the inside."

"So, you tried to open it?"

"Of course. She had sounded like she was in trouble." He blinked at her as if it was all very obvious. "That's when I got out of the train and went around to look in her window to see if she was okay."

"But she wasn't. I'm so sorry for your loss." Craig's voice was soft, tender.

"What it really proves is that I was right to tell her to run, doesn't it?" Iain started rocking harder. "He killed her. If the police had listened to me in the first place, if *she'd* listened, this wouldn't have happened." He beckoned to Roz to move in closer. Craig shook his head slightly. Roz leaned forward a little. "He'll do it again, you know. To someone else. Hurt them, kill them. There's only one way to stop him. Kill him first."

✖✖✖✖

"What do you think?" Roz asked Craig as they walked down the railcar corridor so they could talk without Iain or Grant overhearing.

Craig waited to reply until they were in the next car, and Iain's crying and Grant's shouts for alcohol had faded.

"He's certainly very convincing."

"He is. But I've seen grieving parents and partners appeal for information on their loved one's disappearance or death, only to find they were the ones behind, or supporting, the crime."

"I've seen that too. The betrayal is just…" He petered out, looking off into the distance.

"And he has just placed Grant at the scene around the time of Meg's death," said Roz, "when Grant said he wasn't there."

"Iain's not exactly an impartial witness."

"No, and I know you lot in the CPS wouldn't stand for that," she said before thinking. Was she flirting, negging, or treating him like a detective sergeant on a case? And was she asking him to come to her or pushing him away?

His mouth twitched into a playful smile. "Whereas you lot in the police would be happy with it, right?"

They looked at each other, and it was as if they were the only ones on the train. But they weren't. She broke the stare first. "But whether Iain's lying or not, Beefy's got another detainee. Iain needs to be guarded too. He just made a death threat to Grant."

"We'll get Grant to lock his door from the inside. Just in case."

"Although that didn't help Meg."

Bella then bustled down the corridor toward them from the direction of her driver's cab. "We've got a problem. Several problems."

"What now?" Roz asked.

"I just talked to the police, fire and rescue service, and then our engineers again. They're delayed further due to more trees on the line. If you've ever tried to get Scots pine needles out of your carpet, just imagine how difficult it is to get a trunk off a train track."

"We have no timeline for their arrival?"

"They all said 'as soon as we can,' but could promise nothing more."

Roz thought of Heather in the hospital and her baby. Her heart contracted.

"You said we had 'several' problems," Craig prompted.

"First, the CCTV system is down," Bella said, "and there's no way to retrieve any recordings. At the moment, there's no way to tell if it's another by-product of the derailment or a deliberate act."

"If it's deliberate, would it have to be someone on the train who shut them down?" Craig asked. "Or could it be someone who works for the train line?"

"I don't know. But the cameras were operational when we left London. That would've been one of the safety checks before we departed."

Roz sighed. If someone had deliberately sabotaged the cameras, it suggested premeditation. Murder. She couldn't see Grant undertaking that level of planning or understanding of electrical systems, but maybe she was underestimating him.

"Another issue I've got," Bella continued, "is that the heating system was also damaged in the derailment. I was struggling to keep it going, but now it's stopped working at all. It's going to get really cold in here."

"Are there blankets for these kind of times?" Craig asked.

"We could gather all the duvets from the cabins so that everyone could wrap up warm?" Roz suggested.

"Good idea, although that's not the worst problem." Bella closed her eyes and sighed, as if gathering herself to admit the most repellent of crimes: "We've run out of tea."

Chapter Thirty-One

Roz's phone buzzed. Ellie was requesting a video call. Roz stared at it. She didn't want to have to say that she was stranded, that she may not even make it there tonight.

Maybe Craig heard her heart beating loudly in her chest or just saw her face react, because he said, "You answer that, find out how Heather's doing. I'll go get Liv and her dad. We can interview them in their cabin." He strode off down the corridor as Roz accepted the call.

"What's happening?" she asked. The screen was black at first, with only the sound of machines beeping, then an image formed. Her granddaughter was in the incubator, holding on to Ellie's finger. Tiny face screwed up, her eyes were moving under their lids. Roz hoped the baby was dreaming sweet dreams.

"I thought you'd like to say hello to your granddaughter." Ellie sounded so tired. "She's doing so well, off the oxygen and thriving."

"Hi, little one," she said. "I'm your grandma."

The baby waved her little mittened fists as if boogieing. She was miraculous. This wasn't the time to talk of stuck trains.

"I'll be up there soon as I can to give you a big cuddle," Roz continued. "You're going to tell me all about your journey so far, and I'll tell you a bit about mine. How does that sound?"

Behind the wheezing machines and beeping, Roz thought she heard the baby sigh. She knew that was hardly possible, but her heart clenched anyway. She hated being away from this little one; she could only imagine how Heather was feeling. "How's Heather?"

Ellie turned the phone away from the incubator to show her face. "She's still not stable. They're doing what they can." She was keeping her voice very low, as if not wanting the baby to know. "Her seizures have gotten worse. They're assessing her for risk of coma and stroke."

"Oh God."

"They're talking about putting her into an induced coma to give her body a chance to recover."

Roz covered her face with her hand, as if that could stop the images of Heather in a coma forming in her head. "What about you, love?" she asked Ellie. "How are you doing?"

Ellie shrugged. Her eyes held no expression. "Just get here, would you?" She said her goodbyes, then rang off. Roz felt at once a little bit closer to being there and yet farther away. The mixed blessing of camera phones.

She then remembered Meg's phone, waiting in her bag.

Putting on two more of the gloves that Craig had brought her, she carefully took the phone out of the evidence bag. She turned it on and guessed the password on the third try. Luckily, love-obsessed twenty-somethings were very predictable, especially when their fiancé's birth date was easily available online, which stopped her from having to go into the crime scene and show Meg's dead face to the screen. Roz had been lobbying phone companies to put a stop to that. A killer or abductor could easily open a victim's phone with their thumb or likeness even a short while after death. The phones should at least be able to tell if the owner of that face or finger was alive.

Roz stared at the hundreds of apps that filled the large, cracked screen. She had no idea where to start, so went first for Meg's Instagram account.

The comments under the Meg's last post showed that the news of her death was already out:

Balladmonkey: #RIPMEG

UnionJill: Sleep well. You are among angels now

Meg4Eva: 😭 😭 😭.

CHRISTINEBILLYGOAT: We should've seen the signs.

Woowoomama: She was crying out for love and attention.

AMagicalFaeryWarrior:#Christmasiscanceled

MegFan3987492: I won't believe it till I've seen her body.

Wombat90: Didn't know the girl

HotMess: Where's Grant? What has he got to say?

VisionandSound: MEG WAS TRYING TO TELL US THE TRUTH. EVERYONE WATCH THIS. #domesticviolence

Roz clicked on the link in the last comment, taking her to a recording of Meg's most recent—and final—live stream.

"Hi everyone," Meg said into the camera. It was haunting to see her there, not long before her death. She was in her cabin, big eyes darting around. "Told you I'd be back later. Things haven't gone exactly according to plan. As you've probably already seen, Grant and I have been arguing again. I'd never normally let you see me like this. I'd normally patch myself up and carry on. But not today. Today I'm going to tell you the secrets that lie behind my relationship with Grant.

"First though, and bear with me just for long enough to earn the money I'm going to need, I'm going to talk about what I'm wearing right now. Normally I'd take you through the full process; today, though, I'll show you makeup in the middle of being cried off." Meg's smile was crooked and rueful. "If there was ever a test needed for long-lasting cosmetics, then a broken heart will do it. And I can now vouch for the new makeup I was given to try in exchange for an honest review. It's all natural, organic, homemade, with my eyes made bright and swept a smoky heather, my lips painted in Bad Santa. The lippy stayed on through drinks, snogs, and a fight. Can't say the same for the mascara and liner, but there you go. The brands will appear on screen." They already were, scrolling down in an ugly font that was probably all the rage.

Meg leaned close to the camera. "So this is what I have to tell you. I've already started, in snippets I've got secretly recorded, but now feels the right time to tell the truth. Behind the makeup and photo shoots, the stories in *Hello!* and other places, lies—"

The picture jerked, and Meg's earnest, tear-streaked face turned to confusion and fear. The lights flickered. Items flew around the room, around Meg, like she was Dorothy and it was tornado day. Everything tilted. The camera stayed on Meg's face. As she looked around, her pupils seemed to grow even wider, black pools surrounded by long reeds of hair. She reached for a wall, then fell back onto the bed. The phone sometimes caught her face, sometimes her things moving around the cabin.

As everything settled, the image became steady. Meg smoothed her hair and applied her smile. "Well, I bet you weren't expecting a train crash. And neither was I, though my life has been one for a long time." She breathed in with difficulty, a painful rasping sound. "But Grant will be here soon, so I need to tell you now. I must speak out. Grant was amazing at first. The ultimate romantic. My therapist calls it love-bombing. But soon he—"

Meg stopped talking. She stared toward the door. Her eyes widened, words seemed trapped in her throat. "Grant, oh, it's—" She reached out an arm, turned her head, and the recording stopped on the image of Meg's cheekbones, sharp as the Munro mountains, terror on her beautiful face.

The phone must have fallen and cracked at that point. If Meg were still alive, she'd no doubt have had a free new mobile within a day. But Meg would post no more.

FIREANDMICE: Meg was about to tell all about her abuse, then he killed her to stop the truth coming out.
SandraDeelicious: Meg was dead when she was living.
FarmerGiles: She faked it all
Torrentedsuperheroes: Minx. Always was, always will be
VisionandSound: #megicide

Grant deserves to die. I met Meg once and I thought she was going to open up to me but then he came along and I saw the fear in her eyes. 4real.

Tell me something else that didn't happen

IncellsKing: SHE'S A LIAR

Roz had to look away from the scroll of commentary. Same with the comments appearing below the line in online newspapers. Everyone had an opinion about who was guilty or innocent, lying or otherwise. Never read the comments, she reminded herself—wisdom rarely lay below the waist of people or articles.

The only person who could speak about Meg was Meg, and she was dead. But she could still tell her story. Roz scrolled through the many video files on Meg's phone, stopping on one frozen on Meg's tear-tracked face. Roz's hand went to her heart as she pressed play and watched Meg testify to a time when Grant raped her. "He liked it when I said no," she said.

Chapter Thirty-Two

Roz was about to knock on the door of Liv and Aidan's cabin when her phone signaled the arrival of an email. It was from Laz, with the first results of her info-digging. As Roz read through it, she felt sick. It provided strong indications that Grant was a serial abuser of domestic partners and women. That, plus Meg's video testimonies and injuries, could be enough for even the CPS to take an interest. Now Roz needed that most difficult thing when it was one person's word against another: proof.

Craig stepped back to let her into the cabin, then they moved around each other in a reverse do-si-do. Her Scottish country dancing days had never come with such sexual tension. Roz ended up with her back to the sink under the window, Craig's to the door. His face was as red as hers felt.

Phil sat, head bent, on the bottom bunk. He looked even more tired than the day before, if that was possible.

Liv was curled up on the top bunk, wearing a huge black hoodie. A duvet lay over her legs and a copy of *Bleak House* was splayed next to her, along with a notebook and a bright pink pen that Roz recognized.

Liv saw her looking and picked up the pen, then handed it to Roz. She looked at it with pride. "Meg gave it to me after I said how nice it was."

"Meg always was generous," Phil said. "She gave most of her stuff away to her friends. Seems so unfair that someone so sweet has left us."

"Hopefully you can help me work out what happened to her. First things I need to know are your full names and whether you give permission for me to record our conversation."

"Olivia May Walker and Phillip Randolph Walker from Hammersmith." Phil gave the information slowly as Craig wrote it all down. "Aged twenty and thirty-nine respectively. And sure, tape us if you like."

Roz loved a witness who gave more information than she'd asked for. It usually led to revelation on her part or theirs.

"You wanted to see my phone," Liv said, handing it over. Her hands shook slightly. Being interviewed for the first time was always nerve-racking.

"Thanks, Liv, that's really helpful." Roz infused her voice with softness and gratitude.

The screen showed Liv's photo gallery, starting with a close-up picture of Meg sitting in the booth. Roz scrolled through all the photos of Meg that Liv had taken since seeing her in the first-class lounge. Most were posed selfies of Meg and Liv; Meg, Ember, and Liv; Meg, Grant, and Liv, etc. Meg's smile at the camera was incandescent. Her teeth and eyes shone; she looked the embodiment of modern health and happiness.

In the candid pictures, however, taken through gaps in chairs or from a distance, Meg looked very different. In one, she was staring out of the window, her eyes red, her gaze faraway. In others, she was applying makeup, putting drops in her bloodshot eyes, reapplying concealer, frowning into the mirror that would end up in pieces on her floor. In all of the pictures Liv had taken in secret, Meg looked as if she'd never be happy again.

"These are great. Really useful. If I text you my number, could you send these to my phone, please?" Roz asked.

Liv nodded. "There's my live stream recording too. Of when she ran out of the club car."

Roz felt the familiar telltale tingle she instinctively got when there was, if not a breakthrough in a case, then at least a crack in its carapace. This could be the evidence she needed.

"It's going viral," Phil added, but he wasn't smiling. He seemed sad, if anything.

Liv reached for the phone again and, fingers flying over the tiny keyboard on the screen, found what Roz hoped would be the crucial evidence.

The video was blurred and unsteady, in a close-up on Meg. She was wobbling, arms out, looking out of the window. Roz was reminded of Kate Bush in the video for "Wuthering Heights," playing another ghost of a woman. Liv must have backed off at this point as the shot was wider, showing more of the room. Meg was being turned around on one of the triangular tables by Grant.

"Stop, leave her alone." Liv's voice was barely a whisper, her voice close to the microphone.

"Liv hates to see people in trouble," Phil said. "She's so kind."

"Thanks, Dad," Liv replied.

Grant's mouth was smiling, close to Meg's face, his lips moving as if whispering, but Roz couldn't hear or work out what he'd said. Then, without warning, Meg lurched off the table into Craig, who helped her to standing.

"What were you doing, with her?" Meg said to Grant, pointing at Ember. "I saw you kiss her." The room went quiet. Ember shook her head. She looked like she was in shock.

"You're crazy. Now everyone will know it," Grant said.

Ember stepped forward. "He just said I looked and smelled nice." She shrugged as if to say that was hardly a crime, and, hey, she *did* look and smell nice. "It's not what you're thinking. I promise."

Meg cackled, folding over on herself. Everyone was looking at each other, as if wondering what to do with her. "That's the biggest cliché. Because if you know what I'm thinking, it's probably true."

"You're drunk," Grant snarled, "and God knows what else. You need to go away before you say or do something you regret."

Roz paused the video and enlarged Grant's face. It was etched with hate and disgust. Roz had a flashback to seeing that look on another man. Her rapist. She couldn't remember his face, only that mouth. His cigarette smell. The pain as he tore into her. She felt bile rise and blinked several times to keep in the present. *You're here, you're safe*, she told herself.

"You all right, Roz?" Craig asked. His voice was so full of concern that she couldn't look at him in case she cried.

Roz pressed "play" and tried to concentrate on the footage.

"Sounds a bit like a threat, mate," Craig said. "I'd back off if I were you."

Grant shoved Craig. "Fuck off. Don't 'mate' me. I don't even know you. You're just an ugly old fucker trying to party with young people. What are you, some kind of pervert?"

"Why is everyone shouting?" someone slurred, out of shot. Roz bet that it was Sally.

"You keep out of it too," Grant snapped at her. "Think you can lecture me? Do your children usually see you off your face? 'Cos sure looks like they're used to it. And if you think your husband has been faithful to you, you're as stupid as your children."

"Please, stop," Meg screamed. "I can't take it. I'll go, then it'll all be okay again."

"Meg," Ember said. "I can help you!"

Meg pinballed into a booth wall but didn't appear to feel it. Heading for the door, she seemed to be fighting off people who weren't there. The doors parted, and she stumbled out. There was laughter, some nervous, unsure, and then Beck's cruel laugh cut through.

"Is someone going after her?" Liv asked, her shocked voice close to the phone's microphone. The image whirled around. Craig stood next to a booth, forehead furrowed. Beck was staring at Grant, as was Ayana. Ember moved toward the door, then back to where she'd stood. Only Grant seemed unaffected. The camera stayed on him.

Grant pulled Beck to him, his arm around her shoulders, but she pushed him away, disgust on her face. Grant just laughed, then winked at Ayana. He took out his vape, puffed, then headed for the door. The recording stopped on him going through the door and turning back, puffing smoke in the direction of the camera.

Watch again, the onscreen text said.

Roz turned to Liv. "So what happened next?"

"Nothing, really. Everyone was a bit shocked and didn't say much. Some people talked about going after her." She paused, as if reflecting on what would have happened if they had. "Not long after, the train derailed. Everything fell all over the place. I think we all forgot about Meg, which is terrible."

"What did Grant do after the video?"

"He went out, after a bit, I think. I assumed he was going to check on her. I don't know if he was back during the derailment." She stared at the ceiling as if picturing Grant hurting Meg.

Maybe Iain *was* telling the truth. Craig raised an eyebrow and made a note in his phone. People's memories around the derailment were going to be difficult to unwrap.

"Grant puts his arm around Beck on the video, and she rejects him. Did you see him harass her or anyone else?"

Liv looked to the left, as if replaying the evening. She asked her dad for some water. He passed her a bottle and stroked her hair very gently. She took a swig of water and started talking. "He and Beck seemed to dislike each other from the start. He kept on teasing her. Said she was stupid a lot, which she's obviously not." She paused, thinking some more. "I also went to the toilet at one point and saw him and Ayana laughing in the hallway. She was puffing his vape out the window. They looked pretty close, but I wouldn't say he was harassing her. You never know though." She thought for a moment, doubt flickering across her face. "I mean, I did see her pull away from him, and he doesn't like that." She paused, worry on her face, with a touch of guilt. "I was watching Meg and Grant in the club car, and it looked like he was being lovey-dovey with her, but he frowned after she flinched. So maybe Ayana was trying to leave without making him angry?" She paused, as if reconsidering. Maybe she was wondering if she could have done something differently.

"You're a fan of Meg, right?" Roz asked Liv, trying to bring her out of her reverie.

Phil stuck his head out of the lower bunk and peered up to the top. "She watched Meg win the singing contest again and again. She even sung 'In No Time' on a talent contest on holiday in Majorca."

Liv nodded but still seemed far away.

"You followed her on social media. Did you notice anything that in retrospect could be suspicious?"

"Meg has a lot of trolls. They write disgusting things on her Insta page, Twitter, all of them, about how she should die or be raped. Or both."

Phil held his head in his hands. "God, Liv. And you see this stuff?"

Liv shrugged. "It's everywhere."

"No one says it to you though, do they?" Phil stood, holding on to the bunk ladder. He reached for his daughter.

She shook her head, but did not meet his or Roz's gaze. Roz felt weariness descend. Was there any young woman who hadn't gotten used to this?

"What about you, Phil?" Craig asked. "What's your recollection of the derailment?"

"I missed the whole thing—the conga, the fight, the derailment. Slept through till Roz woke me up. The rhythm of the train sent me to sleep." Phil rocked back and forth on the spot and did a loud fake snore to demonstrate. "Plus, I'm the main caregiver for a toddler and a baby. If I sleep, I really sleep."

"You didn't leave your cabin at any time?" Roz asked.

"No, apart from when I came back into the club car to get the milk from Sally, then I went back to our cabin."

"You didn't go to the toilet?" Craig asked. "These cabins don't have a bathroom."

Phil's eyes slid over to the sink. "I made use of the existing facilities."

"Dad!" Liv said. "That's gross."

"I didn't want to leave the railcar and disturb your brothers, or leave them on their own."

"Did you hear anything from your cabin during the night that, in light of Meg's death, you'd now consider suspicious?"

Phil shook his head. "Sorry. Wish I could help you more."

"Maybe you can. You taught Meg, is that right?"

Phil sighed and got back into the lower bunk. "She was in my class, aye."

"What was she like at school?"

"Clever. Cleverer than she liked people to think. Why do they do that, kids? Hide their brains and what they're thinking?"

"Because we're just trying to fit in and get by," Liv said.

"Anyway, she, er...well, she liked me. A lot. You know?"

That tingle again. Roz was getting somewhere. "What are you saying, Dad?" Liv looked like a bairn. Her voice was high, scared.

"She fancied me, okay?"

"No, she can't have." Liv's hand went over her mouth.

"It's normal for a young person to have a crush on a teacher. Or a youth worker. Meg happened to fixate on me."

"Was your relationship with Meg a factor in you moving down from Scotland?" Roz asked.

"We didn't have a relationship. And why would her fancying me be a factor?"

"Your meeting yesterday was awkward to say the least. Reading between the lines, I'd say something took place. And that seemed to be about the time you moved to London."

Phil rubbed his face. Roz had interviewed enough people to know this often meant a truth, or near-truth, was about to be told. "Another teacher saw one of the notes she wrote me." He went red and turned toward the wall so they couldn't see his face. "I kept them in a drawer in my desk. And then, when I was sick one day, the supply teacher found them and gave them to the head of department. They thought that the relationship was reciprocated."

"Dad?" Liv's nostrils flared in fear and her eyes filled with tears.

"I shouldn't have kept her notes. It was stupid, but I felt flattered. And I also know that's the defense of every man who's had an affair, but we didn't. Cross my heart, Liv. Not one kiss, not a touch. She was seventeen, same age as your brother is now, not that much younger than you in the scheme of things. I didn't write back or even give her so much as a glance in that way." He stared directly at Roz. "All I felt for her was pity."

"Then why move hundreds of miles to a different country and uproot your whole family?" she asked.

"The head thought I'd be better teaching at a higher level. And as there was no room to move upward at that college, she put me in touch with someone at the university."

"Which university?" Craig asked.

"University of London."

"Same as you, Craig," Roz said.

"It's huge," Craig explained. "Split into, what, eighteen, twenty associate colleges, across London."

"I was at Goldsmiths."

"Managed out and upward, eh?" Roz said, allowing her voice to insinuate that Phil had benefited from the situation, and see if that would spark something in him.

"I didn't do anything wrong." Defensiveness shaded Phil's voice. "All I did was be kind to her one lunchtime when I found her crying in my office."

And maybe that was true, Roz thought. If Meg needed a paternal figure, one drop of consideration in a drought seemed like a flood. But keeping the notes said something about Phil's ego and need for attention from young women. And he was hardly going to admit more in front of his daughter. That was one of the problems with being on the force. She had ended up trusting no one.

Roz turned to the window. Snow was climbing up the sill, slowly obscuring the view. Old memories were doing the same. Building up so much that it was hard to see beyond them. If she couldn't sweep them away, she'd never be able to work out what happened to Meg.

Chapter Thirty-Three

"We need to talk to Grant again," Roz said, walking quickly ahead of Craig down the cold corridor. The lack of heating was beginning to be felt. "He said he didn't go after Meg. Liv and Iain say he did."

"He was really pissed, it's possible he didn't remember," Craig said. "I was in the room, and I couldn't say whether he was there or not. He was in and out all night long."

"True. But there's enough to ask him again. Plus, my old DS, Laz, also came back with initial search results. Grant has been charged with affray and assault in the past; also, three complaints of intimate-partner violence have been lodged by separate women."

"Did the complaints progress to charges?"

"No. For the usual reasons, probably."

The door to the next sleeping railcar opened in front of them and Beefy appeared, out of breath. "I need help. It's Grant. He's vomiting, but I can't get in. I've told him to unlock it but…" He put his hand to his chest as if to stop his heart jumping out of it, then turned and ran back the way he came.

Roz followed, moving quickly. Before they'd even got into the railcar they heard Grant's gurgles, spits, and strangled cries, along with the sound of doors being kicked or banged at speed. It sounded as if he were thrashing.

Two doors down, Iain's door opened and his ruffled head appeared. "What's going on?"

"Go back in the room, please, Iain," Roz said, sharply. "And stay there."

Iain ducked back out of sight, shut the door, and locked it.

Beefy tried the key card to Grant's room again, but it wouldn't budge. "Open up, Grant, mate, please."

Grant gave a rasped, rattling inhale, then everything went quiet.

Beefy looked to Roz.

"Break it in," she said.

Beefy backed away, ready to launch his topside at the cabin door. It took several goes, with the lock weakening each time. On the fourth attempt, the door opened but only a few inches. Something was in the way.

The smell of acidic vomit and soiled pants filled the corridor. Gagging, Roz stepped forward and looked through the small gap. The door was lodged in Grant's forehead, blood thickening around the wood. His neck lolled to one side; his tongue was thick, slightly blue and had flopped out of his mouth. His eyes were open and static, and one hand was clenched in a claw against his chest.

Crouching, she managed to reach through the space between wall and door, then pressed her fingers against his carotid artery. There seemed little doubt, but she had to check. No pulse, no life. "He's dead," she said. She hoped for Beefy's sake, and hers, that Grant had been dead before the door opened.

"But I was here all the time." Beefy's face marbled with red veins as blood flushed to his cheeks. "Nobody came in or out. And he locked the door himself when I told him to. I don't understand, how did it happen?" He looked from Roz to Craig, as if hoping they could explain it all away.

"I don't know," Roz said. "And it could be difficult to find out before a postmortem. We can't even get inside to take a look, because we shouldn't move or touch the body."

Taking out her phone, she took pictures of the cyanosis of Grant's tongue and the small number of petechiae in his open eyes that she could see, along with the vomit that covered his face. Scene of Crime Officers would take a sample of the sick when they arrived. And everything would now take much longer.

She knew she shouldn't make this about herself, but her heart still derailed at the thought of not getting to Heather on Christmas Eve.

"We could go look in from outside," Craig suggested. "Break the window, if we have to."

"If someone hasn't already broken it," Roz replied. From this angle, she couldn't see the window.

"You're right, someone could have got through that way and killed him." Beefy shook his head sorrowfully. "Poor bloke. No one deserves that."

Roz wasn't sure she agreed with him, which made her choice to leave the force seem wise.

"We don't know if he was killed at all," Craig said, always the voice of caution and sense. "It could be suicide. He must have known he was our chief suspect for Meg's death. Maybe he couldn't face everyone knowing."

"It's possible," Roz said. While she couldn't see ligature marks around his neck, the vomiting and respiratory distress could point to poisoning, which might indeed be by his own hand. Or, and this was most likely, someone else's. She suspected that if Grant had been faced with a life sentence, he'd have wheeled in the best barrister money could buy and got off with a six-figure book deal. No, she was pretty sure someone else had killed him.

The snow had upped its game, and a blizzard now raged. Beinn Dòrain was hardly visible. Roz could feel its presence though, and drew strength from its solidity and longevity. It was always there, hearing everything, overseeing all, like the ultimate judge in a white wig of snow.

Roz and Craig kept their heads down as they waded through the snow, keeping close to the side of the train. When they reached Grant's cabin, Craig linked his fingers, offering her a lift up.

Roz placed her boot on his palms, and he hoisted her high enough to see through the window. The glass was intact; there was no sign of anyone breaking in or out. Grant, too, had died in a locked room.

The blind was up and, once she'd angled her head to avoid reflections, she could see all of the cabin. Gripping onto the slight sill, she took in as much information as she could. There was so much vomit. Yellow with chunks. On the bed, on the floor, on the door.

Grant lay on his side at an angle; head by the door, feet by the bathroom. His vape cigar was on the bed.

Just in front of Roz, balanced on the side of the sink, was a plate with the remains of a bacon bap, a banana skin, and a packet of crisps. And inside the basin was an opened bottle of champagne, a razor, and a still water bottle.

Roz didn't know if she was shaking from shock, fear, or the cold.

"Can you balance enough to take photos?" Craig said.

Steadying herself with an arm against the train, Roz peeled off her gloves, then took out her phone and pressed it to the glass, hoping there wouldn't be too much reflection.

When she'd finished, Craig helped her down. They stood in silence. Even the wind died down and the snow eased off, as if in respect for death.

"What do you make of it?" Craig asked her eventually.

"Unless he overdosed on something, which is possible, then we could be looking at him being poisoned by someone else."

"In the food or drink, do you think?"

"Seems most likely. He locked the door after it arrived."

"Who would want him dead?"

Roz thought of the remaining passengers and staff, her mind a train whizzing past each suspect as if they were stations. Means, motive, opportunity. "Iain explicitly stated he wanted him dead, but Beefy was keeping an eye on both doors."

"Grant and Beck weren't exactly best buddies," Craig said, "and Phil seemed very angry with him."

"Someone else was very defensive of Meg and distraught at her death," Roz said suddenly. She didn't want to think like this, but she had to.

"Who?"

"Beefy. He was sobbing, blaming himself."

"But why is he so invested? He only met her yesterday."

"Do we know that for sure?"

"True," he said, drawing out the word. Roz could tell Craig didn't want to think Beefy was a killer either. Without discussing it, they both started going back by the longer route, walking all the way around the train rather than opening the nearest door. They were in tune, on parallel tracks.

"Is there any word about your daughter?" Craig asked.

"She's teetering. The doctors are trying to get her stabilized, but her organs seem to be fighting it."

"I'm so sorry. Are you close?"

"I wouldn't say 'close.' We're both private and prickly. And we've gone through difficult times that have meant we haven't stuck together as you'd hope."

"What kind of difficult times?"

"I was twenty when I had her. My mum said, 'at least I won't have the ignominy of you being a teenage mum' and when I pointed out that *she'd* been a teenage mum to me, she said, 'Ah yes, but I was a child bride. That's very different. That's respectable. And anyway, I looked better with a baby bump.' Arguing with Liz, my mum, was impossible. Never-ending. Like painting the Forth Bridge. Get to the end of one argument, and you find it had gone into another layer."

"You said that arguing with your mum 'was' impossible."

"She died a few months ago." Roz thought of her mum's recipe book, all that life and knowledge reduced to a soup of recipes, with bon mots as croutons to add a bit of crunch.

"I know I'm supposed to say 'sorry for your loss,' but that doesn't seem nearly enough."

"It is a loss," Roz said. She thought about what her grief counselor, Toni, had said about the Kübler-Ross theories: grief caused a hole that you grew around. And not just grief; all loss was the same. Loss of adolescence when becoming a young mum. Loss of trust when abused. Toni had brought in a bag of doughnuts to the group meeting and gave one to each attendee. "What happens when you've faced the doughnut and eaten it?" she'd asked.

"It's gone?" someone had said.

"It's become part of the whole," said another attendee, who'd been on the course twice before.

"You're not normally so quiet, Roz," the counselor had said, speaking from her sugar-crusted mouth. "What are your thoughts?"

"We're just eating our grief, aren't we?" Roz replied. "And who here doesn't want another doughnut, right now? Who could go through a whole fairground of doughnuts, hole and all?"

Everyone put up their hand. Roz hadn't gone back to the sessions again. The counselor had gotten it all wrong. Loss was like a Bundt cake, not a doughnut. There was a hole in the middle, but mountains formed around it. At ground level, no one could tell there was a hole. Sugar dust those mountains and even those seemed sweet. Plus, it took a lot of willpower to eat all of a Bundt cake at once.

"Are you okay?" Craig asked, stopping her. "You seemed to go off somewhere."

"I was thinking of grief and what it leaves us with. What about you? What's the hole inside you?"

Craig thought for a moment, then said, "I'm haunted by what I didn't have. What should have been my life." His tone was soaked with sorrow.

Roz's email pinged. "It's from Laz. Next wave of information, she says." Skimming through it, several interesting things struck her.

"Anything useful?" Craig's tone was strange, as if trying to keep it casual, but something was hidden behind it.

"Potentially. We might need to split up, interview one person each at a time."

"I'd rather not separate," Craig said. It felt loaded. "I don't have your skills."

"You're good at it, actually. Astute. Incisive. Kind."

"Thank you, but I bow to your technique. Won't you miss all this now you've retired?"

"I'm trying not to think about the not-working side of retirement. I've worked to distract myself for, well, forever."

"Then what are you going to do?"

"Look after my daughter and granddaughter, read, walk. Find

a part-time job when I inevitably get bored." She realized how that sounded. "Not that Heather and the baby will be boring, just—"

"I understand," Craig said. "You like to fill time till it overflows. Same as me. What about being a private detective? Take the cases you want, make your own hours."

"PIs just go through bins and sit in cars, eating doughnuts, waiting to take a picture of someone having an affair."

"What I'm hearing is that you're paid to eat doughnuts. Sounds ideal."

Roz laughed, but she knew she had to think about her future. She could have thirty or forty years of retirement, alone. "What about you? Do you have any grand career or life plans?" She told herself she wasn't fishing, but she was.

"Nothing specific, as yet. I may be moving house," he said, not taking the bait. "Times like this make you reevaluate your life though, don't they?"

Chapter Thirty-Four

The club car was silent when Roz entered with Craig. Everyone apart from Beefy and Iain was present, but there was no sense that the group was in any way together. They had spaced themselves out as far as they could, keeping their white duvets to themselves. Breath condensed on the cold windows, making the white landscape outside seem even more alien. It was as if they were in a blank room, the only people that existed in the world. Either that or they were in some kind of limbo and they would never be able to leave.

"Have you worked out how she died yet?" Sally asked with more than a trace of impatience. She was in the corner of a booth, wearing dark sunglasses with her coat pulled up to her neck, duvet on top.

"I'm not a coroner," Roz said with matching impatience. "And something has happened that makes things more complicated."

"Oh no," Bella said, leaning against the bar. "What now?"

"Grant has also died. And we think he's been murdered."

Roz watched carefully as each person reacted to the news. Tears, fear, shock, disbelief. But their faces showed nothing especially revealing, each one a mountain summit, veiled in mist. Mountains, at least, were more knowable than people. Their dangers were clear. If you chose to climb them, then you bore the consequences.

Then the quiet broke like ice under an ax.

Voices jostled and jabbed: "What the fuck is going on?"

"Have you called the police?"

"So much for getting home for Christmas."

Their utterances, whether spiced or spiked, plain, nutty, or as dry as raisins, were mixed together into a cacophonous sludge, a Christmas pudding of voices.

Roz stood in the center of the railcar, hands on her hips. "Would everyone shut up? We have to work together." Her voice rang out clear. Everyone shut up. Oli, in the middle of arranging the remaining snacks at the bar, tried not to rustle the packets of crisps and nuts.

She remembered, then, the vomit around Grant's nose and face, and what he had said to Meg in the first-class lounge when she was holding a packet of peanuts: "Are you trying to kill me?"

She didn't know much about anaphylactic shock but knew it could narrow airways and cause respiratory distress, which could in turn cause vomiting and choking.

"Who brought Grant's tray to his cabin this morning?"

"I did," Oli said, putting up his hand.

"And were you the only one to touch everything, other than when you handed the tray to Beefy?"

"No, because I was the only one at the bar. Everyone helped."

"Everyone?" Craig asked.

"Well, I cooked the bacon, Beck opened the champagne when he asked for it, Ayana found a piece of carrot cake, Ember donated a muffin and crisps, Tony gave up his banana... I think that was everything. Oh, and Liv found Phil's water."

"That's very generous of you all, given that he was under suspicion for murder," Roz said.

"But you said he was distraught in his cabin," Liv said, looking confused.

"Why do you ask, Roz?" Tony asked.

"I can't say, I'm afraid."

"You think he was poisoned," Blake said, leaning forward.

"Was Meg poisoned too?" Sam asked. Roz hoped she wasn't detecting something in their tone that suggested that it would be satisfying if poison had been used. As if murder was always as easily wrapped up.

"Well, it obviously wasn't Iain," Mary said. Mousetache was walking over the back of the banquette behind her, curling his tail around her head. "He was in his cabin. Still is. Anyway, he brought back our Mousetache. Even though his breed was built for weather like this, with the thickest fur coats imaginable, he could have been lost for good. That makes him a decent man in my book."

"While that's a laudable sentiment, Mary, it's not evidence," Craig said.

"Do I have to remind you, young man, that I am extremely old and therefore wise? I know people."

"Mousetache is a much more likely murderer than Iain," Tony said. "He has an unfortunate fondness for shrews."

"What are we going to do?" Bella asked. "Two tabloid hacks have already managed to get my number, asking for a quote on Meg's death."

Roz stepped toward Bella. "You didn't—"

"Course I didn't," Bella snapped. "But if they find about Grant too, they're not going to leave me alone. One of them said that it's already going to be the biggest story today, which we should have anticipated. People love a bit of death at Christmas. Look at *Eastenders*."

"That's what I was saying yesterday." Sam clapped their hands. "The solstice, and therefore Christmas, is all about the death of light and the promise of its return. We have to look into the dark to see the light."

Blake leaned his head on Sam's shoulder.

"This isn't the time to be winning your 'Stay Another Day' argument." Beck's face was splashed with sanctimony.

"Keep it down, would you?" Sally was pressing her head against the wall of the booth.

"We should be working out who killed them both," Ember said. She had pulled up her hood and was looking around as if she could hide from the murderer. "There's a serial killer in this room, and you're talking about *Eastenders* and nineties pop music."

"Sorry to be a 'well, actually,' Ember," Sam said, "but a serial killer is usually defined as three or more murders." Their hair fell over one side of their face like the shadow over a half moon.

"Great, Sam," Beck said. "Nice one. Now they'll be looking for a third victim."

"No, no." Sam's eyes were bright, filled with revelation and zeal. "Serial killers have a cooling-off period between murders, so even if another of us dies, it wouldn't count—this, I suspect, would be called a single event, in one place."

"So, what, a spree killer, then?" Beck said.

"That needs more than one location. And we're not moving anywhere. And mass murder requires four or more, give or take. These are generalized of course, FBI based, mainly."

"Four or more murders," Beck said, quietly. She looked unnerved, but Roz couldn't tell if it was due to the talk of death or because she was exposing another weak spot in her knowledge. This was why talking en masse about the murders was useful. Roz was able to observe them all. Watch every move.

"Ember's right," Roz said, raising her voice. "Here are the facts as they stand. It's nearly eleven in the morning. Two people are dead. Most likely murdered. And while it's possible that the murderer could either be someone coming onto the train from the surrounding countryside, or could be a second stowaway we've yet to find, it's probable that the killer is on this train. In this room."

Roz paused, letting that soak in. Phil peered around and held the baby closer to him. She thought of her little granddaughter, waiting for her. If she didn't get these crimes at least partially unwrapped, the Sellotape loosened, then they'd all be here past Boxing Day.

"Right," she said. "I'm not going to do this the nice way anymore. I need everyone to tell me where they were just after the train derailed, and who could corroborate your story. Let's get that sorted first, a really clear picture of where everyone was. I'll then want to know the same— where you were and who you were with—for when Grant died, which was around 10 a.m."

"What, and we say this in front of everyone?" Beck said.

"Why, got something to hide?" Blake smirked.

"What is *your* problem?" Beck stood up and paced with her hands on her hips. A Sloane Ranger gunslinger with Louboutin trainers.

Blake inched forward, chin jutting, Sam at his side. Ayana joined them in a weird nerd standoff against Beck.

"You're all a problem," Roz shouted. "Sit down, this is not the time for petty infighting."

The students shut up and slunk back to their booths.

"I'll start," Ember said. She was looking at Roz with the eagerness and devotion of a Christmas Day puppy. "At the derailment I was in here, and after that too. I went to the toilet at some point in the evening, can't remember when—during one of the answer rounds, I think—but other than that I didn't leave the club car until you came in."

"And can anyone vouch for Ember?" Roz asked.

"I can," Beck said, slightly reluctantly. "She pushed me out of the conga chain."

Ember shook her head. "That's not what happened."

"Anyway," Beck continued, "not long after that, Meg started shouting and ran out, and the derailment happened. I remember seeing Ember afterward, talking with Liv."

"That's what I remember too," Ember said.

"Although I don't remember Liv in the conga line," Beck added, as if she couldn't bear to agree with Ember, or anyone.

Liv nodded. "I felt really tired and was going to go to bed, but got as far as my room, then got huge FOMO and decided to come back."

"FOMO?" Tony asked.

"Fear of Missing Out," Mary said. "Keep up with the times, love."

"My memory of last night is a bit hazy, but I *think* I can account for both Liv and Ember at the time of Meg's death, as well as Sally, Beck, and Aidan." Craig leaned against the booth, arms loosely crossed. His body language was casual, but he kept checking his phone, turning it over and taking surreptitious peeks.

"Yeah," Aidan said. "We were talking about university life. Craig was giving me tips."

"Oh, yeah?" Sally said, surfacing from her hangover. "What kind of tips?"

"Nothing salacious, don't worry." Craig smiled. "The opposite really. I advised Aidan to concentrate on studies rather than on, well, extracurricular activities."

"I thought you wanted to join Footlights?" Phil asked. Bless his vanilla heart. Seeing his face so earnest and blithe, Roz felt for Sally for the first time since meeting her. She bet their sex life was very polite. She pictured him bowing to Sally before commencing coitus, worshipping her yoni, wearing white gloves like a snooker umpire. But maybe Sally was into that.

Roz's mouth twitched, but she managed to stop herself from laughing. "I don't think that's what Craig meant, Phil."

Phil went red. "Oh."

"Mum and I were both in the seated railcar," Tony said, "when the derailment happened. I hadn't gone to sleep, so I can say Mum didn't go anywhere."

"It's unlikely I could have if I tried," Mary replied. She had a collection of date stones on the table in front of her. If someone had drugged or poisoned the dates, Mary would be their Indiana Jones monkey.

Tony smiled and held her hand but said nothing.

"Oli was with me, in the driver's cab," Bella said.

"We weren't doing anything," Oli said quickly. "I was just keeping her company. Keeping her awake."

"Not that I was sleepy," Bella jumped in. "Far from it. I'd had enough coffee to keep my eyes open for a fortnight. And not that I was too wired either. There is no way I could have avoided that tree."

"No one said you could have," Roz reassured her.

"Oh, great. Now I look defensive." Bella looked from Roz to Oli, and back again. "Anyway, I didn't kill anyone. And I was on the phone to the engineer at ten, when Grant died, with Beck haranguing me to come and fix the heating."

"Well, it's unbearable," Beck said, shivering theatrically.

Roz turned to address the whole club car. "So who does that leave without an alibi for both? I think we can assume Mousetache's innocence—of killing humans, at least." Roz looked around the group.

"Me," Ayana said, her hand creeping up. "I went to the toilet after Meg ran out. And I was in there for the derailment. I came out when I was sure it was safe. I was in here at ten though. But then all the passengers were, apart from you, Iain, and Craig."

"Yes, it's more difficult to assess alibis for when we think Grant could have been poisoned."

Phil held up his hand. "I was in my bunk asleep for the whole thing. You could ask this one," he places a hand on Buddy's head, "but all he's saying at the moment is 'no,' so that wouldn't do me any favors. Can you say something other than no, sweetheart?" he said to the child.

"No," Buddy replied and grinned, showing his four teeth.

"There you go. No alibi for Meg's death."

"And he knew Meg," Beck said, shaking her head and sucking through her teeth. "Don't they say that people are usually killed by someone they know?"

"Really interesting you should say that, Beck," Roz said. "I've received information that you did know Grant. He once worked for your parents' company as a car salesman, before he went on telly. Only he was keeping more than his commission."

"That's got nothing to do with me," Beck said. "I bumped into him a few times before they sacked him, that's all. And I was really young when he worked for my parents. I barely recognized him."

"But, Beck, your parents must have known who he was. They would have seen his face everywhere. And you always say how close you are to your mum and dad. Don't they say that people are usually killed by someone they know?" Ayana said. She then put her hands over her mouth, at once shocked and thrilled. She was enjoying playing detective a bit too much.

"You seemed to know him on Liv's live stream. Grant put his arm around you."

"Come on, that's every woman in every town, each Friday night," Beck said. Her scorn was as cold as the air.

"It *is* a bit suspicious, Beck," Sam said. "That you're here at the same time as Grant, when he ripped off your parents. That's motive."

"We're from the same hometown, going home for Christmas," Beck bit back. "The chances of being on the same train go up substantially in those circumstances. We should concentrate on Grant killing Meg."

"He did leave the club car to go after her," Liv said. She looked eager to join in, to be a grown-up. "I saw him."

"So does that mean there's two killers," Ember asked, pulling her duvet up to her nose, "or one?"

"I don't know." Beck's eyes were as spiked as pomanders. "But there's one other person who doesn't have an alibi for both."

"Ah yes," Roz replied. "Me."

Chapter Thirty-Five

"I know you want us to stay in here, Roz," Beck said, standing up and walking into the center of the club car. "But given the circumstances, I think we need to talk about this."

"Okay, but I'm just keen on keeping us all safe and in one place. Not only is the train not secure, but we don't know what danger is faced by the killer or killers." Half the room murmured in assent; the other murmurs sounded more equivocal. "But we should discuss it."

"I meant without you, Roz. After all, you come in here asking us questions and telling us what to do, where we can and can't go, but you don't have an alibi for Meg's death when the majority of us do. You might be the murderer and framing one of us."

"That's a bit strong, Beck," Craig said. He came over to stand by Roz.

"Is it, though? She was quick to point the finger at me, but it could be her. After all, Roz was the one to tell us to bring Grant food and drink. What if she had prepared poison for him in advance and it was a trap?"

"That doesn't seem at all likely or logical," Sam said.

"What possible reason could Roz have for killing either of them?" Craig folded his arms. Roz wanted to put her hands on his shoulders and rest there.

"Who knows?" Beck shrugged. "Maybe her friend can provide

information with spurious links between them. But until we know, do you all think Roz is the right person to be investigating this? I mean, she could be hiding evidence for all we know."

"Roz is a highly trained former police officer," Craig said, "who knows exactly what to do in these situations. She is precisely what's needed."

And now the circus was turning against her. Great. "Thanks, Craig, but I'm more than happy to step down and let the police take over. I've got other things to worry about."

"More than two dead people?" Beck said skeptically.

"Don't get on your daddy's high horse," Ayana said, then seemed shocked at herself. It was always interesting what emerged in times of stress. That part of ourselves that stayed locked inside suddenly finds all the doors and windows are open.

"You asked if she had a 'reason' to kill them," Sam said to Craig. "But do people always have reasons to kill?"

"Few people think when they kill," Roz replied. "They may apply reasons to it afterward, but that is where reason doesn't mean logic."

"Excuses, then." Sam nodded, thoughtful.

"Can we get beyond philosophy?" Sally said. "I want to go to our cabin and sleep until we're rescued."

"I still think it wise that nobody returns to their cabins or the seated railcar," said Roz, "in order to keep each other safe."

"I paid for a sleeper cabin, and I am going to get some sleep," Sally insisted. "You can't stop me."

"Same here," Beck replied. "This is a waste of time. We're going to have to go through all this again whenever the police get here."

"This is a security measure," Roz said. "Look how everything spirals when we can't keep track of each other."

Mary nodded slowly. "We are a collective. There is strength when we're together."

"I see your point," Sam said. "But I would rather no one told us what to do. It's a matter of principle."

"What if staying here could avoid further death," Roz replied, frustration bubbling up and over into her voice. "Isn't that principled?"

"Personal liberty is the highest principle," Beck said, reminding Roz more and more of a young Tory in a debating club, slinging rhetoric and winging it.

"Is all this fighting necessary?" Mary said. Mousetache was picking up on her agitation, tail twitching back and forth. "Roz is trying to help, can't you see that?"

"But keeping us here is kidnapping," Aidan said, seeming to be glad to add something to the debate.

"It really isn't." Roz sighed.

Beck clapped her hands. "I vote that we all go to our cabins and stop talking about all this. Or go out into the snow, wander around. Whatever you want. Free country, right? Stay out of each other's way till the police and engineers arrive."

"You do realize that is exactly what a killer would say to split everyone up," Mary said, shaking her head with sadness.

"Who's coming with me?" Beck's grin had a maniacal tweak to it as Sally, Phil, Liv, and Aidan moved toward the door. The students followed too. Ayana shrugged toward Roz, then walked out.

"You can pop off to bed now, Roz. You're not needed anymore," Beck said smugly before closing the door behind them.

Chapter Thirty-Six

The killer paced in the vestibule, trying to shake off adrenaline surreptitiously, like a prisoner dispensing soil in the yard. Everyone was dispersing across the train. They felt like they could breathe again.

He was dead. At last. Grant was gone. After all this time, all of their wishing it and planning for it, now it was over. But it hadn't gone as they wanted. And that made them want to be sick.

But they couldn't show what they felt. They had to conceal the elation, the pain, the confusion over what to do next and what to do for the best. They had to act normal, whatever normal looked like in abnormal circumstances. At least they knew how to keep secrets. They'd kept secrets for many years. Secrets, though, were like the bees their mum had kept when they were a child. They buzzed inside you and could be made docile with smoke and sugar-syrup words but, at some point, they came out of the hive with a sting, then died.

This was a secret they would have to keep. Forever.

They wished they could talk to Roz about it. She would know what to do. But that was giving up. And they wouldn't do that.

They looked through the window into the railcars—the passengers were returning to their rooms. They all looked in shock, trying to understand what was happening almost as much as the killer was. But maybe that was for the best as well. While chaos reigned, no one would notice the panic that rippled under the killer's skin, or the fear below that, and the relief under the fear. And they must never notice, right at the heart of the killer, the sadness that would never leave and the feeling that they would never make a difference.

Chapter Thirty-Seven

"Sorry about them," Craig said when Roz sat down, exhausted, in one of the booths. "They're scared."

Roz felt the warmth in his tone and saw it in his eyes. He was reaching out to her. And part of her wanted to run toward him. But a larger part of her was terrified of what that intimacy could bring. "I know that," she snapped.

He reared back.

"Sorry," Roz said, rubbing her eyes. "I'm so tired."

"That's why I thought I'd stay. Give you some solidarity and moral support."

"And you'll get a double helping from me," Mary said, sitting very slowly down next to Roz. "Us crones need to sit and stick together. Maidens think they know everything when they have learned nothing. Mothers aren't much better. The crones, though. Crones know. That's why people are so scared of us, try to keep us invisible. But that's when we have the most power. They can't stop us if they don't see us. We slip through the net. We're like ghosts through locked doors."

"You're not like most older women I know," Roz said. "And believe me, that is meant with utmost respect."

"And I return that respect thrice over."

Mousetache jumped up on Roz's lap and started headbutting her hand for a stroke.

"Well, now I know for sure you didn't kill anyone," Mary said. "Mousetache is an even better judge of character than I am."

"It doesn't matter though. I should have left it all alone. Left it for the police." Not her circus. Not her monkey. She might get that tattooed on her wrist in circus script. It'd be her first tattoo. Heather would call it a midlife crisis, to which Roz would reply that she hoped it was, as that would mean she'd live to a hundred.

"You did something. Not giving up, that's what's important."

Roz's phone rang, vibrating on the table between them. Ellie's name appeared on the screen, at last. Craig looked at the phone, then Roz, a question on his face.

"It's my daughter-in-law-to-be," Roz said.

He nodded and Roz stood, heart pounding as she walked over to the corner of the railcar. "Ellie, love, what's—"

"It's me, Mum." Heather sounded breathless. As if her words had been dragged from somewhere deep inside her.

"Oh, darling. How are you feeling?"

"No, Mum. Are *you* all right?"

Now that was a question. "I'm fine. It's you I'm worried about."

"So, you're not on the 'death line,' then?"

"What?"

"It's all over social media. Midwife told me when I said you were coming up on the sleeper. She saw on the news…that two famous people… have died on board an overnight train that's stuck in the Highlands." Heather's breath was ragged.

"Two?"

"So, it's true?"

"I've only just found the other one. But none of this should have gotten out." The young people had been sitting scrolling on their phones during the club car meeting—it could have been any of them. And Craig had been on his phone too.

"You will be okay, won't you, Mum?"

"You needn't worry. I'm going to stop whoever is doing this."

"What do you mean? You're not doing anything stupid and putting yourself in danger are you?" A monitor nearby started beeping an alarm.

"Please don't worry, it's going to be all r—"

The alarm was joined by another, louder one.

Roz heard footsteps run toward Heather. A curtain swished open or closed. Concerned doctors talked over each other, murmuring about doses.

"What's going on?" Roz said.

Someone said the words "seizures" and "coma."

Roz shouted, "*Baby—*"

And the phone call cut off.

"What's happened?" Craig asked, rushing over. "Is Heather all right?"

"No, she's—" Roz stopped. Something wasn't right. "How did you know she was called Heather?"

Craig blinked. "You just said it."

"No, I didn't. And you said her name earlier too." She replayed the events in her mind. "That was after you saw Ellie's name on the screen, but why would you know my daughter's partner was called Ellie?"

Craig looked as if he was about to protest further, then stopped. "I'm sorry, Roz. I've been trying to talk to you since last night, but it never seemed right. Did you not recognize me at all?"

Roz felt as if she was tipping, coming off the tracks. What if it was him, the one who'd raped her when she was pregnant, who had siphoned off so much of her joy and life?

But, looking at him, Roz knew it wasn't—and then she knew who he was.

"Oh, God," she said.

She was looking at Heather's dad.

Roz stumbled out of the booth, tears forming. She ran down the corridors, already getting out her key card. All she wanted was to go to sleep and wake up when the train was in Fort William. She knew there were questions to ask—why was he here? How did he find Heather, or did Heather find him? But she couldn't investigate any of these, not now. Craig had spent all that time with her, asking her questions, and she hadn't even known who he was. Beck was right, she shouldn't be a detective at all.

Chapter Thirty-Eight

"You managed to get away then," the killer said as their blackmailer walked toward them down the corridor. They were trying to appear cool, even though their heart was beating far too fast. The blackmailer had come up to them earlier and told them what they'd seen. They'd seen enough to worry the killer.

The blackmailer smiled. "I think what you're trying to say is 'thank you.' To which I reply, 'You're very welcome.'"

"So, you're doing me a favor by not speaking up?"

"I prefer to think of it as supporting each other."

"Or we could call it what it is: blackmail."

The blackmailer placed a finger on their lips and indicated toward the door.

Two more passengers came in, laughing. While they squeezed by the blackmailer and the killer, the killer looked out of the window. The sun showed through the snow clouds, the blizzard now a light flurry. Beinn Dòrain looked down on the train with icy indifference.

What must it be like at the top? Up there where only clouds and eagles could see it. To be wrapped in snow and cold, like the fleeciest blanket made to kill. It looked like the easiest way to get out of this. Climb and keep climbing. Hope you never reached the top.

When the two passengers had gone, the killer said to the blackmailer, "What do you want?"

"Not here," the blackmailer said, looking around. "You wouldn't want anyone overhearing."

"Sounds like you wouldn't either."

"You've got much more to lose than I have. Or would you rather I marched back to Roz and told her, 'Actually I made a mistake, silly me, guess who I saw tampering with Grant's champagne?'"

The killer imagined Roz's reaction and how, once it was explained, she might even understand and help. But the killer couldn't take that risk. "Fine. What now?"

"We go to my room. I've got the information I need to give you in my suitcase," the blackmailer said.

"I've got something to do first," the killer replied. "I'll meet you there in fifteen minutes."

Chapter Thirty-Nine

The baby is dragged out of Roz, but she cannot see her. She can't hear the baby either. There is emptiness in her stomach and quiet in the room. There are fifteen faceless people, and it feels like none of them are breathing.

"I want to hold her," Roz says, but her voice is stuck behind her mask. She tries to hold out her arms, but they are held back by tubes and machines that heave and hiss. Mum strokes her hair and looks over to where they've taken the baby. Someone is whispering, "Come on, little one. Come on."

When the cry comes, Roz feels her own tears form and her milk come in, her breasts going rocklike. But the midwife doesn't smile. She says, "That cry means she needs oxygen, she can't breathe." The midwife then shows Roz a sparrowlike child in a bundle of blue blankets. The baby smells of orris root and chamomile.

The baby is then placed in a plastic trolley and trundled away, wrenching out Roz's insides. The wheels of the trolley squeak down the corridor, their screeching morphing into Roz's scream.

❧❧❧

"Help!" someone said. "Get Roz!" Feet ran. Doors banged and slammed.

Roz sat up in bed, wrenched out of a fought-for nap Someone was dead. Heather was dead. Or the baby. Or both. She was sure of it.

Roz stumbled to her door and opened it. She didn't know how long she'd been asleep. Not long enough. Ayana was running up and down the corridor, banging on doors. Her eyes were wild. She grabbed hold of Roz's arm and pulled her down the corridor. As they passed Sally and Phil's room, the door opened very slightly, then closed again.

Phil, however, was throwing himself at the door into Beck and Ayana's room. He burst through, falling onto the floor. "Oh no," he cried out. "God, help us."

Roz rushed in. Beck was slumped against the bunk bed. Her mouth was open, giving the unsettling look of an abandoned ventriloquist's dummy. Scissors were lodged in the side of her throat, blood streaming down her clavicle.

Adrenaline bullet-trained through Roz, chasing away the sleep from her tracks. She stepped forward and bent down to touch Beck's wrist. Nothing flowed through her anymore. Not even bitterness.

Phil was rubbing his shoulder, wincing. "That really hurt. I should've gotten Beefy to do it again." He glanced at Beck, then away, wincing even more. "I don't want Liv or Aidan to see this."

Roz assessed how Beck's clothes were rumpled, a sleeve slightly torn as if there had been a struggle. Her hand was covered in blood, and there were prints on the bed, but there were also blooded indentations and marks on her palms as if she'd held up her hand against the scissors. She had probably bled out quickly, but knowing what was happening to her all the way. Knowledgeable even in death.

Roz's gaze then moved around the room. Blood spatters on the floor from where she must have staggered around. The interconnecting door to Blake and Sam's room was ajar. Clothes and quiz books everywhere. It was hard to tell if they were from an altercation or just two young people making a mess. "Has anything been disturbed in here? Something taken or moved?" she asked Ayana.

Ayana looked around the room, but she was mainly checking the upper bunk, standing on tiptoes. "I don't think so."

"What are you looking for?" Roz asked.

"That's my bed. I was just trying to see if my stuff had been taken." She was clearly lying.

"What about the things on the floor?"

"Most of it was like that when I was last here," Ayana said. She was stepping around something important.

"And when was that?"

"Before we all talked in the club car."

"And what happened when you left the club car?"

"I was talking with Liv and Aidan outside, but then I was freezing so I came back to get some more clothes. I found the door was locked from the inside, and so was Blake and Sam's room, so I couldn't use the interconnecting door."

"Blake and Sam are elsewhere, then?"

Ayana nodded frantically. She was also apparently full of adrenaline. "They're having a snowball fight by the ravine."

Funny time to have a snowball fight. But then everyone reacts differently to death. Maybe they were trying to revert to childhood. "Do you think Beck locked herself in?" Roz asked.

"I don't know," Ayana asked, unable to take her eyes off the scissors in Beck's neck. They were unusual, had handles in the shape of swan wings. Roz had seen them before, in Meg's hands as she had cut out the paper dolls.

Ayana wrenched her gaze away and turned to Roz. "I remember Meg saying in the club car that she couldn't find her scissors."

"When was this?"

Ayana frowned, her eyes shifting to the left as she replayed her memory of events. "Not long after the railcars decoupled, I think."

"Did she give any indication that she suspected who'd taken them, and when?"

Ayana shook her head. "Nope."

Roz lodged the information of the missing scissors and changed tack. "From what I've seen, you didn't exactly get on with Beck."

"I suppose we didn't keep that a secret, did we?"

"First thing I thought when I saw the four of you was that those Quizlings are going to be trouble."

"Quizlings. I like that."

"But you didn't like Beck?"

"It's hard to bond when someone doesn't want you to succeed. She even said to me, at one point, that she wanted to be the only girl on the team."

"What?"

"I know. Makes no sense. But she liked to be special in some way or other. She wanted to be famous."

"She will be now." Beck's picture would be all over the Boxing Day papers. Appearing on social media. Meg and Beck's worlds colliding in death. She looked so young now. Roz wanted to comb her hair, tie it back from her face. But she couldn't touch anything else.

"Did you see anything that could help us?"

"Nothing," Ayana said. Which is how Roz knew for sure that she was lying. People always see something, even if it's dismissed as random and irrelevant.

Roz dropped her voice. "You can tell me, you know. If something happened. Tell me and I'll try to help."

Roz saw indecision on Ayana's face. Then she seemed to make up her mind and said: "I'll let you know if I remember anything."

Ayana knew something, Roz was sure. "You do that. Right now, we need to let the police know. So that they're prepared when they arrive." Three dead bodies to remove. And, as yet, no killer to arrest.

"I suppose we'd better tell the others," Phil said.

"Do what you like," Roz said. "I'm not in charge."

"But what are we supposed to do?" He looked lost.

"Not my circus, Phillip."

"You were right," Ayana said. She was rubbing a ring pull up and down her finger. "We should have all stayed in the club car. Together."

"No shit," said Roz.

Chapter Forty

The killer sat in the corner of the booth. Meg was dead. Grant was dead. Beck was dead.

Nothing had gone as they'd planned. All that preparation, and chaos reigned. Death begat death. The killer's mother had always said that. But then Mum had also always said that bad things came in threes. So let that be an end to all the bad things. The killer didn't think they could take any more. No one else must die.

But the killer didn't know if they could be stopped.

Chapter Forty-One

Back in her cabin, Roz's breath condensed into vapor. It was now only slightly warmer inside the train than out. She climbed onto the bed and under the covers. It occurred to her that people never lost the tender toddler logic that, if you were under a duvet, blanket, or fur, then the monsters couldn't get you. But the monsters were sometimes in bed next to you. And they were almost definitely in your mind too.

Two more photos had arrived on her phone. One was of Heather in her bed, asleep, so swollen and full of wires that she looked like a sprouting potato. Roz had cried out when she'd seen it and closed her eyes, as if that could shut out the image.

She had scrolled to the next photo. Little nameless one lay in an incubator. A tube was taped to her nose so she could be fed through to her tiny tummy. In the next picture, presumably taken by a neonatal nurse, Ellie's hand was through the porthole, her hand over the baby's head.

Heather had yet to hold her. Roz knew what that felt like. Heather had been born with her umbilical cord wrapped around her neck and been taken away to get oxygen. Roz knew then, as she did now, that it was necessary. Literally vital. Her heart, though, and her whole body, had screamed. She didn't know if it had ever stopped.

Roz's phone rang. It was Ellie calling. She readied herself and then answered the phone. "Ellie? What's happening?"

"They've stabilized her for now." Exhaustion was breaking through Ellie's voice. "She's stopped having seizures, but she's still critical. Her blood pressure is too high and her kidney function low."

At least that was something. "How's the baby doing?"

"She's amazing," Ellie said. Her voice lifted, infused with wonder. "I can't believe how resilient she is."

That's good, Roz thought. She'll have to be resilient. Out loud, she said, "You're doing a great job, Ellie. Really. I am so grateful that you are there for Heather. I couldn't have a better daughter-in-law."

"Thank you. They are precious to me, you know. Both of them. I'm going between their beds, trying to be the string between them. Feels like I can't get anything right."

"Just keep going. That's all you can do."

"What about you? Any sign the train will be moving soon, or of the killer being caught?" Roz heard the hope in Ellie's voice. She'd probably love to be able to go back to Heather and give good news. Well, Roz wasn't going to give her any more bad news, at least.

"Last I heard, the engineers are a couple of hours away." She changed the subject. "Will Heather be able to hold the baby soon? It'd help, I think."

"Heather still can't be moved. The neonatal unit said that they would be able to bring the baby over to see her tonight."

"Could you put me through to her, do you think?" Roz asked. "I'd love to talk to her."

"Not sure that's wise, after…" Ellie didn't say *after the last time you talked with her*, but Roz heard it. "She's very tired. How about if she rings you when she's ready?"

"Whatever you think best. And anyway, I'll be with you soon enough."

They shared a short silence. Roz was thinking of how difficult it must be for Heather to not be able to hold her daughter. How it was hard enough for Roz to adjust when she had just given birth, how it had episiotomied her memories of being raped. Drugged. Unable to move. Her body being moved by someone else. She had wanted Heather, but somehow it connected as a violation. She'd been sectioned off from her own daughter in her heart. Trauma sticks to trauma. Scar tissue bonding with scar tissue. It was time to heal.

"I've got to go, love," she said. "Kiss my daughter and granddaughter for me."

Roz had barely disconnected the call when Laz rang. "I've got some more research for you."

Roz felt a scissor-stab of guilt. "Thanks for doing all that for me. I owe you. But I won't need it now. I am officially *and* unofficially retired. Someone else has died, and while I probably couldn't have stopped it, I didn't help." Besides, it was Christmas Eve, and her daughter could be dying. What was the point in trying to save the already dead?

"You sure? There's some gems in there."

"Sure."

"I'll send it anyway. And I hope you get home soon. I'll be watching out on the news for when the death train comes in."

"Happy Christmas, Laz."

The sun had won against the snow for now and was at full height, venturing out between the clouds and filling the cabin with pale light. Soon it'd be heading for an early bed like a child waiting for Santa, and the snow would gather its strength again.

Roz curled up on her bed. She'd had so many plans for celebrations that evening, ones that mirrored what Liz used to do on Christmas Eve: threading popcorn in long strands then, instead of putting it around the tree, trying to eat it while only holding one end of the string. Drinking hot chocolate bearded with whipped cream. Staying up till a shooting star had been seen.

There was no reason why that couldn't be done on Boxing Day, New Year's Eve, or next Christmas. It was just that Christmas Eve was the night with magic in it.

Down the corridors, shouts of Beck's murder carried through the train. No doubt one of them would be informing the press that the death train had struck again. Beck would already be being eulogized in obituaries calling her "bright" and a "star in the making." Like all stars, her light was now in the past.

Someone hammered on her door. "Roz?" It was Ember. "Are you coming out?"

Roz didn't answer. She didn't even know what she had to give anymore. She wasn't helping anyone.

Ember's soft footsteps shushed away.

Another, different knock sounded on Roz's door. She didn't answer. Didn't move.

An email from Laz pinged in with the title *Happy Christmas, Death Train!*, but Roz didn't open it. The mirrored cube was in her hand, but she couldn't find the urge to move it. There was nothing left to twist and click into place. The cube was the only thing in the room that sparkled. Clearly—and this was the only thing that was clear to her—she was no longer of use as a police officer. She was no good as a mum either. And now she wasn't needed as a grandmother. And there was nothing to suggest she would be any good at that either.

Not even fifty and Roz was useless. Not wanted anywhere or by anyone.

How had her mum done it? She'd looked after Heather, and the pub, while Roz slowly climbed the police ladder. She'd managed to do it all, while only complaining half the time.

Mum would know what to do in this situation. Just as she said there was a recipe in her book for every occasion or emotion, Mum had had a slice of advice for every event.

Roz took a deep breath and opened it, then reread the last few lines, where she'd left off.

I'm pissed off with you, Rosalind. Really fucking livid. I'm a crone with days to go, my insides eaten by a bastard canker and my heart torn by a daughter who doesn't know how much she is treasured and adored.

I always thought, as you know, that I would live forever. Or at least till 100. A century is a good slice of time. Anything less seems untidy. But life is, isn't it? You can't Mr. Clean your life into submission. Although if a man cleaned my house, I would consider submitting to him! Oh yes. Now, Rosalind, I can almost hear you say "Mum" and shake your head in a way that says "But you're my Mum! You shouldn't say things like that, especially not about a national treasure." Soon, though, you are going to find out that being a grandma doesn't change who you are. Or shouldn't, anyway.

And if you've opened this book as an instruction manual on being a grandmother, then you should know now, you won't find what you're looking for. I don't know anything. Not really. I can put together things I've worked out over a lifetime of shit happening to me, but I don't take my own advice. Never have. You might not have been able to tell, but I admire you. You go your own way. Be the grandmother that works for you and the next little Parker. I am so sorry that I won't get to meet them, but I kinda know I'll be there, in nursery rhymes sung and stories told. And this book. Because it contains everything I made for you and Heather, alongside cups of wisdom gleaned from mistakes. Make lots of mistakes, Rosalind. Make them frequently. And do not give up who you are to be someone else, or someone you think you should be. It never works. Find your strengths and use them. You have many. No one can figure things out like you can. No one stands up for victims like you do, ever since you were in a playground in Kilmarnock on holiday and you got punched while trying to help a little boy. I shouldn't have told you off that day, or any of the other times you came home with grazes on your knees or bruises. I shouldn't have made fun of you being a tomboy. I shouldn't have done many, many things. I shouldn't have reveled in being the one that Heather came to when she fell over. And I gloated. I did. And I'm sorry. I will always feel guilt at that and many other things, but at least I've left something

that tells you this and much more. And that I'm sorry. And that I'm a human who got things wrong, but one that loves you very much. May you make these recipes and think of me. And may you fly high during your cronehood, with love,
   Mum xxx

Roz sat with the book open on her lap. Liz had written her name and the kisses herself. Her last words. It was as if Mum were here, smelling of Dewberry from the Body Shop years after they'd stopped selling it, sitting on the bed with an arm around Roz's shoulders.

Guilt. It ran through everyone who looked after children. And not just those. Guilt ran through a village and a society like a stream, and everyone drank from it. No one is innocent.

She thought then of Ember's copy of *Murder on the Orient Express*, how everyone there was guilty. Including Poirot and the wide-eyed ingenue.

The tingle prickled her neck. She was nearly there. Her instinct was shouting, *Don't give up!* Something to do with Meg's wide eyes.

Roz went back through everything that Meg had posted in the last three months. Clearly, Meg was in receipt of a lot of sponsorship money, but her TikToks, showing sweet and kooky before-and-after makeup looks while dancing, were authentically engaging, and her YouTube channel was like Roz's mum's recipe book. Ostensibly it was just Meg sitting at a table, looking deep into the eyes of the camera, lit and shot well, using high-end cosmetics from her sponsors. But Meg brought something of herself to each clip. Whether that was applying a shade of eyeshadow, mouth wide and tongue peeking out as she concentrated, that reminded Roz of seeing the sea in Greece and understanding for the first time how blue the color blue could be. Or when Meg had tested a lipstick while in the middle of "a fuck-off hangover, I'm telling you, this one was a bastard." A takeaway had arrived while she applied one coat of dark red to her lips, and when she stood up to answer the door, she'd shown that her sparkly designer top was complemented by graying pajama bottoms and sloppy slippers. "So now you know," she'd said, winking at the camera and walking off. She had then returned with a full bag of food, taken out a piece of naan and, after announcing how soft and fluffy it was, placed her face on it. A look of genuine peace was on her face when she lifted her head and the naan was marked with a blurred kiss. She could have edited it out, but instead she'd kept it in, shown her true self. The comments below ranged from applauding her authenticity to calling her "disgusting" and "weird."

Even Roz, whose use of lipstick was limited to an ill-advised shade of white that came free with *Cosmopolitan*, was drawn in by a video where Meg tried on different colors. Meg had also shown her vulnerability and naivety when she revealed the things she hated about herself, to show others that she, too, had problems. She couldn't bear how her eyes could look small (Roz had seen them, they really weren't) and that her tummy "wibble-wobbled," at which point she had pinched her stomach between thumb and forefinger to show how fat she was (she wasn't). It was a move many people with weight or eating issues recognized and led to haterz aplenty in the comments.

None of this took Roz closer to the solution that she could just about feel, like a snowflake melting on her tongue. There was something right in front of her—she just had to click it into place.

Picking up the mirrored cube, she twisted it as she went through the photos taken of Meg and her room.

Another knock on the door. Whoever it was, they weren't giving up either.

"Who is it?" Roz called out.

"Craig. I just wanted to check up on you. And explain."

Roz sighed. Maybe he could help. "Come in."

Craig came into the room carrying a thermos and a flask. He offered them to Roz. "Oli thought you might like some hot chocolate with a jigger of that whisky you like. And I made you a cheese sandwich." He paused and brought out a jar from his jacket pocket. "And a pickled onion chaser with a tickle and a kick."

Roz took them, laughing and blushing. He'd remembered what she said when he first arrived in the bar. Balancing the cup on her lap, she poured out the steaming hot chocolate. The chocolate was a rich, dark-brown color that edged into purple, with whisky running through it like a river in a ravine.

"I know there's a huge amount we need to talk about," Craig said. "And I also know I didn't handle it well when I found out who you were in the club car. I should have told you immediately."

Roz thought back. "It was when I first mentioned my daughter having an emergency C-section. I just thought you looked concerned for me."

"I was. And it all jumped into place. Heather had described how magnificent you are over the phone when she got hold of me. How your hair was now white and gray and gets big on humid days. That it glows like a dandelion clock in the winter light."

"Heather said *that*?"

"Well, no. She said you had temperamental white hair, but I thought that sounded more romantic."

They held a silence softly between them, then Roz said, "How did she find you?"

"You told her that I was called Douglas, and that I studied Music at Edinburgh, and that I was a year older than you. Not that hard, really." He looked down at his hands, twiddling his thumb and forefinger around his ring finger.

"Ah, I see. You're wondering why I didn't get in touch when I found out I was pregnant."

Craig nodded. "I'd have been there for you. For us. I know it was only one night, and I don't remember much of it other than your hair and your laugh and your eyes, and having a *really* good time, but I'd have been a good dad."

"I know you would've been."

"Then why not tell me?"

"I was going to. I was shocked at first, then put off thinking about what to do. I'd only just decided to keep her and find you, when some-thing happened. Something that destroyed everything."

Craig nodded as if he knew. "You can tell me."

Roz felt panic and memories rise. "I can't. Not yet. For now, just know that I wanted things to be very different."

"Whatever it was, Grant triggered it again, didn't he?"

"Yes. And I will say more, but I need to tell Heather first. I've been keeping things from her for a long time. But then, she's been hiding you from me. Wait, how did she find you? Your name's Craig and you studied law in London!"

"Craig was my middle name—Douglas just didn't fit me—and I did my law conversion course in London. Heather must have some of your detection skills, because she contacted the university and went from there."

"Life's weird. We just don't know what's going to happen."

"Sam said something characteristically wise last night about one of the Fates, Atropos, I think, that cuts the thread of life. So we should enjoy our life while the thread is in our hands."

Roz stopped still, thinking. Then she scrolled to the photos on her phone of Meg's room after her death. "Say that again."

"What?"

"The thread of life stuff. I've seen that word somewhere: Atrop-something."

"Atropos. She was one of the answers in the quiz, but I'm pretty sure you'd gone by that time though. One of the three Fates. The Moirai."

"Moirai as in 'grandmother' in Gaelic?"

Craig laughed. "Blake mentioned that, then Sam said there may be a connection there, seeing as Atropos could be considered the Crone of the Three-fold goddess."

"Sam leaves me so far behind I'm at another station."

"And me."

Roz tingled all over. She had all that she needed. She just needed to click it all into place. And then mountain air clarity descended. She seen the word twice, in two different places. She started swiping through the photos that she took of Meg's room.

"What are you looking for?"

"Atropa. It's written on a little bottle on Meg's floor, and I'm sure she's using it in a photo Liv took." Roz went through every millimeter of the photos, expanding them as she examined each cosmetic, unguent, and potion that laid on the floor, as if the whole room were a giant handbag.

And there it was. She closed in on a small bottle with Atropa Beautiful Woman Eye Drops, "for bright and wide eyes." She took a screenshot of the close-up, then went through Liv's photos. And there was Meg, upending the same bottle, earlier, into her bloodshot eyes. If that wasn't enough, it was also listed as one of the brands used at the start of her live stream.

Roz looked up Atropa eye drops online and found a charming website set up by a women's cooperative in Guernsey that handmade their cosmetics with organic and wildcrafted herbs in high concentration.

She showed Craig the page for their eye drops.

His eyes widened. "Beautiful Woman, as in…"

"Belladonna. Yes. I remember reading it was used in the Renaissance, and before, to dilate pupils, to make women look as if they're aroused." Roz couldn't help wondering if her pupils were also dilated. "It was often mistakenly used in toxic quantities and could cause death."

"But not now, surely? It must be safe if they're selling it? You can't just release poison into people's eyes."

"It's not illegal to grow it, and its use would be controlled. But this is a pretty much a homemade, unregulated product. Maybe they got the dilution wrong in this batch. Maybe wildcrafted herb varies in potency."

"Maybe Meg was allergic to it?" Craig suggested.

That telltale tingle again. Roz scrolled through references to belladonna. "It's a nightshade," she said triumphantly.

Craig looked at her in confusion.

"I think Meg was allergic to nightshades."

"How do you know that? Was it on her TikTok or something?"

"Grant asked Oli to get her food that was free from bread, potatoes, and tomatoes. Now bread was probably a staying-thin thing, but potatoes and tomatoes are both nightshades."

Roz quickly googled nightshades and belladonna poisoning. "It all fits," she said, reading about all the types of nightshade and the symptoms of being poisoned by them. "Toxic levels can lead to respiratory failure, delusions, and hallucinations."

"Such as imagining Grant coming through a locked door," Craig said. "So, Meg's death was an accident?"

"I think so. She tried to open her eyes so wide she died."

"What about the other two, they can't be accidents as well? Unless they also died of freak allergies and poisoning."

Allergies. That was it.

"I don't think they were accidents. But you're on the right track. And so am I, I think, with thanks to you and Laz's latest information." Roz stood up, feeling a certainty run through her that she hadn't felt in a long time. "I'm almost there. I'm going to need everyone in the club car one more time to ask them, but before that we're going to need the gloves again. We're going to search the train."

Chapter Forty-Two

Roz was onto them, they knew it, tracking them down one station at a time. She was searching the train now, going from room to room. It gave the killer time to get things straight, to walk in the Highlands while they still could. It was almost a relief that they could be caught. But they still had to make sure that the right tracks were covered and the right ones revealed.

The killer stuck out their tongue and waited till a solitary, pine-kissed snowflake landed and melted. They then crunched through the snow, kicking up a spray of childhood memories. White Christmases had been a regular event when they'd lived in Glencoe. Festive moments of pleasure flashed back: looking out of the window on Christmas morning and seeing white everywhere, as if sheets had been laid over everything, while the sky was painted gray; walking home from midnight mass with incense smoke in their clothes and snowflakes on their skin; going ice-skating in a blizzard and holding on to their girlfriend's hand as if it were the only real thing in the world.

And then other memories came, attaching themselves to the good ones. Out from under the ivy of Christmases past came all the negative memories, and they threatened to take over. The killer pushed those memories down again. Forced them like Jacks back into their boxes, and hoped they would not jump out.

They changed tracks in their mind. Keep it light. Keep it safe.

Christmas here was not like December in London, where you'd be lucky to catch a frost before Boxing Day. Christmases in the South were like affairs: damp, drizzly, and, ultimately, disappointing. This was the snow the killer knew of old, so deep that you don't know where the ground is anymore.

Beinn Dòrain looked down on the killer. It knew what they had done, but it was saying nothing. All those secrets it must keep under its peak, under ice. All it would take would be a landslide or an avalanche, and the train, the deaths, the attack, would all be buried. The killer yearned to fly up the mountain like a witch, to be free before they were locked away.

The train doors opened. "We're having a meeting," Roz called over. "Are you coming?" Her tone seemed light, unburdened. Maybe Roz didn't know what the killer had done, how the deaths took place.

Maybe, just maybe, they'd get away with it.

The killer took a last look at the mountain, then trudged toward the train. "Coming," they said.

Chapter Forty-Three

Roz finished reading Laz's last email and looked around the club car as the passengers and staff settled into the booths and seats. Everyone had their coats and duvets on, some had two. Phil was trying to distract Robert by pretending to be "Daddy Pig" at the same time as changing the baby on the banquette. Ember was reading, hood up, head down. The remaining Quizlings were in a booth, not talking. Aidan and Liv were leaning against each other in another booth, and Oli was behind the bar, polishing already polished glasses. Tony was perched on a swivel chair, and Mary was sitting on a banquette with a benign smile on her face. Roz wondered if Mary would like to adopt her.

"Thanks for coming, everyone," Roz said, striding into the center of the railcar. Every previous station debrief flowed through her, and this wasn't the first time that there was a killer in the room when she'd addressed her team. A few years ago, a grisly case led her to discover that her partner was a serial killer. It had taken her a long time to trust his replacement, Laz, as a result.

"I've had a revelation about the whole event, which is why I brought you back in here, and why, I suspect, some of you are sitting there looking as guilty as Krampus, but without his ability to enjoy it."

Buddy the baby started to cry, and Roz lost her thread. She was chucked like a snowball into the pictures of her granddaughter stuck in a plastic box, trying to breathe on her own.

She shook off the images. Now was not the time. "Where was I?" she asked.

"You were saying that someone here is, or several of us are, guilty," Sam prompted.

"Thank you, Sam. And thank you, too, for illustrating my next point. You say things with such open-eyed clarity and certainty that it's very easy to believe that you are totally innocent. But, as I now know, thanks to your quiz, Quizlings, being wide-eyed only means that you're using the right cosmetics."

"I don't remember that in the quiz," Ayana said.

"Meg was a brand ambassador for lots of small, natural cosmetics companies as well as large ones. On this occasion, on a day where she talked of her bloodshot eyes and looking tired, she used, frequently and generously, as you can see from some of the photos and footage taken last night, a new brand of eye drops with what I suspect has a high concentration of belladonna, otherwise known as deadly nightshade. It's generally safe in small doses, but up the dosage for someone with a sensitivity to it and they'd essentially become psychotic: hallucinating, sweating, heart beating too fast. It's my guess she was already on the way to asphyxiation before the derailment. She would have been unsteady already, then even more so when we stopped. She bumped her head, but the lack of blood suggests that she was already, if not almost, dead by then. I'd also guess that scratches on her neck are her own, maybe as she tried to tear nonexistent hands off her neck."

"So, nobody killed Meg?" Phil said. The relief on his face was clear.

"No. But someone did kill Grant and Beck. And I think this person has been targeting Grant for a while, and killed Beck to cover it up."

"I thought you'd stepped down from investigating," Sally said, probably concerned that she hadn't talked enough in the last ten minutes.

"Things have changed. We need to work together and quickly to make sure no more deaths take place."

"Three deaths in one day. It's beyond careless, it's negligence. This would never have happened if we had the right levels of security on the train," Sally said, staring at Bella and Beefy.

"I am doing my best," Beefy said, defensively. "But I can't guard a whole train at once."

"I don't think there's any need to harangue Beefy," Mary said. "He's broken down more doors and seen more horror today than you have in your lifetime."

Ayana, Sam, and Blake huddled together. They were all looking at each other as if passing psychic messages between themselves. Not that Roz would have been surprised if they were.

And that was how she'd have to think of this crime. She had some evidence, enough to have a suspect, but it felt forced. As if the wrong mirrored stickers were on the Rubik's Cube. Solved and not solved. In a usual investigation, she'd have a team to go through any possible connections between the victims and the suspects. It was like when you got the fairy lights down from the attic, and they didn't work; you had to try each bulb to see what had fried. When the connection was made, their backstories in place, she strung everything together and the lights came on, shining light on everything else. But here there was just her, some information, and her instincts.

In the corner of the room, Craig nodded to her. Time to try out the lights, see which ones shone and which compromised the rest. Get one of them to blink.

"I've received information about some of you and was wondering if I could ask you all some questions."

Looks were shared. Guilty ones. Roz kept tally of them all, as if she were trainspotting.

"What is the source of your information?" Sally said. "Is it reputable?"

The idea of Laz being reputable was laughable. "Impeccable. May I remind you that I was in the Met and therefore have access to an unparalleled network of informants and information."

That seemed to shut Sally up.

"There is one institution that links almost everyone here together," Roz continued.

"What is it?" Craig asked.

"The University of London."

"Oh, come on," Ayana said. "It's massive. You might as well say we were connected by London."

"That's a fair enough reply on the surface," Roz said, "but it's one of the bigger member institutions I'm thinking of: King's College, London. Our Quizlings are there. Mary did her PhD there, studying Edith Morley—"

"Edith Morley was the first female professor in England," Sam said eagerly.

"Thank you, I know," Mary replied drily.

"Sorry, I couldn't stop myself. At least I'm not mansplaining."

"My Phil worked at Goldsmiths not King's," Sally said. "So, he doesn't count, if that's what you're thinking."

"He's also filled in for a tutor at King's College this term."

"You remember, darling," Phil said. "I picked up some extra cash on the Tuesday course."

"I still don't see how it fits together," Blake said with frustration. "A *lot* of people study there."

"And a lot of people work there too," Roz replied. "Including Ember."

Ember nodded. "Yup. I work in IT. But I've never seen anyone else here around campus." She looked around the room. Her foot was tapping up and down.

"It's true—it's so big, I got lost several times," Phil said. Buddy gurgled, and Phil said in a babytalk voice, "Yes, I did, didn't I?"

"How do Meg and Grant fit into this?" Sally asked.

"I'm not sure about Meg," Roz said. "But according to my source, Grant had been accused of various assaults. A police investigation went nowhere, and he threatened to sue when two journalists found more victims. One of these accusations came from an anonymous student or member of staff at King's College, London. My source hasn't yet been able to find out who, but they will."

"I mean, that's all pretty sus, Dad," Aidan said. "Meg fancied you, so we had to move, and then her fiancé finds out, gets jealous and insults you. Maybe you attacked him."

"Aidan!" Liv said. "That's Dad you're talking about."

"There's no evidence linking me to anything," Phil said. But he was sweating despite the cold. Beads formed on his forehead. "Anyway, Tony's also on staff."

"Hardly. I'm on the board. What about the students? Grant seemed to like them young."

"Why do you say that?" Craig asked.

"I heard he was kissing one of our number here," Tony said, trying not to look at Ayana. "And he was toying with Beck and Liv."

"A few people saw you with Grant, Ayana," Roz said. "Was it consensual?"

"Absolutely," Ayana said. "He made me feel good. It was clear to anyone here that their relationship wasn't good, and he told me he was going to split up with her after Christmas. Said it would be cruel beforehand, which I thought was really kind. We were going to go on a date in the new year."

"What about you, Liv?" Roz asked. "Tony said Grant was toying with you."

"I heard him tease her, that's all," Tony said. "Told her she needed to grow up."

Liv shrunk into her brother's side. "Yeah, he said I should be having more fun."

Roz remembered Grant trying to get Liv to sing with him, and her pulling away.

Ember groaned and shook her head. "Good job he died. You both had a lucky escape. Take it from me."

Roz slowly went over to Ember and crouched next to her. She held her hands. "You know why I want to talk to you now, don't you?"

Ember nodded.

"I should have seen it much earlier than I did, and I'm sorry for that. Maybe everything could have worked out better. Perhaps we should talk in private."

"Were you the one from King's who accused him of assault?" Sally asked, marching over to Ember and pointing at her. "Because you need to say so to put my Phil in the clear of any suspicion. It's not fair to have him under scrutiny."

"It's not fair to Ember to ask her that, Mum," Liv said quietly. "If she's been assaulted, she shouldn't have to talk about it in front of us."

Liv was right. Roz wouldn't be able to talk about her rape in front of these strangers. She hadn't even been able talk openly with her own mother, let alone her daughter, colleagues, or friends.

"You're right. That's just forcing her in another way." Sadness weighed her down so much she could hardly dredge up the words. The unfairness of it all. "Could you come with me, Ember?"

Ember followed Roz out into the hallway. They had been here together the night before, talking about how they didn't know how Meg put up with Grant. And now it looked like Ember hadn't put up with him at all.

"Do you have any evidence?" Ember asked softly. "That I killed him."

"Nothing concrete until we searched your room and found a pestle and mortar complete with peanut crumbs that, I suspect, a lab would determine to originate from a packet of nuts. And, of course, Grant was allergic to nuts."

Ember nodded, then turned quickly and pressed the button to open the door.

"Don't run, Ember," Roz called as the cold air entered the railcar. "It won't help you."

Ember jumped out of the train into the snow.

Roz thought for a moment of letting Ember go. Of watching her run off into the snow and hoping to providence, nature, Santa, God, and every other intangible going, to protect her. Failing those, let Beinn Dòrain take her to itself. But that wasn't right or fair. Justice needed to be done, otherwise Roz would not be able to live with herself.

She jumped down into the snow. It was even higher now, up to her knees. The snow was coming directly at her, making movement and vision difficult. Ahead, though, Ember was a thin red target.

"Ember!" Roz called out. "There's nowhere to go!"

Ember sped up. Roz did the same, trying not to think about how neither of them knew what terrain was underfoot, what lay deep beneath the snow. What holes, obstacles, and secrets it kept hidden. Instead, Roz focused on the red coat, repeating a mantra to herself, a train-rhythm prayer of "She will be saved, she must be saved, she will be saved, she must be saved," but not knowing who she was really referring to: Ember, Meg, Heather, her granddaughter, or herself.

Roz's lungs burned. Every ragged intake became harder, as if the cold was taking some of her breath to warm itself. She was fit, but hadn't trained for conditions like this. London could not prepare you for the Highlands. What they gave, what they took. She knew she should feel like she was in her element, that this was the land of her mother and her grandmother before that, a line of wonky-nosed women who railed at the world and tried to make it their own.

She was getting closer. The red splash of coat was nearer. Perhaps Ember was tiring.

Roz forced herself to move faster, to ignore the cold that tore at her skin. "Ember, please! I can help!"

But Ember wasn't listening. Outcrops of rocks were visible now. They were nearing the base of Beinn Dòrain. As Roz stepped to one side to avoid a large rock, her foot caught on another. She fell, crying out. This time her shout echoed around the mountains, as if it were amplifying her pain.

Roz was facedown in snow that filled her mouth and eyes. She pushed herself up, but her arm lit up in a blaze of pain. She'd banged her elbow on a rock. Her head too. Blood crimsoned the snow.

Keep going.

She gently rose onto her scuffed knees and, wincing, eased herself up to standing.

The red coat was only a few meters ahead of her. And it wasn't moving. Perhaps Ember had given up. Perhaps she'd stopped to see if Roz was all right.

Gasping, hearing voices behind that could be the wind or people coming to help or her ancestors' ghosts propelling her on, Roz limped over to Ember.

Only Ember wasn't there. The empty red coat lay huddled on the ground, its arms wrapped around itself. The woman who never took off her coat had shed her second skin and gone it alone.

Chapter Forty-Four

Ember wasn't feeling the cold anymore. She was running up that mountain, flying like a train that would never come to the end of its line. Something must be helping her: an avenging goddess, or just her finding her own strength at last. She didn't know what she was going to do when she got to the top. Maybe throw herself down, give herself up to Beinn Dòrain.

No. That sounded too much like a man's name, as if he were the king of the mountain. She would give herself up to a Munro, but no man. Gamble her life on its kindness.

She could hear Roz calling to her and wished she could tell her everything. Why she did what she did.

But there were no words, and there was no time. She wouldn't burden Roz with the true story. Because that's what it was, if you told someone your story—some of the words stuck to them. It was inevitable. And all those words accrued, one after another, snowflake words that turned into a blizzard of abuse.

Only in darkened rooms, in the smallest hours, in the littlest voices did those who had been treated like pissed-on snow, men's names written all over them, speak.

If she had spoken out when it happened, gone through with

reporting Grant to the police, then maybe none of this would have taken place. Maybe Meg would never have met him. He wouldn't have to be dead.

But Ember knew what would have happened. Every day it happened in courts, victims' words curdled by barristers. The twisting of her life and events and herself into a knot that couldn't be unraveled She would have been left more frayed and flayed than before, and she had protected herself. But no one else. And more would have fallen if he had not died.

Perhaps now he was dead, she could speak.

Perhaps now she could sing.

Perhaps now she could roar.

This was her deal with God. Arms outstretched to the mountain, Ember ran.

She tried out her voice and it was small at first, weak as winter solstice sun. She tried again and it strengthened, gaining in resonance. Then she tried one more time.

"He raped me!" she cried. Her voice seemed to circle the mountain, as if an eagle had caught her words and flew them like a banner. "He raped me!"

Even hearing herself say it made more tears come, but these ones were different to those that she had cried before. These were full of salt, as if she were crying out to Lot's wife. They were from another layer of her, deep down, the strata she had buried deep. And it was flowing like lava out of her on a mountain.

"Grant McVey raped me!"

"I know!" a voice was shouting back. Beinn Dòrain, perhaps. The snow itself, because, of course, snow knows.

Behind her, footsteps came.

Ember turned.

It was Roz, coming toward her, holding Ember's coat, her other arm outstretched. "I know," she said again.

Ember looked back into the swirling snow. It would be so easy to keep running and maybe fall or hide, letting the mountain decide her fate. She was already feeling warm, so she knew that hypothermia was on its way. It was a gentle death, she'd heard, if such a thing could be. Falling into the cold embrace of mother earth.

So. Give herself up to the mountain, to death, or to Roz. At least now she had a choice.

Ember walked toward Roz, then ran.

Chapter Forty-Five

Roz stood mountain-solid as Ember stumbled into her arms. Ember was trembling, her lips blue, her face a gray Roz never wanted to see again. "You're okay," Roz whispered. "It's going to be okay." She didn't know how it would be though. But she would do everything she could.

Roz fed Ember's frozen arm into a sleeve of her red coat, then the other one, triggering strong memories of helping Heather on with her coat when she was small. Of the too-big mittens that had hung off the sleeves. Roz had sewn them on the night after her sergeant's exam. She'd forgotten that. In her mind, she'd done nothing for Heather. But maybe there were a few things. Small acts of caring.

Like doing up Ember's zipper and popping up her hood. Of pulling the toggles gently so that the circle of the hood closed in, protecting her face.

Like taking Ember's hand and breathing on the lilac tips of her fingers to warm them up.

Like saying, "We're going to go down to the bottom now. Slowly."

Below them, the river whispered in the ravine. The Grampians would have stories to tell of this night.

Chapter Forty-Six

Ember sat on her bed, a mug of hot chocolate in her hands. Her fingernails no longer had blue half-moons, and she could wriggle her toes again. She knew that Beefy was standing outside as a security measure, to make sure she didn't run off again, but she felt safer with him there. Especially as the mountain was behind her. It had her back.

As did Roz. She had told everyone that Ember had been attacked by Grant in the past and that she needed time and space to recover from her ordeal on the mountain, somewhere she wouldn't also have to tell her story to a huge crowd. Roz had then come to Ember alone and explained that she was going to record their conversation, and Ember had given her permission. Roz explained everything so well, and so gently. Ember wished she had followed her instinct and told Roz about Grant the previous night, as soon as she had learned Roz was an ex–police officer.

"Let's get started. What do you want to know?" Ember asked.

"Anything that you feel okay telling me," Roz replied. Her voice was as soft as the fleece throw that Bella had placed over Ember's legs. Her Mirror Cube was on her lap, reflecting snow glare from the window. "If anything is painful or uncomfortable in any way, then just stop. You don't have to explain why. I'll also only tell the police what you want me to," she added. "This is not my story to tell, it's yours."

Ember remembered Roz's voice on the mountainside saying, *I know.*
"How did you know though, what he had done to me?" Ember asked.

"As I said earlier, there were signs, but I should have recognized them.
And done something about it."

"Signs?"

"You not wanting to go to bed; that you stayed in the club car to look
after Liv and Meg. And I saw you check on Beck and Ayana. You knew
what he was like and felt you had to be vigilant."

"I *did* have to be vigilant."

"It shouldn't have been down to you. He's the one who should have
controlled himself."

"Of course that's how it *should* have been," Ember replied.

"There were other signs too. You were crying and anxious, wearing your
coat all the time, all things that don't necessarily mean anything—you could
be allergic to carol singers, or get cold easily—but put together with some
of the things you'd said about speaking up not getting you anywhere... I
should have paid more attention to Meg saying Grant was paying attention
to you, but I dismissed it as part of her confusion and hallucination."

Ember rocked backwards and forward. "I should've been braver.
Taken her to her room and then told her what really happened, what
Grant said. At least then I could've tried to resuscitate her or called for
help, when she was hallucinating. Anything. Maybe then she wouldn't
have died."

"I think the postmortem will find that there was nothing you could've
done. If she was delusional and hallucinating, she may even have thought
it was you attacking her. You could both have died."

"But we can't know."

"No, we can't." Roz paused, thinking, then continued: "You said just
now that you would've told Meg, 'What really happened, what Grant
said.' Can you tell me?"

"I can see how from where Meg was standing that it could look like
Grant was kissing my neck." Ember rushed a hand to her mouth as if she
was going to be sick. She swallowed. "Sorry. The very thought of that..."

"Take your time."

"He was holding my waist, hard. And whispering to me, bending down so his face was near my ear." Ember shuddered. Her rocking became more frenetic. "He said, 'I remember you. You're not worth fucking again.'"

Ember watched as Roz took that in. She nodded slowly, but didn't say anything.

"You really don't have to tell me, if it's too much."

"It was five years ago, before he was really famous. I wanted to buy a car, and he managed to sell me an old Nissan and himself. I bought into him completely. He said all the right things. Was sweet. Seemed to be caring, properly charming too, where men make you feel special. He said he loved older women as they taught him things."

Ember swallowed. She was shaking again and Roz held her until she stopped. "We went to an antiques fair the first date and then spent the day wandering around Spitalfields market the next, trying on hats and coats from the stalls, sharing things about ourselves. Bands and TV shows we liked, our first time, that kind of thing. He told me he was allergic to nuts, I told him I hated my boobs.

"Then there was the third date. He picked me up in a convertible, cliché that he was—but it works. That's what I hate: it works for these bastards. And it was a sunny day. Picnic in the back and we were driving south into the Kent countryside. I felt like Bridget Jones on a mini-break." She closed her eyes, but it didn't stop the images re-forming in her mind or shame flooding through her.

"You don't have to say more to me," Roz said. "I've been trained in, and taken far too many, sexual assault witness statements, but I don't want you to be triggered out here, without professional psychological help on hand."

"I want to tell you," Ember said. "Have done ever since I saw you." She took a breath, then began. "We stopped somewhere in the Downs. There was no one around, and that felt romantic at the time. We had the picnic and we kissed for a bit, then he wanted more, but I wasn't ready. His face changed then, like he was taking off a mask. He said that he'd waited and wasted enough time and money on me and that I had to stop being such a coy, prick-teasing cunt."

Ember paused. His words reverberated in her head.

"You're here now," Roz said. "You're safe with me, in the present."

Ember tried to anchor herself in the train, in the now. Her breathing slowed slightly, enough for her to take a deep breath and say it. "He then raped me. Vaginally and anally." Tears were falling now. "Pushed me onto the picnic blanket with everything on it. I couldn't move. I couldn't even scream. I tried but there were no words or sounds. After, he told me to pull down my dress from over my head, then spat in my face. Then he drove me home, talking all the way about the cars he was going to sell to hot women the next day. Before I got out, he said my tits were even more disappointing than I thought. Somehow, I got into the house and didn't get out of bed for three days. I nearly lost my job. Everything changed that day."

Roz put her hand over her mouth as if she was going to be sick. "I understand completely."

Ember looked at Roz then, seeing her for the first time. "You keep saying that. That you understand. And that you know the signs. Why is that?"

"Why do you think?"

"Because it happened to you?"

Roz was holding on to her knees, her knuckles trembling. "Yes."

"I'm so sorry," Ember said, tears flowing down her cheeks.

Roz tried to sit upright, as if a straight back would sort everything out. She had probably been told by someone that it did. "This isn't about me though."

"That's just it." Ember shuffled forward and reached for Roz's hand. "It's about every person who has been made to feel like nothing. Violated mentally and physically. Extinguished. How many on this train have gone through an experience where, at the very best, the next day they have curled up into a ball and screamed silently into a pillow?"

"It's probably easier to say who hasn't." Roz's voice was very quiet. Very small.

"It's my turn to say, to you this time, that you don't have to tell me if you don't want to."

Roz seemed to be taking little gasps of air. Tears fell, but her words seemed stuck. After five minutes or so she said, "I don't think I can. Not yet. I'm so sorry. I can't believe I'd ask that of you and can't myself."

"There'll be a time when it won't feel like you're swallowing moth-balls just as you try to speak."

"That's exactly how it feels. Like they've taken away my voice as well as so much else." Roz paused, thinking of the courage Meg had in her final moments. "Meg wanted to tell the truth. That's what her last live stream was for, but she never got to tell us. But I found a video where she accuses him of rape, and I'm hoping there'll be more saved on her phone or on another device. Then she can have the final word, not him."

"I want that too," Ember said. "When it comes to court, I want to plead not guilty to his murder, so I can stand and tell the world what he was. I will tell them how, after the picnic, he pushed me facedown onto the cold plates that were covered in stars. I have never wished on a star since, although I suppose it worked. I wished he wouldn't kill me."

Ember still felt how very cool the plates were. Felt the slight crack in the one that was under her fingertips. That was what she had concen-trated on, not what he was doing. But she could hear his noises. Smell the aftershave and semen.

Roz squeezed Ember's hand. "Come back to me," she said. Her other hand was placed over her heart. "Try not to get lost in the memory. You're in the present, not the past."

"The thing I hate remembering most though, is that I didn't say anything about it to him. Not that day or ever. I went into a police sta-tion, gave my name and his, place of work, and said I wanted to report a rape. But then I saw an officer laughing—not at me, at something stupid probably, but I couldn't do it."

"Just having done that will help your case," Roz said.

"I could have done so much more though. I just moved on as much as possible, although when people say they've moved on, what they mean is they've packed up their baggage and taken it somewhere else. I've never unpacked it. I fastened it under my coat and never took it off. I assumed Grant had moved on to someone else, and he had. A few years later, I was nearly sick when I saw him on the front cover of something-or-other with Meg. But you know what I also felt? Relieved."

"You were off the hook."

"At first I didn't think of him doing the same, or worse, to some-one else because…" Ember trailed off, still unable to believe her worst thoughts weren't true.

"Because you thought there was something wrong with you, not him. That you set him off. That you were in some way to blame. Is that what you thought?" Roz asked. "Because I did. I still do. And that was thirty years ago. Part of you knew that it wasn't true though. Otherwise, you wouldn't have stayed to keep an eye on Ayana, Liv, and the others." Roz thought for a moment. "The pestle and mortar isn't the usual accessory for a sleeper cabin though. How long have you been planning to kill him?"

"Six months or so. I saw some bruises on Meg in a photo, then a video where she said she'd fallen over. I knew then that she was covering for him, that he would be hurting her and probably others too. And I wanted him to stop raping me in my head."

"So what was your plan, exactly?"

"I knew he was allergic to nuts and that at some point I had to lace his food or drink with peanuts. He'd told me on the drive that he always carried an EpiPen with him, so I knew I just had to remove it. When Meg announced on her Instagram a month or so ago that they were taking the sleeper on the twenty-third, I decided it was the best time to get close to him."

"How did you react to seeing him again?"

"I felt sick. I almost didn't get on the train, and then I saw him on the concourse. His face all screwed up, like this—" Ember scrunched up her face into one of disgust. "He was blaming Meg for the train being delayed. And so I told myself I'd do it. I'd remove him from the world and make sure Meg and people like her never had to be made small again." Ember felt a surge of triumph. That was what she'd intended, and that was what she'd done. She exhaled loudly. "Feels good to say it."

"They say confession is good for you," replied Roz. "I prefer kale."

Ember laughed, then they were both silent for a moment.

The snow had stopped. Nothing moved outside. Ember had never felt such stillness. She wished she could drink it.

She sighed. "They'll want to know why I killed Beck, won't they?"

Roz nodded. "That will be what most people find difficult to understand, yes."

"She was trying to blackmail me. She walked past my room when I was crushing the peanuts and saw when I slipped the nuts into the open bottle of champagne. It was the main reason she wanted us to all go back to our rooms, so she could tell me what she wanted. Can you guess what it was?"

Roz started twisting the mirrored cube. It sounded like a little robot bird, pecking away at seeds. Then she stopped, suddenly. "You work as IT admin at King's. Beck wanted you to make sure that she got onto the King's College quiz team for *Geek Street* by fixing the results."

"She did."

"But why kill her? That's what I don't understand. Why not just do what she said or come to me?"

"That had been my plan, but she started pushing me, telling me I was pathetic. That a man like Grant would never even look at me. I had borrowed Meg's scissors earlier, as I had a pulled thread in my dress pocket, and I just grabbed them. It happened before I knew it. And then there was blood."

"Is there anything else you'd like to say at this point," Roz said, about to turn off the recording.

"Yes," Ember said, sitting up straighter. "I'm doing this, confessing, because I want to speak out at last. I've been quiet for too long. Who knows how many women he hurt between raping me and now. But today, I get to stop other young women suffering because of him." She looked at Roz. "You were right."

"About what?"

"You said to me in the club car, not long after we left Euston, that it felt better to do something rather than nothing. Well, this is my 'something.' My contribution to the cause. I may be the killer, but he's the real criminal."

"Now I understand," Roz said. But would anyone else? "That's everything for now." Roz turned off the recorder and pulled Ember into a hug. "I'll help in any way I can." And Ember at last felt she wasn't alone.

Chapter Forty-Seven

"Now get some rest," Roz said, when Ember had stopped crying.

She nodded and scrambled under the covers like a little girl at bedtime.

Roz gently tucked the blanket around Ember. When she went to leave, Ember grabbed her hand. "What'll happen to me now?"

"I know we just recorded your confession, but you'll need to make an official statement too." Roz looked her in the eyes and tried to communicate everything she was keeping inside, and what would stay inside, if she had her way.

She became very still. Her pupils were belladonna black, her voice very quiet. "How long will I be in prison?"

"I don't know. There are mitigating circumstances for Grant's death, but the extensive premeditation will be a problem. And Beck's death may have been in the moment, but it was covering up a crime."

A knock came on Ember's door. It opened, and Beefy stood awkwardly in the doorway, shifting from foot to foot. He glanced at Ember and said awkwardly, "The engineers will be here soon, on vehicles that can get through snow. Several detectives are with them as they can't get here otherwise, so when they arrive, you'll be under their protection. There'll be an extra stop near the police station."

"Thanks," Ember said. She looked out of the window and, rather than scared, seemed almost serene. Grant's death had brought her peace.

Beefy shuffled in and reached out his big hand as if to touch Ember on the shoulder. When Ember flinched and pulled back, he whipped his hand away. "Oh God, sorry. I don't know any details, obviously. But I'm sorry he did that to you."

"Thank you," Ember said, looking startled.

"If anyone ever touched my daughters or wife, I'd, well, I'd want to kill them too."

"Everyone's a daughter," Ember said.

"And it's not just daughters," Roz added.

"Sure, right," Beefy said, as if assimilating. "Every day's a school day."

Chapter Forty-Eight

After making sure that Ember was set up with coffee and snacks, Roz went around to talk to everyone. Most people were shocked at what mild-mannered Ember had done, but the more Roz explained, the more it made sense. The marble colors mixed and they saw different patterns.

Her penultimate visit was to Phil and Sally's family. From inside, she could hear snoring, Buddy's mumbles, a game of Snap, the sound of a ladder moving, and then a thump as someone jumped onto the floor.

Roz knocked on the door and Liv opened it. Her eyes were as red as Ember's coat. On the top bunk, Aidan sat cross-legged, carrying on the game by himself. "Snap!" he called out, gathering the cards. The door into the adjoining room was ajar, and Roz could just see Sally's snoring face, straggly hair half covering her open mouth.

"I was wondering if I could have a word?" Roz asked Liv.

Liv nodded. She didn't seem surprised. Relieved, if anything.

"I'll give you a word," Aidan said. "Snap!" He thumped another card down on the pack.

"Snap!" echoed Robert from the top bunk of the other room. He then laughed that gorgeous, rolling toddler chuckle.

A bleary-eyed Phil was with him, a protective hand keeping Buddy from toddling off the edge. "Can I help you, Roz? Shocking news about Ember, isn't it? You did well not to get killed up on the mountain."

"I'm glad to be back down," Roz said, half meaning it. "Can I have a chat with Liv?"

"I'll come with you," Phil said, swooping Buddy into his arms.

"It's all right, Dad. I can do this by myself."

Phil looked from Liv to Roz, then back to Liv. "You sure?"

"Let's go outside," Liv said to Roz, zipping up her coat and pulling up her hood.

They went to the ravine side of the train. The snow was now the barely there, snow-mote kind that could still bite. Beinn Dòrain was glowing, reflecting the reddening sky. "If anyone asks what we were talking about out here..." Roz said, looking over to the club car. It paid to be cautious. "Say I was giving you tips on how to do this." Roz took her Mirror Cube out of her pocket. She clicked it a few times, then handed it over to Liv.

Liv shifted the cube around and got into a rhythm of clicking.

"Now is the time to tell me the truth," Roz said.

Liv's face closed off. The shutters pulled down. She clicked the cube faster and faster.

"Don't know what you mean."

"I know it was you."

Liv started shaking. She stared into the cube as if seeing the fractured versions of herself could help. "How?" she asked in the smallest of voices.

"I knew instinctively there was something wrong with Ember killing both Grant and Beck, and I knew you were hiding something, but I didn't know for sure until I was talking to Ember."

Liv pulled back, tears forming in her eyes.

"Don't worry, she didn't tell me you were the real culprit. There were inconsistencies in her story though. She said that Beck had seen her when she crushed the peanuts in her room, but why would she carry out part of a premeditated murder with the door open? Why not just say Beck saw her tamper with the bottle, if she was trying to divert attention from something else? Then she said she'd only meant to borrow Meg's scissors from her bag to cut a thread on her dress, but that didn't seem plausible. Why not ask? Then I wondered if, in fact, she'd stolen them, but that wasn't in her character, which in turn made me find out from Laz that you'd been caught shoplifting many times. You did, after all, have Meg's pen. Maybe she didn't give it to you at all. Maybe you took a few trinkets from Meg's bag, including the pen and the scissors."

Liv looked down at the snow but said nothing.

"And then there was that moment in your interview, when you said that Grant didn't like it when people pulled away. You covered it well, by saying you'd seen him get angry with Meg, but you meant you, didn't you?"

Liv nodded. Her clicking of the cube was slowing.

"But the final thing that made it clear was when Ember said she had 'to speak out at last. To stop other young women from suffering because of him.' That seemed strange, seeing as he's dead and won't attack ever again. That's when I wondered who she would be covering for and remembered you both together so much, talking. Of pulling away from him and wearing a big hoodie, then a coat, even before the heating broke down. Ember was the same, and so was I. For years after I was raped, if I wasn't wearing my police uniform, I wore oversized jumpers, to cover my body. Not all those who are raped do, but I've seen it a lot. And I understand."

Liv broke down then, sinking into the snow. The Mirror Cube fell from her hands, and her thin shoulders shook.

"May I hold you?" Roz asked gently.

Liv nodded. Roz crouched down, and they both shivered together.

"I'm not going to say anything to the police," Roz said, "unless you want me to. And I'm not recording anything. I will support Ember's story if that's what you both want. I'll also say though, that if you wanted to tell the police about what he did to you, even if you kept the rest secret, it would help Ember's case."

"But would it help me?" Liv's eyes were as full of fear as they were of tears.

Roz thought of the number of people who'd come to the station to say they'd been raped or assaulted. Of being with them in the rape suite.

Hearing their stories and holding their hands if it helped, not touching them if that was what they wanted. Men. Women. Non-binary people. Trans and cis. Straight, gay, bi, pan, asexual. Attacked by partners, relatives, or close friends, acquaintances or strangers. So, so many stories of bodies and souls torn. And how many of them saw the rapist end up in prison?

In her last case, a young woman had been raped in a nightclub and Roz had done everything she could to get evidence for a conviction. She'd stayed on as a Met detective, at the expense of delaying going up to Scotland to her pregnant daughter, in order to still be in active service as an officer, while testifying in court. And the rapist had been found innocent. Roz could still hear the young woman's sobs as the verdict was read out, and the rapist's laugh as he left the courtroom a free man. "I wish I could say it would," Roz said.

"Aren't you breaking the law by not saying what you know?" Liv asked.

"I am aiding, I am abetting, I am concealing evidence. Yes, I am breaking the law."

"Why would you help me?"

Roz took a breath of air so cold that it seemed to cut through the thing that stopped her talking. "I was raped. I know what it does to you. And I don't see why someone as young as you should have their life further ruined by prison."

Liv held out her hand and placed it on Roz's. "What happened? Can you tell me?"

"I'm not sure that's a good idea. It might trigger you." The very thought of opening up to this young woman was terrifying.

"Please," Liv said. "I don't want to feel alone."

Roz looked at Liv's face, full of questions and confusion. Perhaps telling her would help Liv cope. Perhaps it would help Roz too. "You, love, are not alone. You have joined one of the largest and most isolated gangs in the world."

"Then tell me. Please."

Roz sighed. Tried to quell the usual nausea. "I was four months pregnant with my daughter, Heather, and out at a club. I hadn't come to grips with having a child at the point, I was only twenty myself. So while

I wasn't in complete denial, I was out most nights. This was an indie club, and I remember 'Boys Don't Cry' coming on. I ran onto the dance floor, and a young man started dancing with me. Flirting. Bought me a drink. We danced some more, and then I started feeling woozy. I wasn't drinking booze, so I knew something was wrong. The lights were too bright. It felt like they were shouting at me. Swallowing me. I remember someone hurrying me to the door, helping me, I thought. Then I only remember glimpses. Like a flip-book that gets stuck on certain images. A man on top of me. Heavy. Smelling of dry ice and Marlboro lights. Of not being able to move." Roz felt like she was in the flip-book, then. Squashed between pages, reliving the same memory over and over, and—

"Come back," Liv said. "Come back to me." She was so gentle. The look in her eyes older than her years.

"I'm so sorry," Roz said, shaking her head. "This should be about you."

"Is that why you became a police officer? To help people like you?"

"I wanted to make a difference," Roz said. Her sobs felt like they came from deep inside her and many years ago. "And I didn't."

"You have to me. Already."

"But Ember. If I hadn't been so keen on proving I still had worth, that I could control things, maybe I could have helped her too."

"Someone would have been found guilty. And it could've been me."

"Not with your dad's alibi. He knows, right? He was covering for you, saying you were with him till you were playing with Ember. But you didn't tell him straight away."

"I couldn't. I was in a daze after, and Grant was acting like everything had just been normal. It was when we'd stopped. At Edinburgh. After he…" Liv closed her eyes briefly, unable to say the words. "After, Grant said to me, 'I'll go back into the club car first, then you follow in a wee while.' He then winked at me and left, as if we'd just had a quick Christmas fumble not him…" Liv started rocking back and forth. "And I did. I did what he said."

"It's all right, darlin', it's all right." But Roz knew it wouldn't be all right, not for a very long time.

"I don't know why though. They'd say I wanted to be with him, that

I can't have objected that much. I hated breathing the same air as him, but I didn't want to be alone. So I was just there, in the club car, while he carried on as he had before. He even tried to dance with me and make me sing with him."

"When did you tell your dad?" She hoped that mentioning Liv's dad would help center her.

"Somewhere between then and the derailment. I don't know when. It's all a bit confused. Especially as when I got back, he wasn't in the room with the little ones, he was in mine and Aidan's room. With Ayana. Having sex."

Roz blinked a few times as she processed the new information. She then thought of Phil protesting, too much as it turned out, that he couldn't have been involved with Meg as she'd been almost the same age that Liv was now, yet Ayana was the same age as Liv. Maybe he *had* had an affair with Meg while she was his student.

But Meg wasn't here to tell her story anymore.

"He was trying to explain himself, obviously. Then he realized something was wrong, and I couldn't stop myself telling him. He believed me, straight away. So did Ayana. Dad was all for going to kill Grant, but Ayana stopped him. She's been great too. I told them, and Ember, after what I did to Grant, and then Beck. They've all been protecting me since."

"But you didn't tell your mum?"

"What do you think?" Her sardonic tone broke Roz's heart. "She'd only blame me for it happening and say it had ruined her Christmas."

Roz knew she was right, and felt the fear of Heather ever having felt that way.

"What can I do?" Liv asked. "To make everything okay?"

Roz thought through all the permutations, twisting and clicking to try and remove Liv from the picture. It was going to be difficult. And against everything that she knew as a police officer. But she wasn't in the police any more.

"If I've guessed right, Grant wasn't poisoned with peanuts at all. It was with tobacco in the form of vape juice, that you administered. And not only do I understand why you did, I'm going to help you get away with it. But to do that, I need to know everything. Okay?"

Liv nodded. "Ember and me were helping with the breakfasts, including Grant's. I saw her put peanut dust on the rim of the bottle, but she then changed her mind and wiped it away. But it gave me the idea. How did you know what happened?"

"Two things. I saw it on the nightshade list when I was researching Meg's death. And then I was having a flashback of the man who raped me blowing smoke in my face, which made me think of Grant constantly vaping. Once I'd thought of it, it was the only poison that would account for his reaction." Roz didn't want to go into details, but she could still hear the frenetic hitting of Grant's shoes against the bathroom door as he was thrashing. See the clenched fist as his muscles tightened.

"What did you do?" Roz continued. "Take one of the bottles of vape juice from his jacket at some point and tip it into the half bottle of champagne that Grant ordered, along with his breakfast? Sixty milligrams of nicotine could kill someone."

Liv nodded. "And I put in two bottles, so that would do it." There wasn't a trace of remorse on her face. Roz wondered if letting this young person go free was the wise thing to do, then she thought of the rapists who went free every day.

"Your DNA will probably be found on the champagne bottle probably; you'll need a reason to say why it's there, like you handed it to Ember, to give to Oli to take to Grant's cabin. And, I am so sorry to ask this, but could your DNA be found on him in another way?"

"He used a condom." Liv vomited then, onto the snow.

Roz rubbed Liv's back gently and wondered if, one day, crones and mothers wouldn't have to comfort maidens in this way. She prayed to Beinn Dòrain that that time would come.

When Liv had stopping being sick, Roz said. "I'm glad he did, in many ways. And if anything else turns up, they'd know you were potentially in contact with him in the club car, by being on his quiz team. When the police ask about him, say he was friendly. That should cover transfer of DNA."

"Thank you."

"What about the door into Beck's cabin being locked? I couldn't work out how anyone could get in or out. Then I wondered if it wasn't locked at all. Your dad and Ayana said it was locked, but they were protecting you. You dad could have faked the door being locked from the inside. After all, he broke down the door a little too easily. If it takes Beefy several goes, then your dad doesn't have a chance. No offense. Am I right?"

Liv nodded. "Ember came to get me straight after Beck said she'd seen her rub crushed peanuts onto the mouth of the bottle, but it didn't look as if she saw her wipe it off, or see me tip the bottles of vape juice in. I had to be sure though, so I insisted that I was the one who met Beck in her room."

"And was she surprised to see you?"

"She looked really confused for a moment, then asked if Ember had asked me to do her dirty work."

"So she had no idea you were involved?"

"No. She then said that Ember had to use her position in IT to guarantee that Beck got onto the team for *Geek Street*. When I said that wasn't going to happen and that Grant had been killed because he'd raped Ember, she just said, 'With men like that, you just kick them in the balls and walk away. I don't know what her problem is. You don't have to kill them.' She then laughed really hard."

Roz was saddened but not shocked. A *lot* of women bought into that way of thinking and thought a short skirt, or any skirt, was "asking for it."

"What happened then?"

"I felt this white rage, grabbed Beck, and started shaking her. I wasn't even thinking. Beck pushed me away into the sink, calling me pathetic, which is what Grant had said to me afterward. I reached in my pocket for Meg's scissors. And then Beck was bleeding but not breathing. And there was so much blood. I don't even remember stabbing her, or when Dad, Ember, and Ayana appeared. They cleaned me up and I just stood there, like a doll being dressed."

"Oh, Liv," Roz said. "Why did you take the scissors with you?"

"I don't know. After what happened with Grant, to make me feel safer." She was quiet for a moment. "Do you think the police will work out what I did?"

"Well, I did, but I'll tell Ember to say that she added the vape juice in case the peanuts didn't cause an allergic reaction. With a confession, evidence, and no reason, or finances, to dig further, I hope you'll get away with it."

"Thank you," Liv said and hugged her. Roz felt something inside her melt. She picked up the Mirror Cube from the ground. She clicked it again and again, as if that could take the sadness away, sending reflections of the red sky onto the snow like a bloodied glitterball.

Chapter Forty-Nine

Roz popped in to see Ember again, before the police arrived and everything changed. "I talked to Liv," she said, holding eye contact.

Ember grabbed her hand. "You can't tell the—"

"I'm not going to tell anyone. What good would it do?"

Ember smiled. "That's what I thought. If the only positive thing to emerge from all of this is that she lives a life protected from what happened, then it's worth it."

"If they decide you should be charged with murder, for both Grant and Beck's deaths, with no assessment of diminished responsibility, you could be in prison till you're, well, much older than me. A crone. You'll always be known as the killer, but you're not."

"But she would be free."

Roz understood. "She's going to need help though. Getting over it. All of it. If she doesn't, it'll hollow her out."

"Like it did you?" Ember was looking at Roz with the eyes of a mother.

Roz said nothing.

"At least she'll have you to help her, if she needs it." Ember paused. "She will, won't she?"

"Of course. I should have looked after her before. I should've noticed what had happened. I should have stayed in the club car."

"You shouldn't have to be a bodyguard. *We* shouldn't need them. And it's time we stopped saying what we 'should' or 'shouldn't' do. They should stop raping us."

They were silent for a moment. They knew that wouldn't happen.

"Tell me what happened," Roz said after a while. "Liv told me some, but I didn't want to press her. The more I know, the more I can help both of you."

More tears fell as Ember said, "He had attacked her earlier in the evening. Took her into the toilet, offering to share his cocaine, then he pushed her to the ground, held her down, and raped her."

"How did you know something had happened?"

"I had been watching him since we got on the train, looking for a time when I could lace his drink. But I hadn't had a chance to grab his EpiPen, until she followed him out for one of his vape breaks when we stopped at Edinburgh Waverley. He left his jacket behind and no one noticed me take out the EpiPen."

"Have you still got it?" Roz asked.

Ember plucked the device from her coat pocket and waved it.

"Keep it, and hand it to the police when they arrive. It'll be a key piece of evidence."

Ember nodded. "He came back a while later, his usual self. But Liv was acting differently. Keeping to the side of the room, holding her arms over her chest. She sat down in her booth really carefully, and winced."

"Oh, God." Roz remembered that sensation. Of feeling torn and that she would never be okay down there again.

"I asked her if later Grant had done something. And she told me. I replied that I'd keep her close and look after her. I didn't intend for her to see me try to poison Grant. It didn't matter that I changed my mind; she got the idea from me. Although I'd never have thought of using the vape juice. A very modern poison." She looked almost proud of Liv.

"Is that why you told her you'd take the blame? Because you felt responsible?"

"Without me trying to poison him, none of this would have happened."

"And without him, none of us would be in this situation. All of this comes back to Grant. All of it."

"Do you think he was bullied or abused too? And that's why he did it?"

"Maybe. But most people who abuse do not go on to be abusers. That's a myth."

Ember was sobbing now, back to rocking. "But look what we've done. Look what we are after what he did to us."

"And you're torn apart by it. Do you think he was? Should be simple, shouldn't it? If you've been hurt, don't hurt others. But it's not. I haven't attacked anyone, but I've pushed people away for the slightest reason. Even my own family."

"Maybe you can make a new start with them?" Ember's eyes seemed amber with the hope she had for Roz, as if she was pouring her life into her and the woman she was protecting.

"I hope so."

Roz bent down and gently kissed Ember on the forehead. She went out into the corridor, closed the door behind her with a soft click, smiled at Beefy and Bella, then ran to the railcar toilet, her hand over her mouth.

Inside, she retched and retched, bile burning her throat. Her tears were molten too, as if her whole body was trying to rid itself of her ice-hot rage. Her throat felt torn, her hands trembled. She'd managed— she hoped she had anyway—to keep an almost professional, calm facade throughout talking to Ember, but inside she'd been screaming. All she wanted to do was kill Grant all over again.

Assault and abuse changed you. They couldn't not. She thought then of how tablet was made. Of how sugar was mixed with other ingredients and heated. The sugar became grainy at first, then disappeared. The heat was turned up and the mixture boiled. It bubbled and rose, fizzed and spat. And it could boil over at any time. Burn. Scald. Scar. Cause permanent damage.

At the end of the process, the mixture cooled and hardened. Became solid again. It was scored, then broken into pieces. Fundamentally changed.

Roz didn't know what she'd be like if she hadn't been raped at twenty, while already pregnant with Heather. Ember would never be the same person she was before she met Grant. And neither would any of the other women Roz was sure he had assaulted. But she could try and help one in particular.

Chapter Fifty

Ember watched from her window as the tree was lifted from the path of the train. It was huge. She imagined it as a Christmas tree, covered in homemade ornaments and lights. Perhaps the tracks breathed an iron sigh of relief. The engineers had arrived with the mechanics, paramedics, and police to enormous cheers from the passengers. They were already working on getting the train back on its tracks. She wished that lives were that easy.

The train jerked. She and the police officers on either side of her clanked in time with the handcuffs. From elsewhere in the train, she heard whooping and clapping. They would be able to carry on with their Christmases with a tale to tell. It would keep the country occupied in schadenfreude, just as last year when the news of the murders of Endgame House became public. These things kept countrywide gossip burning on the darkest nights.

Paramedics were carrying body bags to the train. Ember thought of Grant's body, encased first in plastic, and then in the grave. And she was glad.

She looked out of the window. The sky was swirled in pink and orange. She may change her mind, but for now she felt proud that she would always be known as the killer. She would have done something with her life after all. Ember wondered if she'd have a view from her prison cell, if she'd get a glimpse of the big sky.

Chapter Fifty-One

The sun was beginning its evening descent, dipping into the space between mountains, a slice of orange in a martini glass.

The train was at slow speed, cautious as though aware of black ice beneath snow, but they were moving on. Those that could move on, anyway. Roz had given a statement to a police officer who smelled like cigarettes smothered in strong mints. She told them about Meg's accidental death, her live stream, the possibility of more recorded testimonies that would point to Grant's abuse. She talked about Ember's breakdown and confession to killing both Grant and Beck in a rage.

Now she could begin to think of what came next. All she'd had for hours was a picture of her little granddaughter in a tiny woolen Santa hat. She was off the oxygen and doing well.

The train chugged to a stop at Roy Bridge, the stop for the police station. Ember disembarked first, accompanied by two police officers. Beefy helped Mary off the train, and both Mary and Tony waved to Roz. She'd promised them that she'd pay them a visit and bring them tablet. Tony turned around so she could say goodbye to Mousetache too. She was sure the cat placed a paw against the mesh in salute.

Iain, followed by Phil, Sally, and their kids, also got off at Roy Bridge.

Liv placed her hand on her heart as the train moved on without her. Roz's own heart was back on track.

"Your stop is next, right?" Roz said to Sam.

"Yup. Being picked up by my dad."

"Are you going to be all right? Beck's death must shake the equilibrium of the team a bit."

"If anything, it'll strengthen it. We won't be working and competing against each other anymore to get on the show. And we might even win the whole thing."

"And be on TV. I'll watch. I love a quiz."

They laughed. "Yes, but I'll avoid getting famous. I've seen what can happen."

They were both silent for a while, each thinking of what had taken place over the last day.

"I was going to get Christmas presents today," they said. "But I can always give people facts. How old are you again?"

"Nearly fifty."

"Then my present to you is the knowledge that fifty is a harshad number."

"And what is that?"

"A harshad number, as defined by D. R. Kaprekar, can be divided by the sum of its digits. So five plus zero is five, and fifty divided by five is ten." Sam paused, and when Roz must have still seemed unimpressed, said, "Harshad means 'joy-giver' or 'great joy' in Sanskrit, which seems appropriate for a festive occasion."

"Well, that's festive, I suppose. Thank you, Sam."

"That's not all. Fifty is also a Stirling number, named after Scottish mathematician James Stirling."

"Now you're talking. A good Scottish number. Fifty is to be relied upon."

"It's a foundation for your future."

"Whatever that is."

Craig appeared. He stood next to her, nibbling his cuticles. "You okay?" he asked her.

"I will be when I see our daughter," Roz said.

"I'm due to see her tomorrow. Maybe we can meet up, have a Christmas Day drink?"

Sam looked from one to the other, grinning. They gave Roz a quick hug and walked away, singing, "Stay Another Day."

"So," Roz said.

"So," replied Craig.

The distance between them seemed too short, too deep, and too wide at the same time.

Roz looked at Craig, searching his face. The only specific thing she remembered from the night she conceived Heather was her dancing closer and closer with a man who made her laugh. They'd had sex in a bus shelter, and two cars had beeped as they went past. That was it. No picture of his face had stayed in her head, other than that she remembered she'd liked it. And that his skin was soft, and his accent even softer. And then, months later, she'd been raped. She had been folded, cut, and snipped like one of Meg's paper dolls. That night with Craig was still hazy, but maybe it would advance as the other, darker memory retreated into the past. Maybe the happier memory would also be her present.

"It's New Year soon. Good time to start again." There were layers to his voice. He was suggesting more than reigniting her relationship with Heather.

They journeyed on in perfect silence, watching the rivers and lochs and hills pass by. There a farmhouse, there a hare, there a count of sheep: a traveler's prayer.

The sky over Loch Linnhe was the color of embers when the train pulled into Fort William. Mountains and hills surrounded the town, swaddling it. Roz was home.

It had been an epic journey, but it wasn't over. Not till she had made things right with Heather. The last moments before the doors opened felt the longest yet. She hoped the taxi she'd ordered was waiting for her, ready to take her to the hospital.

"Would you like to come with me?" Roz asked when they stepped onto the platform, dizzy with the hometown memories that rushed by.

Craig nodded. She took his arm, and his eyes glowed.

Beefy, Bella, and Oli walked toward them on the platform. They looked as weary as she felt.

"We got you home, then," Beefy said when he reached them, placing his big hands on Craig and Roz's shoulders.

"But you're not," Roz replied.

"It's not Christmas yet," Beefy replied. "And you never know, if they clear the roads enough, I might just get home to see my boy before the end of Boxing Day."

"So not by train then," Bella said.

Beefy grinned. "*Definitely* not by train."

The three crew members wished Roz and Craig a happy Christmas, then walked away, their arms around each other.

Roz had thought, yesterday morning, that she couldn't be surprised anymore. That she was too cynical to be caught off guard, pleasantly or otherwise. But here she was, walking to the taxi stand with a man she'd known for one night, thirty-odd years ago. And, somehow, it felt right.

❦❦❦

"I'm going to stay around reception," Craig said as they entered the hospital. "Give you all some time together."

"Are you sure?" Roz touched his arm. Felt electricity flow as if they were the third rail.

"She's been through enough in the last twenty-four hours. Give her a day before she deals with properly meeting her 'long-lost dad.'"

"Then I'll see you tomorrow too," she said, trying to conceal the wrench that leaving him made her feel.

"I'm not going anywhere," he said. "I'm waiting here in that chair, having a bad coffee from the machine and reading my book till you come back down." He pulled the copy of the Christmas poems book out from his jacket pocket, his thumb holding it open on the page of "A Visit from St. Nicholas."

✗✗✗✗✓

Heather in her hospital bed, hardly recognizable. Swollen, balloon-like, as if filled with water. On her chest, skin-to-skin, was the baby. The baby was so small, with such perfect little features. Her eyes were like little clam shells, yet to open. Her skinny, spider monkey arms grabbed on to Heather's chest. She was tucked in with small knitted blankets and was wearing a teeny Santa hat.

On one side of the bed was a wee cot on wheels. On the other, in a hard chair, Ellie was looking at Heather with such fierce love it burned. Her skin was the gray of someone who had seen too much that day. It had been a very long day for them all.

Roz approached the bed slowly. All the words that she wanted to say fought in her head but wouldn't travel to her mouth.

"It's all right, Mum, you don't have to stalk me. I'm not going to bite you or shout at you."

"I'm so sorry," Roz said, standing at Heather's side. "For everything. For not being here before. For being distant in every way. Not telling you what was hurting me. Not helping you find your dad. Everything." She took Heather's hand. It was so swollen that even the gentlest touch left a mark that didn't go away.

"It's all right, Mum," Heather said, and Roz's heart filled to the brim. "There'll be time for us to talk about everything."

"How are you feeling?" Roz asked, feeling the inadequacy in her words.

"Like a magician's assistant cut in half."

"At least they pulled out a baby instead of a rabbit. That would have been alarming."

Heather laughed, then her face scrunched in pain. "Don't make me laugh. I don't fancy breaking my stitches."

"Sorry, love."

"This is your granddaughter," Heather said. She looked so tired, but her eyes were oxytocin bright. "We've called her Eve." She very carefully, wincing as she moved, gathered Eve and held her out.

Roz took the baby into her arms. "Hello, Eve," she whispered. She hoped her heart was only beating loudly inside her; she didn't want to wake Eve. The warm bundle was at once light and yet so heavy in her arms. Roz looked down at Eve's little face, sleeping under the woolly Santa hat. Even now, in her nose and brow, Roz could see the long line of Parker women running through her granddaughter's face. She felt an instant connection.

"Welcome, little one." Roz bent and placed a snowflake kiss on Eve's forehead. "I'm your granny," she whispered. "And I am going to protect and love you with the fierceness of whisky, the sweetness of tablet, and the wrinkled longevity of raisins."

"Talking of which…" Heather said, eyebrows raised and expectant.

"In my rucksack," Roz replied.

Ellie slipped out of her chair and rootled around in Roz's bag. She pulled out the last box of tablet with the glee of someone who's found treasure at the bottom of a stocking. Tablet was a surefire way to win anyone around. She took out a piece and placed it gently on Heather's tongue. Heather's eyes closed, and only her mouth moved as she chewed.

"I'm surprised you've gone for 'Granny,'" Ellie said. "I thought you were weighing up 'Nana' or 'Seanmhair.'"

"I decided 'Granny' was more archetypal. As in GILF. I'm owning the Crone."

"Which makes me the Mother now, I suppose." Heather looked dazed. "Doesn't feel real."

Roz pushed a damp piece of hair away from Heather's eyes. "It takes time to adjust to a new role, but it's already happened. In time you'll align with yours, and I will with mine."

The baby stirred, turning her little head and kitten-mewled. "She wants her mum," Roz said, carefully placing her granddaughter in her daughter's waiting hands.

"And I want mine," Heather said, soft as cotton wool.

"Really?" Roz said. Her heart veered off its tracks and back again.

Heather slowly rested her head against Roz's side. "But you can't just step into Gran's shoes—there's no way you can raise Eve."

"I'd never want to take that from you. I'll be here when you need me and will slip away when you don't."

"Find something else to do as well, won't you? You'll get depressed if you're not busy."

"Time for you to stop worrying about me. You've got wee Eve to take up all your worry brain. And that won't stop, you know."

"You could join the force up here. There's a new station on the Blar, between Lochy Bridge and Banavie."

"I don't think policing is for me anymore."

"But all those skills you have. You can't just leave it."

Roz thought of how everything had clicked into place, and the peace she had felt when it happened. "I might go freelance."

"Be a private investigator? You always said that was fishing in people's bins and eating doughnuts."

"I know. But I'm a big fan of doughnuts." Maybe she could perfect a doughnut recipe and make it the first in her own life recipe book to give to Heather. "And perhaps I could help people too."

❦

Craig was in the hospital waiting area when Roz came out of the lift. Carol singers, dressed in their hospital uniforms, sang of a baby laying down his sweet head. Craig looked up and saw her. The book, forgotten, dropped to his lap.

"We have a granddaughter," Roz said, hardly able to understand the words as she said them. "Called Eve."

"Eve!" He started crying and laughing. He didn't try to stop the tears, just let them fall.

Roz took out her phone and showed him some of the pictures Ellie had taken. He put his little finger to the screen as if to stroke Eve's cheek. "She's so tiny and perfect."

They stood staring for a whole verse of "Away in a Manger," then Roz's practicality snapped into place. "Soon as the shops reopen, we need to find her some premature baby clothes and nappies. And get Heather more clothes as she's going to be in here until her blood pressure is under control."

"We?"

"If you'd like to help, that is." Roz felt an urge to look away, so instead she faced him.

Emotions crossed his face like the aurora borealis. "I am here, however you want, however you need me, for however long."

In the taxi, Roz took Craig's hand. It was smooth and warm and squeezed hers. She didn't know what was going to happen, but it would be okay, one way or another.

As they drove into Fort William, Roz felt lit up inside, like every house they passed. The sun stood behind the mountain. This was her town, this was her circus, and the people in it were her monkeys. And she was going to protect as many of those monkeys as she could.

Roz looked at Craig, and their eyes were a locked room. It was the night before a new life. December *would* be magic again. Happy Christmas to all, and to all a good night.

Anagram Solutions

"Adlestrop" = "read plots," p. 60

"Charon" = "anchor," p. 214

"From a Railway Carriage" = "AMagicalFaeryWarrior," p. 146

"Ghost Train" = "Grant, oh it's—" p. xii and p. 147

"The Marshalling Yard" = "A hanged martyr's hill," p. 107

Murder on the Orient Express = "Torrentedsuperheroes: Minx," p. 147

"Orient Express" = "sex nor respite," p. 54

"The Railway Library" = "braille. Hairy, warty," p. 37

The Signalman = "He's malignant," p. 71

Stamboul Train = "barman Oli tuts," p. 63

"The Stopped Train" = "TaintedProphets," p. x

Strangers on a Train = "arranges transit on," p. 5

The Trains = "Tin hearts," p. 123

Train Song = "Grant is no," p. 86

Violet = "love it," p. 28 and p. 238

"The Way My Mother Speaks" = "swept a smoky heather, my," p. 146

Murder on the Christmas Express Quiz

Round One—A Question of Christmas

1. Who wrote the poem, "A Visit from St. Nicholas," popularly known as "The Night Before Christmas"?
2. Who directed the film *The Nightmare Before Christmas*?
3. Who invented the Christmas cracker?
4. When did the "Elf on a Shelf" tradition begin?
5. Which monarch is supposed to have begun the tradition of decorating gingerbread biscuits?
6. What is the full name of the composer of *The Nutcracker*? (Half a point for just the last name)
7. The film *It's a Wonderful Life* came out in which year?
8. The 2021 Christmas Price Index estimated that if someone bought all of items in "The Twelve Days of Christmas," it would cost how much, to the nearest thousand dollars?
9. In which decade was the first Christmas card sent? (For an extra point, guess the exact year)
10. Estimate to the nearest fifty calories the number of calories if you ate ALL the birds in "The Twelve Days of Christmas," minus the energy expended doing all the activities in the song (i.e., milking, dancing, leaping, etc)?

Round Two–Christmas Around the World

1. Before the tradition changed to Twelfth Night, when did Christmas decorations used to be taken down in Great Britain?

2. Ordering from which U.S. fast-food chain has become a Christmas tradition in Japan?

3. Which method of transport do people tend to use to attend Christmas church services in Caracas, Venezuela?

4. Which Welsh festive ritual features a horse's skull, white sheets, and a pole?

5. Which insect features on Ukrainian Christmas trees?

6. Which illustrator was commissioned by Coca-Cola in 1931 to design the now ubiquitous image of Santa Claus in a red coat?

7. On what day is Krampusnacht held in Central Europe?

8. In which Australian cricket ground is the tradition Boxing Day cricket Test Match held?

9. What is the Icelandic name for all the books that come out in the run-up to Christmas, often given as presents and read on Christmas Eve?

10. What meat is traditionally eaten in Hawaii at Christmas?

Round Three–Christmas Music

1. Which carol, since 1919, has traditionally opened every year at the famous annual King's College Festival of Nine Lessons and Carols?

2. In what year was the first official Christmas number one? (for an extra point, what was it and who sang it?)

3. What was the original first couplet, written by John Wesley, of "Hark the Herald Angels Sing"?

4. How many Christmas number ones have Christmas (or Xmas) in the title? (Plus half a point for every one named)

5. How many physical items are requested in "Santa Baby"? (Plus half a point for every one named)

6. What was the original German name of Gruber and Mohr's "Silent Night"?

7. On which album did Chris de Burgh's "A Spaceman Came Traveling" first appear?

8. What song does Jovie, and then Buddy, sing in the bathroom in *Elf*?

9. Who does Tim Minchin address in the second half of his brilliant "White Wine in the Sun"?

10. What is the French version of "Rudolph the Red-Nosed Reindeer" called?

Murder on the Christmas Express Quiz—Answers

Round One: A Question of Christmas

1. Clement Clarke Moore
2. Henry Selick
3. Tom Smith
4. 2005
5. Queen Elizabeth I
6. Pyotr Illyich Tchaikovsky
7. 1946
8. $41,205.58 https://www.pncchristmaspriceindex.com
9. The 1840s (1843)
10. 2,384 calories. (For a full breakdown, and fascinating information, look at Olga Khazan's brilliant article in the *Atlantic* www.theatlantic.com/health/archive/2013/12/health-consequences -of-actually-living-the-12-days-of-christmas/282313/)

Round Two—Christmas Around the World

1. Candlemas—February 2nd

2. KFC
3. Roller skates
4. Marie Llwyd
5. Spiders
6. Haddon Sundblom
7. December 5th
8. MCG (Melbourne Cricket Ground)
9. Jólabókaflóðið
10. Kalua pig (cooked in an underground oven called an imu)

Round Three—Christmas Music

1. "Once in Royal David's City"
2. 1952 ("Here in My Heart," Al Martino)
3. "Hark how all the Welkin rings,/ 'Glory to the King of Kings'"
4. Eight—"Christmas Alphabet," Dickie Valentine (1955); "Merry Xmas Everybody," Slade (1973); "Lonely This Christmas," Mud (1974); "Do They Know It's Christmas?," Band Aid (1984); "Merry Christmas Everyone," Shakin' Stevens (1985); "Do They Know It's Christmas?," Band Aid II (1989); "Do They Know It's Christmas?," Band Aid 20 (2004); "Do They Know It's Christmas?," Band Aid 30 (2014)
5. Eight (taking "checks" as one item)—sable; convertible; yacht; platinum mine; duplex; checks; Tiffany decorations; ring
6. "Stille Nacht, heilige Nacht"
7. *Spanish Trains and Other Stories*
8. "Baby It's Cold Outside"
9. His baby daughter
10. "Le petit renne au nez rouge"

Answers to quiz questions in the book that went unanswered, as that would irritate me!

Question 2, p. 60: "Jingle Bells" (Wally Schirra and Tom Stafford; bells and harmonica)

Question 4, p. 62: Santa Kurohsu

Question 10, p. 62: candy corn

Christmas Tablet—From Mum's Recipe Book

4½ cups of superfine sugar
1¼ cups whole milk
½ cup butter (I prefer salted)
14 oz condensed milk
2 tablespoons Scottish whisky
1 teaspoon cinnamon syrup
1 ounce raisins

— Soak raisins in whisky overnight. Obviously, you'll have ice cubes in the freezer for cocktail hour, but check anyway.

— Butter up a baking tray like I do our pasty Celtic skin with sun lotion. Or you could line your dish with parchment paper, but buttering is more fun.

— Pop the sugar, butter, and milk in a big pan and heat on a low heat, very slowly.

— Stir every now and then but not too much. DON'T LET IT BOIL YET! Patience, Rosalind, is important in all things, but especially relationships, orgasms, and fudge.

— All the sugar needs to dissolve, so scrape a little mixture against the side of the pan. If it still feels grainy, keep it on a low heat until smooth. When the sugar has completely dissolved, add the condensed milk. Stir in slowly, making sure it doesn't stick.

— Then fold in the whisky that the raisins have been soaking in. Make a Christmas wish while adding another slug of whisky. Make it a good wish—really go for it. No point asking for something small.

— NOW is the time to boil! This is your moment! Let it bubble on a high heat for twenty minutes, stirring regularly. Be careful though, it is very dangerous. Have an adult do this bit, and yes, I do mean you, Rosalind. At around fifteen minutes, put cold water in a bowl and add a handful of ice cubes. At twenty minutes, drop a small amount of the mix into the iced water. Pluck it out and see if you can roll it on your palm. If it goes into a wee ball, the soft ball stage, then tip in the raisins and stir through the cinnamon syrup.

— Take off the heat and leave for five or so minutes, then whisk thoroughly until it feels thick and set. Pour into the buttered tin and gently score squares with a knife.

— Pop in the fridge for a couple of hours. Then cut into cubes.

— Leave out a couple of pieces for Santa with a glass of the same whisky. She'll really appreciate it.

Acknowledgments

1. Who is the very best husband and writer in all of time and space?
2. Our daughter, namesake of the founding producer of *Doctor Who*
3. Brilliant editor to whom this book is dedicated
4. My daughter calls her my "angel"
5. The brilliant group that steams ahead with this book
6. My wonderful new in-laws, who have looked after our daughter during work hours so this book could be written (Clue—a late princess and a frequent Almodóvar actor)
7. Their last name is blessed, their first names shared with Harlow and Evans/Pine/Hemsworth/Pratt respectively
8. An organization that really likes facilitating authors
9. My first best friend, and namesake of this book's protagonist; and my best friend since university (also a fabulous writer)
10. My criminal besties, a.k.a Lady Sushi Oil and Barb Throb Spied

Answers

1. My new husband, the glorious Guy Adams
2. Verity, our wonderful three-year-old
3. Katherine Armstrong, editor extraordinaire
4. Diana Beaumont, my fabulous agent
5. Team S & S (including wonderful assistant editor, Judith Long; brilliant publicist, Sabah Khan; marketeer extraordinaire, Richard Vlietstra; Emma Ewbank, designer of the beautiful cover; Matt Johnson in design; Francesca Sironi, overseer of production; copy editor, Saxon Bullock; and proofreader, David Callahan.) I'm so very glad to join you all at Simon & Schuster!
6. Di and Antonio
7. Jean and Chris Benedict
8. RLF (Royal Literary Fund)
9. Roz Davies; Karen (K.E.) Minto
10. Susi Holliday and Steph Broadribb

Thanks also to: my glorious brother, David Benedict, his wife, Carolina, and my niece, Sofia Maia; Dame Margaret Rutherford; my wonderful extended family; my magnificent Hastings friends—Judith, Michelle, Boy Sam, Girl Sam, Nigel, Lou, Steve, Caroline, and Kirsty; Paul and Marie; John and Lin; Ceejay; Heidi Heelz; Jamie Holliday; Tracy Fenton; Jamie-Lee Nardone; Neil Snowdon; Caroline Maston; Nick Weekes; Susan Watkins; Linda Broomhead; Claire Lees Ingham; Ciara and Kelly; Holly and Matt; Stephanie Roundsmith; Steve Shaw; Brian Showers; Colin Scott; Writing around the Kids; writers who have provided support, solace, sanity, encouragement, and/or inspiration including, in very random order, Marnie R, Katerina D, Derek F, Hayley W, Martyn W, Steve S, Louise V, Caroline G, Cavan S, Mason/Alex, Alexandra S, Anna Mazz, Sinead C, Cate G, Cally T, James G, Jacqueline F, Ruth W, Catriona W, Sophia B, Rhiannon T, Emma R, Roman C, Charlotte B, Luca V, Paul B, George M, Tom W, Amanda J, John D, Justin L, William R, Claire McG, Maggie B, Sarah H, Clare Mack,

Jennifer J, Paul C, Wendy M, Tiffani A, Jonathan B, Carol H, Natascha L, Elizabeth H, Syd M, Alex C, Laura S-R, Mark E, Erin K, Johnny M, Paul F, Fergus McN, Maxim W, Steve V, and so many others; Leslie; Angela; Zo; Emma O'Leary, for sorting out my writer's back; Russell T Davies; Black Phoenix Alchemy Lab for the olfactory accompaniments; every blogger who has reviewed my books; and Val McDermid, Empress of Crime, for the lovely quotes on the cover.

Finally, huge thanks, and my eternal gratitude, to the staff at Medway Maritime Hospital's Maternity Emergency Unit, Pearl Ward, and Oliver Fisher Baby Unit. I was admitted with severe preeclampsia, and Verity was born seven weeks early—they saved our lives.

About the Author

Alexandra Benedict is an award-winning writer for novels, short stories, and scripts. As A. K. Benedict, she published the critically acclaimed *The Beauty of Murder*, *The Evidence of Ghosts*, and *The Stone House*. Alexandra has also composed music for film, TV, and radio, most recently for productions on BBC Sounds and Audible. She taught and ran the highly successful Crime Thrillers MA at City University and now mentors, coaches, and edits writers. She lives by the sea with writer Guy Adams; their daughter, Verity; and dog, Dame Margaret Rutherford.